From

The Wom
34 Great Sutton S

Michèle Roberts

Michèle Roberts was born in 1949 of a French mother and an English father. She currently divides her time between England, Italy and America.

She has co-edited and contributed to several collections of feminist prose and poetry, including *Cutlasses and Earrings* (poetry, 1976); *Tales I Tell My Mother* (stories, 1978); *Smile, Smile, Smile, Smile* (stories and poetry, 1980); *Touchpapers* (poetry, 1982); and *More Tales I Tell My Mother* (1986).

Her first solo collection of poetry was *Mirror of the Mother* (1986). Her first two novels, *A Piece of the Night* and *The Visitation,* are both published by the Women's Press (1978 and 1983). *The Wild Girl,* her third novel, was published in 1984, and her fourth novel, *Mrs Noah's Diary,* will appear in 1987.

About *A Piece of the Night:*

'Miss Roberts' prose has the distinction of Colette'
Sunday Times

'A new writer of talent and energy' *Guardian*

'A landmark in the British Women's Movement and women's writing' *Women Speaking*

MICHELE ROBERTS

The Visitation

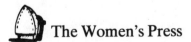 The Women's Press

Published by The Women's Press Limited 1983
A member of the Namara Group
34 Great Sutton Street, London EC1V 0DX

Reprinted 1986

The Visitation is a work of fiction. Any resemblance
to actual persons, living or dead, is coincidental.

British Library Cataloguing in Publication Data

Roberts, Michèle
    The visitation
    I. Title
    823'.914[R]   PR6068.0

    ISBN 0-7043-3903-X

Typeset by MC Typeset, Rochester, Kent
Printed in Great Britain by Nene Litho
and bound by Woolnough Bookbinding
both of Wellingborough, Northants

This novel is dedicated to
Marguerite Defriez, Sian Dodderidge
and Sarah Lefanu

I should like to thank the many people who read and criticised the manuscript in its various stages, and in particular: Ros Carne, Marguerite Defriez, Sian Dodderidge, Judith Kazantzis, Sarah Lefanu, Sara Maitland, Chandra Masoliver, Rosie Parker, Ruthie Petrie, Reg and Monique Roberts, and Michelene Wandor.

I also want to thank Ros De Lanerolle and everyone at The Women's Press for their encouragement and support. I am especially grateful to my editor, Faith Evans.

PART ONE

Genesis

Then God said, Let us make man in our image, after our likeness . . . in the image of God he created him; male and female he created them

GENESIS, *chapter 1, verses 26–27*

One

The first thing of which she is aware is the dark. Formless, seemingly endless. Inconceivable space within which she hangs. Then, that there is life, and light, stirring somewhere beyond her in the blackness and changing its boundary.

The first thing that she sees is an enormous pale face, close to her own. Not having seen her own face yet, she sees the other's. It swims, flat and round, like a mirror with fins. Like a moon at the bottom of the sea. Blank. White. Shimmering.

They touch one another through curtains of skin. They dance in the womb, within their separate sacs, tumbling gracefully over each other like Chinese acrobats. They stretch out their tiny arms, and waltz in slow motion in their world of darkness and fluid. Two loving punch-balls, each a balloon for the other.

Their mother's body divides them. It calls them out. From their happy room where they float and kick like waterlilies swaying on stems, they are expelled. The world, their underwater cave, is after all the belly of the whale. Twin Jonases, they shiver, unable to distinguish between earthquakes, indigestion, death. The walls of their sanctuary contract. A disaster is set in motion.

She loses him. He is sucked away from her; he escapes through the hatch, small perfect astronaut shooting towards a cold foreign star, the outside, where gravity rules and he can no longer fly and freely dance. Brother, come back. Come back.

She has no choice. Where he goes, she must follow. She plunges after him. Wildly, awkwardly. She is crying her way out, her feet slipping in blood, in mucus. She does not want to leave. But muscles, hands, and the season of birth, propel her. And the determination not to let go of him.

Two

There is a tenderness in the London suburb of Edgware in spring. The air carries the warm chirrup of birds, the scent of flowering redcurrant, a haze of pollen and dust. Helen aged ten walks home from the primary school playing fields, tired, sweaty and content after the last hockey match of the season, her knees bare under grey flannel shorts cut to look like a skirt. She comes, mindless and voluptuous, down the long gentle hill of Broadfields Avenue, through the long tunnel of ornamental cherry trees clotted with pink, unable to see the sky, a thick litter of pink petals under her feet, a mass of pink blossom over her head, raftered with reddish-brown.

The suburb has only recently been snatched from the open countryside, as the street names attest: Bullscroft Road, Harrowes Meade, Bushfield Crescent, Hartland Drive. From the top of the hill, where Helen's primary school stands, you can see beyond the compact loops and crescents of the suburb, beyond the council estate at its boundary, to the green fields, farms and woods that stretch towards Hertfordshire. Helen, unless accompanied by her twin brother Felix, rarely ventures that far. She confines her childhood mainly to the back garden of her home and the streets immediately around it. Run into the garden and play, their mother constantly urges the two children, and Helen obeys.

Felix makes forays into the unknown, climbing over the high wooden fences espaliered with fruit trees separating their house from the street and from the council estate at its end. He makes friends up there, returns, eyes glowing, for scolds at his trespassing, with stories of derelict cars, waste-sites, bomb-shelters, children whose parents do not know where they are for whole hours at a time, who swear and who steal. Felix comes home with new words, dangerous knowledge, toys swapped or picked up casually in Woolworths, to be told off for being so late in, to Helen who never is, and who waits for him.

Today, she is alone out on the street, on the half-mile descent between school and the front garden gate of home, safe and familiar territory crossed four times a day. On either side of the road are houses in rows, detached, some done up with timbered fronts in fake Tudor, others glazed with pastel gravel chips, with tubs of miniature fir trees set on front yards of coloured concrete; others bulge with bays and sunset gates and stained-glass window-panes.

On either side of the pavement, under the trees, is a continuous green strip, as neat as the front gardens and their flower-beds. The wide road is swept and garnished every week; nevertheless, in this spring weather, the gutters are choked with pink blossom, with furry flower dust. Well-dressed children venture from their homes to build the clean rubbish into castles and heaps, squat to poke at the drains with budding green sticks. The prams are out, pale frilly battleships done up with bows, and with nets to keep cats and birds away. Some are parked in front gardens, and whether occupied or not it is hard to say, since here babies do not seem to cry; others are wheeled along the road by au pair girls, and again, whether it is the pram or the baby which is taken out for an airing, no one can say, for the pram's sunshade is down, and its front veiled in gauze.

It is three in the afternoon, that peaceful, somnolent, after-lunch time. Helen pads down the hill, her blue aertex sports shirt flattening agreeably against her tiny sprouts of breasts in the warm wind. She is dreaming of sports day next term, when two hundred parents will see her win the girls hundred yards race; she is dreaming of teatime today, of marmite and cream-cheese sandwiches in the back garden under the apple trees, the sofa swing newly out from its winter sleep in the shed, and her mother, in a flowered cotton frock, settling the wide wooden tea-tray on the shabby wrought-iron table under the kitchen window. Her mother will perhaps have driven the big white family saloon up the hill to Grodzinski's to buy egg bread in seeded plaits, or, for a special treat, soggy dark chocolate cake flavoured with black cherries and rum, or vanilla ice-cream topped with walnuts and golden syrup. Her mother will listen raptly, utterly spellbound, to Helen's tale of the match; she will drink tea from a blue willow-pattern cup with a slice of lemon floating on the top; she will turn to her husband and son, full of pride in her daughter, to await their applause.

Then, as Helen turns the corner into her street, she sees the crazy man waiting for her.

She clutches her hockey stick tight. He dances on the pavement between her front-garden gate and the little square busy with shrubs which separates their house from the road, the folds of his open overcoat flapping loosely, his arms outstretched to catch her.

This has been happening regularly for six months now, on those afternoons when Helen walks home alone. It is a favourite game of Helen's, this encounter: enjoyable, because kept a secret from her brother and parents; daring, because played with a stranger; safe, because she always manages to get away. The sense of herself as agile and strong, which she has begun to develop through netball, hockey and tennis at school, is here confirmed, with an excitement added for which she has no name. Invincible and perfect, she dodges him cheerfully, bounds under his arm and runs through the privet arch framing the open gate, up the path bordered with neatly tended lavender bushes, and around the side of the house to the back door. Words are already spilling off her tongue: Mummy, our side won, I scored a goal, Miss Parry said I've improved.

In the same second, she realises that the house is empty.

It confronts her blandly, enquiring why she should be so surprised to find doors and windows locked, all motion of curtains stilled, the garden hushed. The shock of this unexpected setback sets her heart racing, her knees trembling, blood rushing to her face and banging in her ears. She is going to be sick. She has been abandoned by her family. They have gone somewhere far away without her, have forgotten all about her. She has lost them, and will never see them again.

Then sanity returns. She remembers that it is Saturday, the day that the family goes off for the traditional afternoon tea at her grandparents' house a mile away. She was supposed to go there straight from the match.

With this realisation come shock and dismay. She will be late, she, the triumphant heroine of the hockey match. The glories of the playing field drop away; she is merely a child feeling frightened, feeling a fool at the thought of being late, at the thought of her parents worrying about where she is. Helen is never late home from anywhere; by being perfect in her obedience she manages to feel superior to the rules that require it. Now, for the first time in her life, she has let herself down: her parents have no idea where she is.

Hasty with panic, she turns to run back to the front of the house and on to the street again, but hesitates, remembering the crazy man lurking there, suddenly no longer her friend. She is uncertain, this time, that she will be able to get past him. She turns back and climbs the low fence by the back door into the back garden, dodges through rose bushes and under young weeping willows, hauls herself over the fence into the neighbour's garden, and climbs their fence in turn to bring her out into the crescent enclosing her own street and from which she can escape without being seen.

She flees along flowery roads with her head down, tears forcing themselves from the corners of her eyes, praying that she will not meet anyone she knows, or that if she does, they will not recognise her as she gallops past. She wishes that she were inside a pram veiled with gauze, or hidden in a house behind crisp net curtains, anywhere but outside on the neat street which she disturbs with her thudding feet, her red face, her muddy knees and her hockey stick which bangs clumsily at her side. On the playing field earlier in the afternoon she ran with her head down, confident, smooth, her eyes on the ball which she dribbled expertly through a ballet of hostile boots, her stick an extension of graceful and powerful arms, her lungs raw with running but her heart pounding with pleasure as her team urged her on. Now she climbs the gentle green slope between the main road and her grandparents' house with great tearing gasps, and, when she has rung the front door bell with one last effort, leans exhausted against the ivied front porch feeling the blood thunder in her ears and throat.

Her mother is a tall woman, blonde and sturdy, whose face and bearing usually suggest the repose of confidence and capability. Today, opening the door, this has fled; she tucks a strand of hair worriedly behind one ear and then pounces on her daughter, distraught, her voice pitched in a high key.

– Thank God. Where on earth have you been? You're nearly an hour late, look at you, the state you're in, whatever have you been up to? Where have you been?

Talking and exclaiming, she leaves the child little space to answer her, of which Helen is perversely glad. She is shepherded inexorably down the cool, dark hall towards the kitchen and thence out into the garden where the rest of the family is gathered, seated in deck-chairs pulled into a circle around the low tea-table which has suddenly acquired the appearance of the dock in a court of law. Faced with four adults' curiosity and tension, she is certain that they will be angry with her and jeer at her. She remembers the game they had to play last Christmas, the game called the Pope's Blessing. Each child was brought into the room in turn and made to kneel down, surrounded by an audience of relatives, in front of a tall effigy of the Pope, which turned out to be her uncle standing on a chair, draped with a blanket from chin to floor. As the child knelt, the Pope raised his hands in blessing and bowed his head, and a cascade of water gushed from the concealing brim of the bowler hat he wore as papal tiara to soak the child at his feet. How everybody jeered and roared, as did the victims once they were safely part of the audience and able to mock at the next unsuspecting child to be brought in.

Her parents hadn't tried to stop the horseplay. They had laughed too. Helen marches up the steps in front of her mother, and faces the family. Her grandmother plies her with questions, her grandfather removes his pipe from his mouth and stares at her, her father looks up from his newspaper, her brother gazes in surprise at her crimson face.

– It's all right, Helen drawls: nothing really happened. A man made me go with him, that's all.

– *What?*

Having chosen the first lie that came into her mind, she is totally unprepared for the ensuing hubbub. Her father and grandfather start up to get the car out and search for the perpetrator of the assault, and her mother and grandmother clasp her by the arm and throw anxious questions at her.

– But it was all right, Helen assures them, ashamed and guilty: I ran away again.

Useless now to try and deny what she has said. She feels forced to invent in detail a story of what has happened, and to reassure them, in the only vocabulary she so far possesses, that she is untouched and unharmed.

– But are you all right? they ask desperately: are you *all right*?

Helen does not understand this question, but she sees that for them it is of vital import. Her lie has taken over, to recreate her a heroine, but this is a doubtful triumph suddenly, for the threats to send for the police, to have her interviewed for an exact description of her assailant, to make her cruise all afternoon through the suburb in a car full of detectives in the hope of pointing him out will preclude any possibility of enjoying tea and sinking back into the warm bath of family, will end, almost certainly, in her tearful confession and total disgrace.

It is her grandfather who comes to her rescue, putting his arm around her and hugging her. She subsides with immense gratitude into his forgiveness and comfort.

– She's all right, he pronounces, his pipe going back towards his mouth signalling the resumption of normal life: luckily she's too young to understand. Just thank our lucky stars she ran fast enough. That's what matters.

– Leave her alone now, her father advises: better not dwell on it, it'll only do harm, put ideas into her head.

Her mother and grandmother subside, still looking worried, murmuring to each other while the two men resume their sipping at tea and newspapers. They have lost interest in her, and part of her resents it.

8

– This weather, her grandfather says softly, his voice droning like one of the aeroplanes overhead: isn't it lovely? Just like summer.

– She's getting to be a big girl, her mother says fondly, reluctantly, looking at Helen's height, tiny breasts, hips.

– Has she, you know, *begun*? her grandmother whispers to her mother across the cake stand, does she *know*?

– No, Catherine Home says, shocked: she's too young.

– Well, if you ask me, her grandmother says in her straightforward way: it's time that she did.

Helen stares at the two of them with horror. The family has suddenly divided itself into two camps, male and female, and so far she has hung on to her ignorance of the rules governing entry into the latter. She backs away, sensing the beginning of one of those low voiced feminine conversations which she pretends bore and disgust her but which in reality she feels threatened by. She has her own mysteries, her own universe of play, her imagination, interior land-scapes, inhabited only by plants and beasts, in which she can fly and roam at will. She wants no other. She moves away from the tea-table and the circle of deck-chairs which suddenly have re-formed, divided into opposite, separate rows. Why has she never noticed? Blue deck-chairs for the men, red ones for the women. Pain and apprehension strike at her heart. Her mother and grandmother are obscene, witch-like, muttering spells she does not want to hear. Their lowered voices are the signal for a listening child to depart. Her mother looks up.

– That's right, darling, she says: run off and play.

Helen has always loved the Saturday teas at her grandparents' house. Her grandfather teaches the two children how to butter the loaf clutched under one arm and then shave off wafer-thin slices with the worn sharp breadknife. Her grandmother teaches them to tip their tea into their saucers and blow waves across it until it is cool enough to drink, how to cut oranges in half crossways and pack a sugar lump into each half and then suck out orange juice and sugar together. They roll up the delicate slices of bread to eat them with shrimps, watercress, celery stacked in a glass jug, fish-paste packed in tiny squat jars, flan made from the different soft fruits grown against the fence separating the end of the garden from the park beyond.

In May, the garden will be a jungle of bluebells, but by midsummer her grandparents will have it tame again, fifty yards of earth between wooden fences bearing docile rows of fragrant sweet peas, hollyhocks and roses, an ex-army rug spread on the shaven lawn for the children to sit on for tea outdoors. In autumn there are fat blackberries, and hard crisp apples and pears tasting of sweet rain, and in winter they build snowmen at their father's direction, Hitler and Mussolini seated on the rustic garden bench. Now, in early April, just before Easter, the daffodils are out in the flower-beds under the trees, but there is still enough bare and pleasingly damp earth for Helen and Felix to mould roads and walls beyond the beaded stone edging of the path.

Felix looks up impatiently from this occupation as his sister wanders down the path towards him.

– Come on then, he says, beaming at her: come and play with me.

– That's right, their mother repeats: you children run off and play.

Helen sidles after her brother towards the garden shed backing on to the park. At week-ends, this wooden box becomes their den, magically unknown to the grown-ups. It is dusty and untidy, another part of its charm, crammed with gardening tools, coils of rubber hose, boxes of earthenware flowerpots, seedling trays. Helen picks her way over hairy sacks and bags of potting compost to the far wall and leans against the little window, drawing her index finger gloomily through the dirt on the window glass pane. She feels large and clumsy, as though like Alice she has drunk a potion to grow huge. Giant blooms, says the empty packet of sunflower seeds at her feet. She brushes her hand over her hair, convinced it is touching the roof.

That was another of the family's Christmas games. The children, blindfolded, were seated on chairs, which were then lifted and swung about by the grown-ups. Once the child was completely disorientated, her head was tapped with a book to make her believe she had hit the ceiling. Her cry, followed by the laughter of the watching grownups, was the signal for the game to recommence with the next child. Helen looks at her brother and feels her guts whirl with anticipation and fear. He is radiant and seraphic. He has been taught a new game.

– Watch me, he crows: watch me.

He pulls down his shorts and pants and rotates gravely in front of her, his head flung back, his arms stretched out. His gym shoes delicately scuffing the earthy floor with precise and graceful steps turn him into a temple dancer, a little god.

– Now you. Go on, it's your turn.

Helen sees him as her brother again, because he has stopped dancing and has opened friendly eyes. She sees his small pink bum, the small pink penis dangling at his front. This item, long familiar from bathtimes, has never seemed significant. She shrugs, but pulls down her shorts and knickers and turns round and round in front of him, looking at him questioningly.

– D'you see? Felix cries out in an ecstasy: I've got a bum and a penis and you've only got a bum. I've got two, and you've only got one.

Their games and experiments have usually been carried on in silence up until today. Not so much because of the need for secrecy allied to certain forms of play as because there is no language necessary to describe their experience, discoveries locking them into a silent subjectivity they always knew each other shared. They have been pirates, mothers, doctors, sheikhs, sailors and wild beasts. Always together. Identical. Equal. Now, tears rush into Helen's eyes and slide down her cheeks. She feels cold, and pulls up her clothes again.

– You're horrible, she weeps furiously: I hate you. I'm not going to play with you any more.

At the door of the wooden shed she turns, in order to receive indelibly the impression of him prancing in his naked pink delight.

– You're bad, she cries out in despair: you're stupid, you are, all boys are horrible.

She lifts the latch of the wooden gate set into the fence and passes into the park. This is another place that she has always shared with Felix. They stand together in the long and tangling grass, watching the men build bonfires, feed and stir and contemplate them through long afternoons. They sniff the smoke at dusk of burning briars that hides them from the adults calling them to suppertime; they plunge together into beds of daffodils and lie there with the cool juicy stems rearing above their heads; they squat by the fish-pond stroking its scummy surface with reeds; they dare each other to tiptoe across formal rose-plots and steal buds; they climb trees, run races, explore the air-raid shelters smelling of urine and decay. Now, Helen runs clumsily along the narrow path between the allotments, her eyes so swollen with crying that she cannot see properly where she is going and so lurches, trips, bangs into sacks of manure and heaps of thorny weeds.

Panting, she makes for the bumpy green field still set with football posts and unrolled as yet for summer cricket matches, the line of tall elms just beyond. It's the nearest goal; she is running away from home but doesn't know where to go.

No one is about. She is completely alone in the park.

She is a dot in the enormous field, whose green is darkening. Shadows begin to creep out at her from the elms massed blackly far away and yet somehow feeling very close. A wind springs up, tossing

11

their branches. When she looks up, the sky has lost its blue and become turbulent. It is too big. Grey and white clouds race across its expanse, reaching down to touch her. Standing stockstill, feeling very small, hearing her heart beat in time with the wind, and looking up so that the clouds are all she can see, she loses all sense of balance.

She begins to run again, crossing the field after what seems an eternity, and reaching the line of elms where they thin out to a hedge of scrub. Here she plunges in, roots and branches tearing at her clothes and scratching her knees afresh, wildly parting the undergrowth, not daring to look round and face whatever it is that scrabbles behind her, moaning and calling her name. Bolting through the bushes, she comes to the deepest part of the hedge, a small green cave, and sinks down, gasping with relief, on to earth and grass and stones, her breath raw in her throat, her head bent, her hands tightly clutching her knees drawn up to her chin. Nobody, she determines, will ever be able to find her here.

And yet she lifts her head in terror and delight, and listens for the trampling of the crazy man's boots.

Three

Helen and Felix always enjoy staying the night at their grandparents', enjoy feeling special, spoilt. The treat is based on difference. The house, to begin with, feels strange, having been built in the twenties rather than in the fifties like their own home. The outside of the house is all comfortable bulges and curves, rather like their grandmother, with stained glass in the windows, a little white wood porch covered with rambling ivy, and a front garden full of hollyhocks, roses and forget-me-nots.

The sitting-room, at the back of the house, is dark, its french windows veiled first by the softest and thinnest of cream linen curtains, and then by long red velvet ones that reach to the ground. On wet afternoons, the children hide behind the drawn curtains, pull the thick folds around them, whisper stories to one another of ogres who grind human bones for bread.

The armchairs and sofa look and feel like solid clouds, and have lace antimacassars and pale pink squashy cushions embroidered with baskets of flowers and ladies in crinolines. A tall cupboard with a diamond-paned door holds a hundred miniature jugs and pots, crested mementos from Worthing, Southend, the Isle of Wight, Herne Bay and Torquay, all the resorts shown in the photographs of their grandmother with funny bobbed hair, soft bosom under droopy crepe frocks, mouth laughing in the shade of a huge floppy hat.

The dining room is at the front of the house, its walls and furniture the colour of freshly sawn wood, so that when the sun pours in through the big bay window and the children look down at the main road at the bottom of the sloping bank on which the row of houses stands, they imagine they are on a ship racing along between waves and sky. In the old days, their grandfather tells them, the houses fringed an avenue of limes, along which he would dawdle home on early summer evenings to enjoy the strong scent of the lime flowers; the trees have long since been felled to make way for the widening of the road.

Their grandmother gives them food that is distinctively her own. From the stone shelf in the thick-walled pantry she brings them shallow bowls of custard, paler and thinner than the custard their mother makes. She gives them fruit pies baked in a glass dish, not a china one like at home, the pastry held up by the beak of a white china bird, the blackberry and apple beneath both sugary and sharp. She indulges them when they clamour for their favourite bowls, the green and black ones patterned at the rim with scrolls and arabesques; she watches with pleasure as they devour her suet puddings, her steak and kidney pies.

As the children sit at the table covered by an orange chenille cloth, their grandfather sits in his armchair by the fireplace, busy with pipe, matches and pipe-cleaners. His love, like their grandmother's, never needs to be questioned; quiet, warming, solid, it can be taken for granted with delightful selfishness. He tells the children funny stories; he twists words around and tells them of dribs singing strange songs, yeknoms gambolling in trees; he refers to certain cakes as kill-me-quicks and as tonsils-on-toast; he accepts the drawings that Helen does for him and enchants her by tucking them seriously into his breast pocket, over his heart; he lets the children rummage in the gothic glass-fronted bookcase and laugh at the moral tales he received for school and Sunday school prizes sixty years ago.

The floor of the dining-room is slippery brown linoleum covered in a blue and brown patterned carpet. The children's feet drag across it as the little wooden clock on the mantelpiece chimes out bedtime. But the night too has its charms. The stairs twist up rapidly from the hall, a crimson turkey runner railed into each steep step with a smart brass rod. The bedrooms, for children used to modern furniture in light wood, are out of ancient history. The beds are high and narrow, with plain dark headboards, deep soft mattresses and coverlets. The quilts on the beds are of cool slippery silk, padded and faded in pink and blue. Each room has a wash-stand and dressing-table, highly polished and strewn with little lace mats on which stand pots and utensils in flowered china whose uses are incomprehensible: hair-tidy, shaving-rest, trinket tray. Felix and Helen lie in separate rooms in their foreign beds, watching the crack of light where the door has been left open to comfort them, waiting for their grandparents slowly to mount the stairs and come in to kiss them goodnight.

Then Felix creeps across the landing and clambers into Helen's bed.

– Tell me a story, he pleads: go on, go on from where you left off last night.

In the morning, there is the funny old bath set on curly legs, the feel of sitting on a rough patch where the enamel has worn away, the plain white paint on the bathroom walls, the marbled linoleum in green and white on the floor, the enormous loofah, the tin mug of false teeth, the indigestion pills in the little cabinet on the back of the heavy door. Breakfast too is a novelty: cornflakes, which they don't have at home, a striped blue and white jug of milk rather than coffee or tea, toast cut into neat crustless triangles and arranged in a pewter rack.

This particular morning feels different from other visits. The two children remain silent while Mr and Mrs Home discuss what they might like to do today, whether accompany them to the shops, or play in the park allotments, or in the garden. Felix and Helen have heavy and anxious hearts. Today two brown envelopes will slip through the letter-box of their parents' house, informing them of the children's results in the eleven-plus examination. Felix and Helen refuse to be fooled by their grandparents' kindly assumption of unconcern and normality. Neither can think further than the opening of the envelopes; neither can think of anything else. So Felix petulantly refuses his favourite green bowl, and Helen concentrates with immense care on the exact amount of sugar and milk she adds to her cornflakes.

– Go on then, you two, Mrs Home says at last: George and I'll wash up. Run off and play.

– They look, those two, says her husband, watching them through the kitchen window: like a couple of pensioners stuck in bath-chairs at the sea-side.

Helen and Felix sit primly side by side on the coal-bunker. Where they would normally swing their feet, they keep their knees pressed together, and they stare straight ahead, their hands interlocked in their laps.

– Come on George, says Mrs Home, unable to bear it: come and help me with the breakfast things.

They attack their task with energy. When in half an hour's time Mrs Home glances out of the window again, the children are still in the same attitude, unmoving.

– Here, she calls through the window: you two miseries, stir a stump. Give these crusts to the birds, will you? Grandpa's robin wouldn't get any breakfast if he had to depend on you. You've forgotten all about him.

It's usually one of Felix's favourite jobs. Listlessly, he and Helen climb down from the bunker and come down the steps and the short flagged path, up to the window-sill where Mrs Home is placing the basket of stale bread. She cocks an ear at the deep burr of the telephone behind her.

– That's probably the butcher. Here you are then. Now come on, you two. Let's see all those crusts gone by the time I get back. I shan't be a minute.

Helen looks at Felix.

– Perhaps it really *is* the butcher.

– No, he says, with a gloomy sort of satisfaction at his grand-mother's dishonesty: he's already rung.

They make no attempt to pick up the basket of bread from the window-sill. They are thinking of the telephone, which sits on the hall table next to the front door, wedged between a china cat with a tartan bow round its neck, a mug full of pencils, a large pebble weighting a pile of football coupons, shopping lists and messages. Cautiously their imaginations approach the telephone itself. This is massive and black, squatting on bakelite haunches, the ends of the receiver drooping like the heavy ears of a spaniel, the thick flex coiling stiffly like a tail. If the spaniel barks ten times, Helen prays, we'll be all right. It barks eleven times and then stops. She sees Mrs Home's plump wrinkled hand picking up the receiver and speaking to her daughter-in-law, her forehead frowning in concentration.

Silence for the next ten minutes. It is their grandfather who emerges from the house to end their eternity of waiting, closing the back door behind him gently, coming round the corner of the house to face them, looking at them shyly, pleadingly. They look back at him dumbly, pleading with him in their turn. They are asking him to spare them, not to lie, to tell them they have passed. His hand, brought out from his trouser pocket, just happens to contain two half-crowns. He presses one each into their palms. They don't look at the money, or thank him, they just go on looking at him. Like executioners, he tells his wife afterwards.

– There you are, my dears, he says awkwardly: I'm sure you both deserve it, you've worked so hard.

Mrs Home, emerging a moment later, and seeing their faces still questioning, gives them precise information. Helen has passed with flying colours, winning a scholarship to the local girls' grammar school. Felix has failed, and is therefore destined for the boys' secondary modern in the neighbouring suburb.

The children return to their bunker and sit on it again in their former places, not looking at each other.

– Does Dad know? Felix asks finally.

– Yes, darling, his grandmother says: he opened the envelopes when they arrived.

– Can I stay here tonight? Felix asks quickly: I don't want to go home.

– No, pet, Mrs Home says: Bill's coming to fetch you in the car this afternoon, after lunch.

– I don't want to go home, Felix says breathlessly: why can't I stay here with you?

I'll protect you, Felix, Helen wants to say. But she senses dimly that this is not possible, that the ferocity of Bill Home's disappointed ambition for his son will be expressed to Felix in private, will exclude both her mother and herself as unimportant. It began long ago, the special training for manhood that Felix receives. Helen has failed too, by passing when Felix hasn't, and she can think of no way to comfort him.

– Let's go and play in the park, Felix, she ventures: let's go and jump off the air-raid shelters.

He is too tight with fear to respond. It is Mr Home who intervenes successfully.

– We'll go and do some weeding, shall we, Felix? he suggested: and we'll make sure those birds aren't getting at my peas. Come on, Felix, be a good chap, now.

The two of them vanish up the path. Helen, desperate that everything should return to normal, and seeing that it won't, bursts into tears.

– Helen, Helen, her grandmother sighs, putting her arms around her: don't take on so. He'll be all right. They won't be angry with him for long, they'll get over it.

She shepherds Helen inside with her, and gets her busy with little household jobs.

– That butter's grubby, she says: could do with a new dish. You do that, love, while I peel these potatoes for lunch. We're going to have a lovely piece of beef, as a special treat for you children. And little Yorkshire puddings, the way you like them. Did I ever tell you about my sister Ellen, the one who married the Frenchman and went to live in Paris? Every Sunday, she used to make the most delicious Yorkshire, she wrote and told me once, and she'd weep into the batter all the time she was making it. Dear me, that's not a very cheerful story, is it?

– You needn't worry, Nana, Helen says in a cool, grown-up voice: I'm not a baby, you know. I don't like roast beef and Yorkshire pudding, anyway. Margaret Douglas at school, she says it's old-fashioned.

– Dear me, her grandmother says again, hurt: you're growing up into a real little madam, aren't you? I hope they won't teach you things like that at the grammar school. In my day, we were taught parsing, we girls, and spelling, and our tables. I expect I shan't be able to understand all the subjects you'll be doing.

– I shall have lots of homework, I expect, Helen says: Margaret's sister has to spend all the week-end doing homework.

– You're such a dear little girl, Helen, Mrs Home says, sighing: and you've always been so loving. Don't grow up *too* fast.

– Oh, Nana, really, Helen says, with a hard laugh: just look at your face. You've got bits of mud from the potatoes splashed all over it.

– Well then, her beloved grandmother returns more sharply than she has ever spoken to Helen in her life: we'll stop chattering, then, shall we, and get on with our work.

Helen bends her head over the butter dish so that Mrs Home won't see the tears spilling down her cheeks again, and they finish preparing the lunch in silence.

– Well done, Helen, her mother says to her later that day: I'm really proud of you.

And then both of them turn their faces towards the sitting-room door, behind which Felix is in conference with his father.

Four

The day is all white, a cool moist gauziness under the mossy old cedars on the lawn where the sun cannot reach in very far, a dry shimmering whiteness in the open air above the lawn and around the house. This is built of white stone, graceful and square, a Victorian fantasy frilled with wrought iron at window and door, scalloped with grey tiles curling along the steeply pitched roof. In front of the house, at the end of the drive running a quarter of a mile to the gates, is a half-circle of white gravel, all different shapes and textures of little stones, quartzy, a cloud of chalk and rough cream, all scraped together. In the stillness of afternoon the air trembles with heat. The flower-beds droop with crumpled white velvet, the pale labrador sprawled by the front door is asleep, and iron chairs, their white curls complex as lace, glint on the lawn with bright dust, and with spiders' webs.

The noise of a car engine disturbs the peace. A gleaming Ford Consul grinds and skitters up to the front door, small stones flying as it comes to a skidding halt. The labrador begins to bark, nearly choking itself at the end of its chain, its front paws scrabbling at the air. Mr and Mrs Home, Felix and Helen, peer through the dusty panes of the door into the gloom beyond. Then Bill Home presses the bell, stabbing his forefinger at the white enamel nipple half obscured by the roses clambering around the porch. Three seconds pass, in the heat, and then they hear the bell jangle, far off.

– Remember, darlings, Catherine Home says: you're going to come in just for a little while. And you must keep very quiet. Aunt Felicity's very ill, and she's not used to children any more.

Bill inserts a finger into the collar of his white shirt, tugging at it, overly stiff and tight because it is new and not yet softened by washing and wear. He's a big man, with sensual features: brown eyes, fleshy nose and lips, and thinning dark hair trained into crinkles with brilliantine. He is too hot in his summer outfit of cream linen suit, coffee-coloured socks and heavy brown shoes. Catherine is hot, too. She pats at her face with her powder puff and glances at her white box-pleated skirt and terylene blouse. She wishes she hadn't felt it was necessary to put on a girdle and stockings. The old lady would probably never have noticed.

18

– It's too hot, Felix grumbles, scuffing the tips of his new sandals against the step: and why can't we stay outside and play?

– Don't spoil your new shoes, his mother warns him: and don't start acting up. You'll upset Aunt Felicity.

– She's not your aunt, Felix says, dancing up and down on the step: she's Helen and my godmother.

This is true. Catherine Place worked in a nearby factory during the war and met Miss Gettering at a charity concert in the village hall. The two women, so different in age, class and temperament, struck up a friendship which endured after the war had ended and Catherine had met Bill and married him. She went on finding the time to visit her every few months, retaining an affection for the eccentric older woman who ordered her about in a manner that did not discompose her, for an old-fashioned, upper middle-class lifestyle experienced in this house, and for what, although here too the suburbs begin to encroach, is still the countryside.

She tells the children stories about it. How they dressed for dinner every night, and how they would warm their evening frocks at the fire in the huge drawing-room and then scuttle back upstairs with them to dress in their rooms at the ends of icy corridors. The dresses sit up stiffly in front of the flames, pale net ghosts.

Helen, who has never lived in the real country, feels scared of this house which she has never visited before, scared of the dog which is still barking hysterically, of the noise and smells of the farm behind the house, of the lack of visible barriers separating the estate from the surrounding rural landscape, of the shadows that suddenly move, even of the heat, which is like a chain on her limbs.

She squints at the shuttered front of the house, listening to the maid fumbling with the handle on the other side of the door, and tries to decide behind which rectangle of peeling white paint her godmother lies propped up in darkness. She tries to imagine the smell of ageing and death, but is too frightened, and can only summon images of medicines and lavender water. She herself is all bursting life, twelve years old and sturdily built. In the eyes of her newly awakening sense of femininity, fat and unattractive, awkwardly maturing, and resentful of this. Her pleated skirt, white terylene like her mother's, bulges out over well-rounded hips; her breasts spread out sideways in a pointed brassiere beneath her clinging ribbed white nylon top. As the front door opens and Miss Gettering's aged maid beckons them to follow her up the dark stairs to the first floor, she scowls with irritation.

She stands with Felix in the doorway of their godmother's room, with their parents in front of them, and the sound of the maid's footsteps clacking away back down the stairs. She strains her eyes towards the crack of light between the closed shutters. After the glare of the sun outside bouncing off white stone, it is difficult to get used to the dimness inside the house. It's very quiet. Perhaps the old lady is asleep and they can all tiptoe away again. But then Catherine and Bill brush confidently past the chest of drawers looming beside the door, stride forwards and are swallowed up in the gloom. Felix plunges after them.

Seeing nothing, and furious because she is afraid, Helen advances into the bedroom after her parents and brother, stumbling on the edge of the frayed carpet, banging into a low chair. She blushes, she can feel the blood surging into her cheeks in a tide of crimson, staining them; she glares in what she imagines to be the direction of the bed. A pale hump of pillows glimmers in one corner, the sheen of a silk counterpane becomes visible like a shoreline in fog, and like a traveller she must cry land, land, and go eagerly towards it. The air in the room is stuffy and sour, as though the windows are rarely opened. At home, the outside world retreats behind locked sheets of double glazing, but the air inside the house is always sweet. She edges a little further forwards on reluctant feet.

Nobody speaks. She doesn't know how much time has passed, whether a few seconds or five minutes. She must have reached the bed by now. It's as though there is no one in the room but herself, just like the game called murder in the dark, when you wait shivering in blackness, trying not to breathe, so that you can distinguish the heartbeat of the killer crouched behind the door or underneath the bed, waiting to stroke the back of your neck with a chilly, an unexpected hand, and declare, in a sudden whisper, that you are dead. Her knees shake. Stupid old git, she says to herself, borrowing the language of Felix's boys gang to anaesthetise terror: dried-up old cow. She remembers Felix describing the breasts of his middle-aged form teacher at school: a pair of long floppy bags, he imagined them, wrinkled and empty, hanging down to her waist. He wanted to grab one by the grey nipple and pull it right out; then he'd let it go, ping! and watch it flop back like the elastic on his catapult. Helen was shocked at the time by his cruelty and his curiosity; now she summons them for her own use.

– Well, you children, snaps a voice near her face: and so what have you got to say for yourselves?

20

Helen jerks with guilt, convinced that her evil thoughts have been overheard.

– Hello, Aunt Felicity, she and Felix stammer in duet.

– Open the shutters for a moment, the old woman commands: I want to see what you look like. Haven't seen you for over a year.

Usually the annual meeting takes place in a hotel lounge in central London, over tea, on one of Aunt Felicity's trips up to town. The children wait, heartless, patient and greedy, for the last cucumber sandwich to be grasped between mottled fingers, the last scone to be coated with jam, for the plump, beringed hand to reach into the crocodile bag and extract this year's present, usually a cast-off from their godmother's store of knick-knacks and ornaments. They receive odd, splendid, intriguing gifts which they do not appreciate in the least: inlaid Burmese boxes, silk handkerchiefs, postage stamp collections, backgammon sets. They sit back, satisfied by the pound note usually accompanying their booty, their payment for good manners clasped in buttery hands.

– The shutters, Catherine exclaims: I'll open them.

– Let me do it, Bill says, starting forward.

He has been hovering between the door and the bed, his big hands dangling at his sides, feeling out of place and looking it. Now he darts to the window, unexpectedly agile, so pleased is he to have something to do, and fumbles with paint-encrusted catches and hooks. With a creak and a wrench, the shutters fold back, letting in a slab of sunshine that falls across the bed to illuminate Miss Gettering's face, pasty white, the sharp cheekbones jutting up through the flesh wrinkled like soft rubber. Her body under the bedclothes looks as though it has collapsed, the cancer puddling the muscles across the sheet. Catherine draws in a sharp breath of dismay at the change in her old friend, but Bill and Felix look away again, and Helen, shameful Helen, locks her hands into one another behind her back in a hastily invented magic sign, waggling her fingers against old age and decay until the fear threatening to liquify her stomach subsides under her control.

– I'll talk to Helen first, Aunt Felicity decides: come here, child, where I can see you properly.

Helen inches closer to the bed, still appalled at the difference in her godmother, stripped not only of health but also of make up and elegant clothes. The old woman's eyes, pale blue and watery and almost lashless, wander over her, and she stiffens like a new recruit on parade, awaiting the inevitable comments on her hair, complexion, clothes. She can't get used to it, the way that adults now comment on her appearance: a shame about her large feet, she's not taken after her mother, has she, in looks? But today Aunt Felicity has no interest in her godchildren's deficiencies; she sounds weary, as though it's an effort even for her to speak.

– So, she enquires courteously: and what are you going to be when you grow up?

At the moment, the book privately circulating amongst Helen's coterie at school and occasioning their derision and mirth is a text called *It's time you knew*, filched from the school library and giggled over behind desks. By those possessed of superior knowledge, that is; Helen, savagely innocent, unwilling to learn from her mother or anyone else, is scared by it. It is specially written for girls by a doctor, mixing clinical descriptions of reproduction and menstruation with moral warnings about the danger of accidentally arousing the over-whelming animal passions of men. One of the most bewildering stories concerns a girl of Helen's own age who takes part in a game of strip poker with a group of boys. This is loss of purity enough, but there is worse to come. At the moment when the gleeful boys watch the wretched girl forced to remove her skirt and reveal her under-wear, she nonchalantly whips it off and displays a pair of sturdy shorts. Cock-teaser. A word that Felix has already learnt at school and relayed to his twin.

– I'm going to be an explorer, she tells her godmother: I'm going to travel around the world and not come back for years.

The image is indistinct, but it concerns a safe place, far away, warm and fertile, inhabited by a troop of girls clad in shaggy skins who will elect Helen to be their queen. This happens less in the playground than it used to. Helen's contemporaries, who betrayed her at primary school by turning to the ambiguous pleasures of being pursued by boys who planted wet kisses on their mouths during games of kiss-chase and pressed india-rubbers heated at the gas-fire on their coy bare knees, now abandon her frequently for huddled discussions of brassieres, suspender belts, coming on. The race to be first. To be top in new approval stakes.

– She's very bright, Catherine says proudly of her daughter: we're very pleased with her progress at school. She's usually top of the class.

– I'll never get married, Helen says desperately: and I never want to have children.

She squints out of the corner of her eye to see the puzzlement on her mother's face. But Miss Gettering laughs, a whispery cracked

22

echo of a laugh that issues from between dried-up lips, flies up the chimney and down again, and clambers into Helen's pocket. She looks at her godmother's female body again. Once and for all, she repudiates it. She herself will never grow old and never die. She knows the secret of eternal youth, and will not relinquish it.

– So, says her godmother unexpectedly: I like that. I've pleased myself, all my life long, plenty of money and no one to tell me what to do.

Helen has a sudden vision of her, young, imperious, beautiful, refusing offers of marriage right and left and then coming downstairs to dine with her widowed father. The lamp gleams on the massive silver epergne in the centre of the table, on her bare shoulders as she leans forward to peel her father a peach. The dessert service is made from fragile white porcelain circled in gold, no less delicate than Felicity's fingers paring the soft sweet flesh of the fruit. After dinner, she cuts her father's cigar for him, reads to him from the newspaper, and then plays him soothing tunes on the piano until it is time for bed.

– You might go far, her godmother remarks with a faint smile: who knows?

– Far away, Helen corrects her: to explore foreign lands. Places no one's ever been to before.

– I'm tired now, Miss Gettering says, coughing: you've tired me out with all your chatter. Run away now, go and play outside while I talk to Felix.

The door closes heavily behind Helen, and she moves cautiously down the stairs, out of the front door and into the sunshine again. She looks warily around, uncertain what to do next.

Above her, a window flies open, banging against the shutters creased up against the white stone of the house. Into the black space thus revealed pops her mother's head and shoulders, the rest of her body invisible in the room behind. The house could be a cardboard cutout, it seems to the child, with holes cut in it and her mother standing on a stepladder on the other side.

– Darling, Catherine calls: I forgot to give you your tea. Here is is. Catch.

A plump paper bag sails down, passing too rapidly between mother and daughter for clumsy Helen to catch it, so that it bursts squashily on to the gravel, just beyond the reach of the labrador leaping at the end of his chain. He scoops with his front paws in a hungry arc. Nothing. The windows, and the shutters too this time, bang closed again.

23

Helen tears open the soggy bag. Thin slices of white bread soaked and glued into sandwiches with lemon curd. A large pear, pale yellow, bruised by contact with the ground. A custard tart, crisp pastry crumbling under the shiny skin speckled with nutmeg. Redcurrants, translucent scarlet globes still on their spiky stems. She seizes the fruit in her fist and crams it into her mouth, smearing her lips with red sweetness, bubbles bursting sharply against her tongue. Then she drops the rest of her tea on to the ground again, where the dog can reach it this time, and the chickens stalking around the side of the house.

She's not really hungry. She has a stomach ache, a grinding pain deep in her guts. She feels too heavy to climb the cedars spreading temptingly low and wide at the far end of the lawn; she must not dirty her new skirt by crouching to pick daisies or grub idly at the roots of weeds. She allows herself to move within an area only as large as that of her own home and garden, from the front door down the white gravel path to the gleaming tin car and back again, sideways as far as the flower-beds edged with white rocks. She paces her self-elected prison cell doggedly, sullenly. She is close to tears of inexplicable misery when she hears with relief the barking of the labrador signalling the exit from the house of her parents and Felix. She comes slowly across the drive to meet them and watches the dog leap forwards the length of his chain as the stiff and squeaking door is wrenched shut. Doesn't it ever learn, she thinks scornfully: stupid animal.

Catherine hides her grief under briskness.

– Come on darling. Hurry up.

Helen glances at her twin, sees the blankness pulled down over his features like a visor. She is becoming used to this, his retreats into himself which bar any communication, but it never ceases to give her pain.

– We didn't stay too long, her father says heartily: did we?

– But look at the state you're in, exclaims her mother: redcurrant stains all down the back of your skirt.

She seizes her daughter by the arm.

– That's not fruit stains. Oh Helen, lowering her voice out of concern for the listening males: what a time to choose to begin. Come back inside and let me clean you up.

In the car, going home. If you walk in the green suburb in summertime, your bare feet slip and slide on the flat base of leather sandals, the spaces between toes receiving the wetness of roads after showers of fine rain, the cool stems of grasses and weeds in the cracks of the pavement. But inside the car, Helen is dreary, her thighs clinging to the hot plastic cover of the seat, sticky, uncomfortable. Felix, cocooned away from her in his comic and a silence he will not break even when she tries to pick a fight with him, reclines in a far corner.

Helen doesn't want her mother to mourn for Aunt Felicity, her approaching death. She wants to be mourned for herself. And that night when Helen awakes crying out from a nightmare of monsters with Aunt Felicity's face her mother does come to sit by her bed and stroke her hair and croon to her: never mind, you'll get used to it.

Five

Helen opens the cloakroom door slowly, dreading what she will find inside. Five third-formers huddle in front of the small, spotted mirror hung above the row of sinks, putting on make-up. Their faces, as they spin round at her entry, are both hostile and complacent. Pale lipstick, black mascara and eye-liner, purple eye-shadow and thick powder make them women, painted ready for the battle with the authorities.

Helen grasps the lapels of her grey and purple gown. The five younger girls stare back at her, waiting for her to say something ridiculous. She practises this confrontation nightly, before falling asleep. She's not up to it. When the nuns tell her at the beginning of term, the start of her last year at school, that she has been selected by them to become head girl, she is stunned and then appalled, stammering out her dismay, her lack of fitness for the role. All the pupils hate the head girl, whose job is to demonstrate the power vested in the staff and deliver the punishments, arranged in a complicated graded system, chosen by the nuns. They smile at her, pleased with her modesty. My dear Helen, it is God's will. He has chosen you, as His instrument. They use the same language for describing the religious vocation. To refuse is unthinkable. God seems to swoop, with unerring accuracy, on those who don't want Him; it's the indifferent ones he passes by. Other girls in the class read D. H. Lawrence, Henry Miller, Norman Mailer; Helen is locked into an uneasy love affair with St Teresa of Avila, Julian of Norwich, Margery Kempe, the string of women mystics down the centuries pursued by God and eventually succumbing. Make me holy, she prays, paraphrasing St

Augustine: but not yet. First of all, she's convinced, she wants a proper adolescence, yet while her contemporaries shorten their serge skirts above regulation length, swap the prescribed ribbed woollen stockings for nylons, back-comb their hair and abandon their ugly velour hats, Helen inexplicably ends up concealing herself in the head girl's voluminous and unbecoming gown.

She clears her throat.

– You know you're not allowed to wear make-up. Take it off or I'll have to send you to detention.

The five girls go on looking at her, their eyes mocking through the delicate, bland masks of paint. She knows what they see, sees herself night and morning with their eyes as she gazes despairingly into her bedroom mirror. A sturdy body tending to plumpness, a round face with full, pink cheeks, shiny nose, and acne marring the forehead and chin, short curly hair badly cut and sticking out in two lumps of irrepressible frizz. She looks very young. Other eighteen-year olds manage to add years to their age through a combination of growing their hair long, using a great deal of skilful make-up and choosing colourful, provocative clothes. Above all, they have unashamed shape. Helen sees herself as an ugly blob. She pretends she doesn't care, throws herself fiercely into her books.

She can feel her cheeks growing hotter and redder with every second that passes, sweat starting up under her hair and her arms. She gives in.

– If you're still here when I come back in five minutes time, she warns them, turning to go, her fingers searching gladly for the door handle: there'll be trouble.

Back outside in the corridor, she leans against the wall, shaking, waiting to hear the condemnation she knows she deserves.

– Silly cow, she hears one voice say with a giggle.

– It wouldn't do her any harm, a second voice remarks: to use a bit of make-up. It could hardly make her look any worse.

Set into a recess on the opposite side of the corridor is a statue of the Virgin, her hands clasped together on her breast, her eyes, half closed, rolling upwards in ecstasy, her stone veil fluttering with the intensity of her rapture, her naked feet treading on golden roses. There is a lily between her hands, a rosary over her arm, a cherub supporting her. Helen moves nearer to the statue, sinking down on the pri-dieu in front of it. She forces herself to recognise the banality of the plaster features, the simpering mouth, the crude pink and white colouring of the face, the pierced and bleeding heart coyly revealed

26

between two chipped folds of the blue robe. You're not really like this, she tells the statue in passionate silence: don't you *care*?

Back at home, she eagerly discards her tie, bulky blouse and skirt, thick stockings and lace-up shoes, putting on her dressing-gown instead. It's not worth getting dressed for supper and then changing again afterwards. She looks uncertainly at the dress laid out on the bed. Blue lurex, sleeveless, with a scooped neck and slightly A-line skirt, specially cut to minimise, she hopes, her rounded hips. She chose the material herself from the draper in the high street, searched fruitlessly for a pattern she liked, ended up taking a sketch of what she wanted to Mrs Morgan, the lady who runs up all Catherine's clothes. She stands in her white nylon slip while Mrs Morgan lassoos her with the measuring-tape.

– You've got a lovely figure, dear, the old dressmaker tells her: you're just right.

Helen looks at her in surprise, and then at her reflection in the long mirror. She sees the warm flesh of her arms and neck, her naked shoulders, the tops of her full breasts above the lace edge of her skimpy petticoat, and holds her breath. Suddenly, she dares to have great hopes of the blue lurex dress, the Halloween dance at the church youth club.

– What time does the dance end? Catherine asks over supper: what time will you be home?

Helen starts out of her dream of dancing hip to hip with Mike Thomas, Felix's best friend, the back of whose head she adores weekly as he serves at Sunday mass, and focuses on the plate of cold meat and salad in front of her. It's half empty, but she can't remember tasting any of it.

– Eleven o'clock, I think, she replies: the same time as they always shut the club on a Friday.

– I'll come and fetch you in the car, Bill says: at ten-thirty. You shouldn't be out any later than that.

She loves having her father as chauffeur. He drives her to school in the morning, picks her up from visits to friends' houses for tea, gives her lifts to the public library. They don't talk much to each other on these occasions, but she cherishes the contact, the time spent alone with him. But, since that day at Mrs Morgan's, she feels differently.

– Oh *no*, she beseeches him: no one else's father will be picking them up.

Mike Thomas will despise her for ever if her father turns up. Her tentative dream of being walked home and kissed lies shattered in front of her.

– Some parents, her father returns heavily: don't worry about their daughters. Your mother and I do.

– But I could come home with Felix, she pleads: that would be all right, wouldn't it?

Her brother moves restlessly in his seat opposite. She concentrates on him fiercely, willing him to come to her aid, trying to catch his eye and convey her message: you don't *have* to see me home; I'll come back on my own, I'll be all right. Felix, as so often these days, refuses her attempt at telepathic connection. Sometimes she thinks it's his height that takes him away from her. He has flowered into six-foot masculine beauty, with broad shoulders and long legs, taller than Bill now, able to look down on him when they fight. He wears his tightly curling hair cropped very short, close to his skull, which suits him, and is all leanness and lurching grace, his eyes scowling above his bony cheeks. Unwillingly, he looks back at Helen, hunching his shoulders inside his black leather jacket which his parents hate and which he therefore never removes.

– The church youth club dance, he says contemptuously: I'm not going to *that*.

– Where are you off to tonight, then? Bill demands.

Felix immediately assumes a pose he knows his father dislikes, leaning back in his chair, tilting it, spreading his palms wide on the table.

– Just *out*, he says: I'm off *out*.

Bill reddens. Helen throws herself into the breach, desperate to avert another of the rows they seem to find necessary these days. Don't provoke Dad, she implores Felix silently: don't make life difficult.

– I could come home with one of the other girls, she says quickly: we'll all come back together.

She knows Felix despises her, if he bothers to think about it at all, for the way she constantly seeks to avoid trouble. She can't bear watching him square up to Bill, fighting ruthlessly with any weapons available for his independence, taking pleasure in beating the older man with all the pent-up energy of his youth. He's not a tyrant, Helen wants to explain to her brother: if you handle him right. She watches miserably as Bill reaches a decision.

– I'll pick you up in the car at half-past ten, he pronounces: that's final.

28

Catherine, glancing tight-lipped at Felix, starts to clear the table. Helen jumps up to help her. Neither of the two men makes a move. The room cleared of the women, they can take up their battle from where they left off last time. Their voices batter at the wall separating the kitchen from the dining-room.

– I don't know what's come over Felix, Catherine sighs as she piles the dirty plates in the sink: girls are so much less trouble.

The church hall is a concrete hut behind the recently built church, its bleak lines not yet softened by the beds of shrubs bordering the asphalt path that circles it. Helen clops up to the door in her new stiletto heels that pinch and give her blisters but make her feel deliciously sophisticated, the chilly night air sneaking up inside her fur-collared, purple bouclé coat and making her shiver. She's glad to abandon the coat in the Ladies and check her appearance again. Her spots are hidden under patches of Clearasil, her shiny nose and cheeks thickly powdered, her hair back-combed and lacquered into a semblance of straightness.

Viv's there too, smoothing highlighter under her brows, a pearly sheen that matches the skinny sharkskin dress hugging her from delicate shoulders to knees. Viv's knees are lovely, arches of darkness behind them as she bends to pat her sheer nylons into place. The whole of Viv is lovely, from the shoulder-length dark hair that swings in an effortless bell around her cheeky face to the small feet encased in white sling-backs. A nymph out of *Honey* magazine, she fills Helen with aching, envious awe, a jumbled interior babble about patches of moonlight and white blossoms falling on the grass of a garden at night. Viv accepts Helen's admiration as her due, just as she now accepts the loan of her comb, just as she accepts her chaperonage on those occasions when it's convenient not to be left alone with a boy. Helen looks down at herself and feels like a man in disguise. Her feet are too big. What must it feel like to be a real girl, a girl like Viv?

– Your brother coming? Viv asks casually.

– I don't think so. I don't know what he's doing.

Viv flicks the ends of her hair under, spins round and hands Helen back her comb.

– Never mind, she says in a careless tone that doesn't deceive Helen for a second: plenty more fish in the sea. Out there.

She jerks her head at the door, then turns back to the mirror to contemplate her image one more time before picking up her tiny white shoulder-bag and grinning at Helen.

– Let's go.

Bill Home admires Viv for her prettiness and gaiety, the witty way she chats with him when he collects them from the youth club and gives Viv a lift home. Such a nice young girl, he says appreciatively, watching her saunter up the path: that's the style of beauty I like best, that Spanish look. Helen slumps in the back seat, a bag of flesh.

She takes refuge behind the bar counter at one end of the hall, gladly volunteering to dole out instant coffee in smoky glass cups. She's left alone, the other girls relieved to have the chance to escape back to the little tables ranged all round the walls. They have covered the harsh fluorescent lights in bands of pink and green crepe paper, so that the atmosphere is softer and darker than usual, the holy pictures and the big crucifix in shadow, the ugly aluminium windows similarly swathed in makeshift blackout rendering the hall endless and mysterious.

She busies herself turning over the records stacked next to the record player on the formica counter-top, stopping as soon as a boy approaches to select a new record. The Beatles, the Stones, the Kinks, the Supremes, each blaring melody seduces her hips to sway, her feet to tap, her arms to rise into the air. Embarrassed, she seizes a tea-towel and begins to dry ashtrays. No one is dancing yet. The few boys who have so far turned up huddle at the far end of the hall, their bodies clenched into tight suits, their hands in their pockets, while the girls billow and seethe in one sparkling feathery mass of laughter, cigarette smoke, lurex, powder, gleaming legs. When one bold boy decides the time has come to switch off all the centre lights, the dance begins.

Blessed darkness, which lets her relax, leaning on the bar counter and watching the others, unseen, unjudged, no one to declare her a failure, a wallflower. She half-closes her eyes against the smell of beer, sweat and nicotine, slowly wriggles her shoulders in time to the thump of 'Nineteenth Nervous Breakdown'. She is dancing with Mike Thomas. Her body moves in the stuffy hall as lightly as the strands of sound, she floats, her arms, hips, legs articulating in constantly changing patterns of delight. She invents a new body at every step; one moment it is her left wrist that dances all on its own while the rest of her rocks and taps, watching it circle at the end of her arm; the next moment she forgets herself completely and is simply a flexing vessel through which music is poured. Then she experiments with movement with her head down, her hands laid lightly on her thighs as she crosses and criss-crosses her feet in a complicated counterpoint with the music; then she shimmers and glides; then she twirls and bounces, throwing out her arms.

The darkness and whirling patterns behind her eyelids are slashed by spears of noise and light. She opens her eyes, just as the hall door crashes to behind Felix and Mike. They stand like cowboys, fingers in belts, pelvises jutting forwards, faces carefully expressionless, so that the octopus throng on the floor can note their arrival. Then Felix plunges up to Viv where she sits in good view of the door, and becomes a shy boy again, ducking his head, jerking his shoulders in the direction of the dancers. She rises from her plastic chair and follows him. Helen follows both of them with her eyes, unable to refrain from disrupting the fragile privacy of their arms around each other. They don't care, inventing their own inviolable sanctuary of hips grinding into hips, hands wrapped around shoulders and backs, mouths pressed against necks and then tongues plunging down throats. Fifty anonymous couples sway and lurch in the shadows between the statues of the Sacred Heart and Our Lady of Perpetual Help.

Helen's tired, her eyes stinging from cigarette smoke, her feet aching from standing up for so long. Surreptitiously she bends down and slips off her stilettos, welcoming the cool lino on her nylon-covered soles. She rubs the elastoplast covering her blisters and looks around. No one's going to need coffee at this late stage of the evening. She makes her escape unseen, slipping out by the side door at the far end of the bar which she opens a crack and closes noiselessly behind her.

She tiptoes forward into the night, exploring the world with her unshod feet: the gritty asphalt of the path, the damp grass bordering it, the dry earth of the flower-beds. Her sore feet contact bottle tops and broken glass; she comes back on to the path and starts slowly to circumnavigate the hall. Gradually, outlines become clearer against the grey sky, and shapes swim out at her. The rigid silver of the dustbins, their lids askew revealing deep wedges of black, the corrugated iron of the roof like a blanket knitted in metal, the hangar-like side of the newly-built church. Halloween, the nuns explain, means the eve of All Saints, the night dedicated to the holy souls in purgatory. You can get a soul out of purgatory for every visit to a church that day. Helen tries the church door handle. Locked. She shivers, surrounded by pleading ghosts pressing up against her in the glass and chrome porch, begging to be let in to heaven. Outside again, she looks up at the sky, and gasps. It is an infinite expanse of stars.

She cranes her head back, to see better, losing all sense of her size, shrunk to a dot in that vastness, feeling she will tip over, fall off the edge of the planet, as the stars grip her and whirl her off and up and she's dimly aware of her self effortlessly falling away, her mind going.

– Hi.

A male voice, from somewhere close at hand. It's Mike, whom she's forgotten all about, doing up his zip. She gulps and blushes, not having heard him approach. He must be wearing crepe-soled shoes.

– Star-gazing, huh?

That silly song they used to sing at primary school. Catch a falling star and dip it in the Omo, call it Perry Como, hang it on the line to dry. Make it stiff and starchy, call it Liberace, that'll make the girls all cry.

– Want a cigarette?

He proffers a packet of Piccadilly. She's glad she's begun practising this art on the dog-ends discovered in Felix's bedroom, so that she doesn't cough and splutter as the acrid taste hits the back of her throat. They stand together in friendly silence, looped together by strings of smoke, a wreathing Helen has no desire to break. She's managing this better than she thought she would. Mike grinds his butt underfoot.

– Like to come and see my motor-bike? he asks: it's over by the front of the church.

They pick their way across the gravel, hand in hand, more relaxed with each other now, but unable to think of anything to say. Helen can't help worrying: why do I always have sweaty palms?

There's a car turning in at the main gate, its headlights cutting white swathes through the darkness under the deep overhang of the church roof. In the bright light, you can see that someone has carelessly left a pair of trousers hanging there, a pair of white stockings. Then, as the beam moves upwards, you see the two bodies stabbed and transfixed by the glare of Bill's enormous eyes, God's eyes: Viv with her white dress pulled down from her shoulders, rucked up around her waist, her glazed face as white as her thighs, and Felix with his face hidden in Viv's neck, his trousers open.

Put the light out, oh put the light out. Give them back their privacy, their blanket of darkness, their innocence, Viv's good name, God's approval. Too late. Bill is out of the car, and shouting, and the priest, a red-faced gibbering voyeur, has inexplicably arrived from nowhere to send all the dancers home. Helen freezes in terror, but God's gaze swivels in her direction and pins her down too, petrified and shoeless, clutching the leather-jacketed assassin of her virginity, her pink lipstick smeared all over her flushed face. She sees it in the bathroom mirror, later, after the terrible journey back in the car, the father she has betrayed hewn of stone and not speaking to her, the memory of the priest, wound up on whisky nightcaps, shouting hysterical abuse at Viv and herself, Felix and Mike escaping with a roar of exhaust like the devil going down into hell, red eyes blazing.

She can't sleep. You're whores, nothing but whores. She's too hot, clammy between the sheets. If she dared, she'd take off her nylon nightdress and sleep naked. The nuns teach her how to compose herself for sleep: lie on your back, arms folded across your breast, and think of the four last things. Death, judgement, heaven and hell. She sits up, switches on the light beside her bed, grabs her notebook and begins to write. The dictates of the male saints will keep interrupting her, will intervene, cancelling her apocryphal words. O felix culpa, says St Augustine, O happy fault of Adam's, necessitating the advent of the Christ, O happy fault from which the world was then so gloriously redeemed. Helen's pencil trembles between her fingers. The man will go on looking at the woman, in her poem, and the woman at the man.

The main mass on Sunday is at ten o'clock, the mass with singing, a flock of choirboys, a long sermon, and the congregation chatting in the porch afterwards before drifting across for coffee and biscuits in the church hall.

Catherine always sits in the front pew, a position earned by her hours spent arranging flowers, cleaning the church brass, arguing with the priest about points of doctrine she considers him mistaken on, organising church committees, outings, fetes and bazaars. Helen drags behind her up the aisle, her head bent, her cheeks burning. Everyone's looking at her, she's convinced, pointing the finger, whispering. The stuck-up prig, thinking herself better than all of us, she's taken a tumble since Friday night. The humble families from the housing estate cluster in the pews at the back of the church. She is sure she can hear their derision. Helen and Catherine occupy their pew on their own, right under the nose of the priest as he approaches the lectern and clears his throat preparatory to delivering his sermon.

She tries not to hear a single word he says. She looks at the tabernacle behind him, and reminds herself that God dwells not only inside that green brocade tent, as bread, but everywhere in the church, in every atom, every particle. But God has chosen Father

Briggs as his mouthpiece, has ordained that his words represent the Law. There is no escaping it. The priest's words boom between the brick walls bare except for the Stations of the Cross. Friday night. Holy souls. Disgusting orgy. Lack of decency. Young girls behaving like prostitutes. The priest's mouth works up and down in a frenzy, spittle-flecked, his thin lips a pair of shears cutting Helen into pieces and scattering her to the four winds. She retreats inside herself as far as she can go, mutters over and over to herself all the incantations and litanies she can remember, clenches her hands together in her lap, willing herself not to hear a single word he says. But his red face swells to fill all the space between her and the altar, so that she loses all consciousness, all experience of God, and is left only with her hatred of Father Briggs. She wants to kill him, she realises. Her only choice: to destroy him before he destroys her.

She doesn't go to Holy Communion. How can she, filled with needs for murder and revenge? There can be no consolation for the likes of her, cutting herself off from the sacraments, their saving grace, fleeing into the outer darkness where there is weeping and gnashing of teeth and no God. She will die here, like a fish taken out of water, like a bird denied oxygen. Unless some saviour comes.

PART TWO

The Visitation

And Mary arose in those days, and went into the hill country with haste, into a city of Juda; and entered into the house of Zacharias, and saluted Elisabeth. And it came to pass that, when Elisabeth heard the salutation of Mary, the babe leaped in her womb; and Elisabeth was filled with the Holy Ghost: and she spake out with a loud voice, and said, Blessed art thou among women, and blessed is the fruit of thy womb.

ST LUKE'S GOSPEL, *chapter 1, verses 39–43*

First Visitation: Autumn

One

Even though it's after sunset and darkness hangs above the city like a cloth, the air is no cooler and the humidity no less. Sweat starts up along Helen's skin with every movement that she makes, so that by the time she has traversed the short distance between the crowded bus setting her down at the high gates to her apartment compound and the foot of the white concrete staircase that zigzags thirty floors up, she is running with water, her skimpy dress soaked. Climbing the sparkling stairs slowly, she leaves behind her the wail of transistor radios and the roar of motor-bikes as the servants' children return home for supper cooked and eaten in the cell-like quarters at the back of the courtyard, and gains a view, through the open shaft up which the staircase coils, of the landlord's orchid house roof, hears the rustle of trees in his secluded garden. She is looking forward to having a shower, donning a sarong, drinking iced water and smoking a joint of Buddha grass before she settles to the nightly business of typing out her notes gathered during the day, and jabs her key eagerly into the lock of her front door.

She looks incredulously around as she steps across the threshold. The room has been completely stripped during her absence, patches of dust marking where chairs, desk, bed formerly stood. Not a single one of her possessions remains. She blinks with shock.

Presumably the thieves got in by the window. The mesh of the mosquito net stretched on a frame to fit tightly across the square opening has been slashed. Then she sees the litter of porcelain fragments lying under the window, the only relic of the treasures she has gathered together so lovingly over the past few weeks. Her little goddess, a squatting figure in greeny-blue glazed Sukhothai pottery, lies there smashed. Somehow this is the worst blow, to see the little figurine, her arms curved around a bird, her face a mask of peace and strength, and her posture that of a Buddha, lying shattered on the floor under the window-sill.

37

Helen picks up the pieces and cradles them in her palm. She can't see how she'll ever fit them together again; there are too many of them. Nor can she remember the original shape. But she must do something.

She has no glue. She'll never be able to reconstruct the dismembered parts. Tears begin to roll down her cheeks, and she squats against the wall, her head bent over the shards clutched in her hand, weeping bitterly.

Helen wakes sharply from her dream and feels warm tears on her face. She's crying, as though she's been grabbed by her feet and swung upside down in the air and smacked soundly to make her bawl and breathe. She lies panting in the darkness of her room, while her tears splash down. She puts her hand out, to find George, the comfort of his body, but there's no one there. A chilly hollow where his body should be.

The face of the alarm clock glimmers green like phosphorescence next to the wide bed. Her finger tips brush the rug as her hands scurry back and forth searching for cigarettes. Then she remembers: she has given up smoking. She groans, and opens her eyes a little wider and switches on the lamp by the bed. It is still almost dark, although the sun must clearly be up. It is pressed in by clouds. She sits up in bed, the morning air cool on her naked shoulders and the cotton duvet warm on her belly and legs. The duvet cover is patterned in pale green and blue, a formal Indian design of fish, flowers and birds. It always gives her pleasure to look at it, to wake up and see it swirling around her waist as she erupts from the night and sits up.

She contemplates the day. Through the panes of the window, the maple tree outside looks like a fern under glass, like a green fish swimming past. She can hear the hush-hush of the rain, as it beats softly on the pavement, and the swish and trickle of water along the gutters and beneath the tyres of cars. She smells the scent of the roses that she bought herself yesterday and put in her blue and yellow jug on the wooden table that she keeps her typewriter and all her bits and pieces on. There they are, a dim pink bush burning with perfume in the corner. The smell of earth and leaves blows in through the open window from the street. She props her pillows behind her back against the bed-head and reclines against them, silent, and suddenly, inexplicably happy, floating in her large bed in her white and green and blue room, darkness and roses and rain and leaves. She remembers now. It is Saturday morning. Beth is arriving this morning. Beth is coming to stay for the whole week-end, right through to Monday morning.

Meeting Beth for the first time, at university. Helen is lost in a labyrinth of basement underground corridors, carpeted and walled in grey so that her sense of gravity is gone; she might be walking on her head, or swimming, like someone out in space at the end of an umbilical cord. Silence reigns. Her first day in college and she hasn't made anybody's acquaintance yet. You walk into the junior common room five minutes after everyone else and instantly assume that they have known each other all their lives.

Round the corner of the maze tunnel comes a young woman. It's almost like walking into a mirror, for this newcomer sports a grey mohair skirt and twinset very like Helen's own. It is the fashion this autumn. The richer students add cream lace blouses and strings of pearls. Helen surveys the other woman skimming soundlessly towards her over the grey carpet. She has long curly hair the colour of fire, vividly blue eyes under pale brows, a pointed chin. She is small, no more than five foot two at a guess, yet she propels herself along like a shooting star, like an archangel on a mission.

– Excuse me, Helen asks, clearing her throat nervously: do you know the way to the library?

The archangel halts, and contemplates Helen with a frown.

– I've just come from there, she complains: ten minutes ago. I'm trying to find my way out of this bloody place.

– Oh, I know that, Helen says eagerly: I've just come from there. I'm sure I can find it, if I retrace my steps. I'll show you, if you like.

The archangel finds nothing odd in a total stranger's willingness to turn back and find the way out. She is used, Helen decides, to people falling in love with her at first sight.

– Well, the other woman says with some amusement: let's find the way out together. Then if we're lost for ever, at least we'll have each other for company while we starve to death. My name's Beth, by the way. Short for Eliza.

– Mine's Helen. Long for Nell.

Within moments they have found a staircase leading upwards and then a door opening on to the fresh air of a Victorian quadrangle, and are discussing the horrors of the education system, already friends for life, in a cafe in the neighbouring street.

Beth's words thirteen years ago ringing in her head and the cotton of sheet and duvet enclosing her make Helen feel like a letter in an envelope waiting to be read. The workmen have arrived early at the house next door. One of them is singing in a tenor voice, and the other is banging away with a hammer. They don't seem to mind having to work on a Saturday. She hopes, her pleasure embracing the entire world, that they are getting double time. She leaps out of bed, and puts on her nightshirt, leaving her feet bare in order to have the pleasure of feeling the shabby rugs under her soles. The cats swirl about her ankles as soon as she opens the door into the kitchen. Her nightshirt is only kneelength, so that the cats turn into furry socks wrapped around her legs. She goes into the kitchen, grumbling affectionately at them, and opens a tin of catfood. In their immediate, absorbed attention to feeding, there is silence except for the sound of munching and swallowing. She watches them for a moment, and then goes through into the bathroom and throws open the back door to observe the day from the little balcony.

It's satisfactory for mid-September. The rain has stopped, and mist lies threaded under the bushes and trees. The garden is not hers, her brother explained carefully when she took over his flat, but the landlord lets all the tenants use it. She shoves on the wellingtons she keeps by the door, and wanders out to inspect the flower-beds. She plunges her nose into wet greenery, and is given back the harsh, sour smell of marigolds. Their colours, yellow and orange, are as hot as turmeric, and their scent as spicy. It makes her sneeze. Their hearts, tightly packed, are a dense green that is almost yellow. The morning is as wet, fragrant and sweet as the apples hanging on the trees. Helen picks one, which she is not supposed to do, and wanders back to the flat munching it, enjoying the bursts of tart juice on her tongue as her teeth pierce the rough, almost scarred skin, the hard white flesh.

She potters about the kitchen that is just large enough to hold a table as well as stove, fridge and cupboards, taking sips of orange juice in between making coffee and toasting bread. She switches on the radio and does a little dance to the music of horns and flutes. Her delight in Felix's flat and all its appurtenances corresponds exactly to how she felt when given a dolls' house one Christmas. There is the same sense of astonishment: I waited, and all this happened; all this space just for me.

She picks out her new cup, saucer and plate from the cupboard and sits down at the table, facing the window so that she can look at her plants while she eats. She curls her feet over the bar of her chair, wanting to slide them up and down over the cool, smooth wood, and discovers she is still wearing her wellingtons. She kicks them off, and they bounce to the floor, to become green rubber nests for the cats.

She pours her coffee. Her cup is wide and shallow, and patterned, like the saucer and plate, with a wreath of flowers enclosing a man and a woman, all painted on in orange, dark blue and pink. George brought it back for her from France, along with a bottle of olive oil and some brandy. First he told her the bad news, then he gave her presents.

He went away for a whole month. Having recently moved and bought second-hand all the furniture and equipment her brother's flat lacked, she couldn't afford a holiday, she was convinced, and wouldn't let him pay for her, and was adamant that in any case she couldn't take time off work. Not now. Perhaps later. So he went off alone.

August has been very long. But today, the end of the month, as she goes to the market to buy vegetables, and cleans and tidies the flat, she sings to herself a silent refrain of gladness, forgetting all their difficulties: George is coming home, George is coming home, and moves dusters and brooms to its rhythm.

At five o'clock, she leaves the house by the back door. On the lawn there is a soft, bright litter of leaves, and the flowers, dahlias, carnations, late roses, gladioli and marigolds, twinkle like little warm stars. Despite the sunshine, the air is chilly. But it tingles and fizzes and snaps, and brings the blood singing to her cheeks, and makes her heels want to click together and dance. She goes through the gate in the fence at the bottom of the garden and comes out into the alley that snakes down the side of the little hill between the backs of houses. It is the hour at the end of summer that is still only afternoon but hovers like twilight, that hour of subtle colours mixed with flares, the steely glint of the sky, wind rushing in the dense masses of the trees, golden lights going up already in kitchens.

She arrives early at Victoria, so she goes into the buffet and sips weak tea from a ribbed cup in plastic so thin it burns her fingers. She rejoins George as he rattles along in the train, seeing Michaelmas daisies and bay willow herb seeding along the railway lines, chalky cliffs disappearing behind him, and in front of him fields opening up, with horses galloping. The trees are turning bronze and rusty at their tips and the sun hangs low and heavy like a yellow plum. The cottages along the sides of roads have dahlias for sale, big bunches stuck in plastic buckets. He passes through woods and over hills, and then he begins to race above the city, its warehouses and factories and huge old-fashioned signs advertising hostels and bedding and soap. He is gliding in, past gas-works and chimneys and tower blocks, to come to rest just in front of her.

She comes to with a start, as the tannoy booms into her ear the arrival of the boat train from Newhaven. She hurries across the concourse. Late. There is George by the barrier, looking around.

– I thought you weren't coming, he says, hugging her.

– You look, she blurts: different, somehow.

He has leather gloves on, which feel cold as they clasp her hands. He is wearing a long heavy greatcoat of dark serge, the collar turned up. His eyes sparkle, his cheeks are thinner, he has a two days growth of beard, his hair is curly and cropped. He is dark and glittering, like frost at night on city streets. She has walked along those streets to come to him, and, reaching him, stands in front of him in the great railway station, vaulted with iron struts and dirty glass clouded with pigeons' droppings. It throbs with busy life, and she and George shine in its midst, amongst throngs of hurrying passengers, porters, guards.

She and Beth escape from the college library one afternoon in September in their second year. They have come up early, before term starts, to work, but today they go blackberrying, in the thickets near Port Meadow, where the streets peter out and the river and the marshy fields begin. They leave behind them the white marble fountain at the intersection of two red brick streets, the warehouse gates crowned with eagles and the pubs slapped on one side by the canal, and arrive, via a rickety wooden bridge, at the entrance to the meadow.

They stay out till the late afternoon, when it begins to grow cold, and the colours grow dim. Lovingly, greedily, they pick the ripe purple fruit, straining through deep nests of brambles to reach the big, plump ones, which always seem to hide at the very heart of the bush. A chill and a mist wander in from the river and wrap themselves around the trees. Their feet trample dead ferns. Their mouths are stained crimson with blackberry juice and their cheeks red with cold. It is silent where they stand, in the deep hollow, surrounded by scrub, under the bridge, except for the occasional chatter of birds, the rattle of a distant train.

Beth gazes at Helen, and she at her, both of them speechless in the face of this mystery, the joy produced by a chilly, dark September afternoon in which to be alone together and silent and feed upon blackberries offered in each other's palms. They pass blackberries back and forth, their feet planted in cold ruts of mud, their faces white and red, their hands scratched and bleeding from reaching through thorns. Beth, Helen remembers, takes Helen's torn hand in hers, and looks at the red of it, intense in the light of almost sunset, and then raises it to her mouth to suck the blood away.

– It's sweet, she exclaims, licking at blood and blackberry juice: it tastes sweet.

George kisses Helen. His lips are soft, his cheeks are cold. They brush one another's mouths very slowly, George with his arms around Helen, she with her hands laid upon his sleeves, and then one hand raised to stroke his grizzled face. Time can be measured by these simple things: George's unshaven chin grown bristly, Helen's hair grown longer, and the distance between them while they were apart for a month is overcome through the touch of fingers on faces and necks, exploring.

There is the time, that winter, when Beth and Helen both have gastric flu. They mope in their attic flat, awaiting visits from friends. They are bored by their confinement, yet also pleased, inventing games to play together in bed, reading to each other as they begin to feel better, and then fooling about. On the night of November 5th, they sit close together, warmly wrapped in thick dressing-gowns, curled up on the window-seat of their little sitting-room, with the curtains pulled to behind them. They are suspended in their own little world, pressing their noses against the glass. In the dark, they see the party down below, the little hills of bonfires, black cones bursting into fiery life. They see flowers and fountains and necklaces flame, pour and explode, they watch rockets dart, hiss and sizzle up, leaping in arcs, in showers of petals and tongues.

– Helen, George says: look at me.

She looks up. She sees his eyes like leopards, long and dark, deeply flecked with green, and furred with lashes. She wanders towards those eyes, suddenly nervous.

– There's something, he starts: I want to tell you.

The station tannoy booms again, just above their heads this time, muffled, dull. Helen begins to feel the draughts sweeping across the concourse and blowing a tide of litter, tins and cigarette stubs and empty plastic cups, against her feet. She remembers suddenly a

43

paragraph in the newspaper that morning, describing how a stretch of coastline in a conservation area is littered daily with tampon applicators washed ashore, pink tubes curved into claws at one end. Little pink plastic prawns, crabs, lobsters, with claws that crack, strange seafood spat out from whose jaws in the deep?

She shivers, and presses herself against George till he opens his greatcoat and pulls her inside it, wrapping it round her so that she is pressed against his chest, hearing his heart beat against his pullover, feeling his sturdy ribs and spine with her fingers. Wool under her hands, and beneath that bones, skin, blood, nerves. And her own, answering.

After half a minute, he stiffens.

– All right, she says cheerfully: I suppose we'd better be making a move.

In the bright grey steel and plastic tube that spins them north, where they sit under the glare of many eyes, her mood is speedier.

– Tell me your adventures, she urges: all of them.

He perches on the edge of his seat, looking at all the new signs and advertisements that have appeared since he has been away, darting his eyes from one side of the compartment to the other, up and down, drumming his hands on the arm-rest.

– Well, he says finally: I spent a lot of time in Aix-en-Provence contacting the members of the Flamme Rouge collective. It took ages tracking them down because most of them were on holiday and the office was closed.

Helen remembers travelling in Provence with her lover Steven on one of his leaves from his job in Bangkok, six years ago. She remembers how they spent a lot of time sitting alone together and very still, as you have to in that heat pressing down on you and baking your limbs and telling them to relax. She remembers the colours of the hills around the village of Bonnieux where they stayed, which had scarlet and pink mixed into their green as they saw when they looked carefully, and the colours of paths, which were not grey but purple and yellow and blue. They watched the sunsets from the little high back terrace of the hill-set house Steven had rented, skies of lemon and rose smeared across gleaming lavender.

– They introduced me to several of their comrades, George goes on: and one of them had a girlfriend, sorry, I mean, knew a woman, and this woman could speak English really well, so she translated for me. They took me over to Grasse to see the perfume factory there, because they've been organising among the workers.

44

Helen remembers sitting with Steven on the wall overlooking the village street, listening to wasps, the bubble of water, the voices of the old people, looking at the colours of the peeling shutters, grey and dark blue. She remembers how they walked in the feathery green and yellow hills and over the mountains called Luberon and down again between fields of olive trees whose trunks twisted up quivering like shouts in the still heat, how they came to a village called Cucuron in whose square was a cafe with orange plastic chairs and red geraniums, with a double row of mighty plane trees enclosing a vast rectangular pond that was green, cold and deep. Their room that night looked out over the dusty rose and apricot tiles of the church roof, and had blue shutters, a floor tiled red, a straw-seated chair, a hard mattress, and a tall white jug stencilled with burgundy flowers.

– Is that all you did? she asks incredulously: tour factories?

George looks angrily at her, and then straight ahead. There were fetes in all the villages, one by one, she remembers, with dancing at night under strings of fairy lights hung in the plane trees, and bands, and much drinking and fighting in the cafes. Wild children underfoot, and shooting-ranges, everyone in their gala clothes, and, at night in bed, Steven giving her the presents he had collected for her during the day: a bunch of wild flowers, a pebble from Camus' garden, a feather, a glove of bark.

– Well, there was, George says, looking at Helen with dislike: as I told you, this absolutely amazing woman I met.

He pauses to light a cigarette. Automatically she grabs for one too, forgetting that she has given up smoking.

– Oh, he says, blowing out a cloud of smoke: we ended up going around together, to markets and fairs and so on. You know.

He looks down at his feet.

– It's all your own fault. You made me tell you.

Helen chokes on her cigarette, and on jealousy that tastes of thyme and lavender and dust, sitting in her throat as heavy as the red and yellow rocks of Roussillon. At the same time, she is detached and efficient, and sees that the tube has arrived at Oxford Circus.

– Come on, she says sharply, grinding out her cigarette underfoot and wrenching at one of his bags: we've got to change.

They take the tube eastwards to Bethnal Green in silence. They stand at the bus stop opposite the Bethnal Green Museum, waiting for a bus that will take them up to Stoke Newington, to George's flat. The museum, and the wide, tree-lined streets converging at the junction with its traffic lights and railway bridge, are spangled with the reflections of cold stars. Dark green and dark blue breathes the night, dotted with silver and with gold. As though it were Christmas already, and they were in the city centre strung with decorations flashing like ice.

She is waiting for something to happen, a thrill of anticipation mingled with fear. Like being a schoolgirl again, participating in the Christmas carol concert. The dark corridors around the assembly hall are lined with rows of girls in white frocks waiting to go on stage, silent, an occasional nun swishing like an angry ghost between the long files of girls in glimmering white, hissing to them to stand straight and not to giggle. The girls are ghosts too, speechless, invisible. Until they process decorously out of the dark and on to the stage and open their mouths like doves to sing in pure soprano, in sweet descant, of the Saviour's birth. Israel has mourned while she waited for him through centuries; now she trumpets forth joy, and sings of the man who has arrived: matchless: her redeemer.

– So you're here, Helen says, sighing with pain.

George leans forward, his mouth brushing her ear.

– Germaine took me walking. There were caves in those mountains, hollowed from the rock. I wanted to explore them, but I was afraid of getting lost. So we went together. That was when –

He hesitates.

– When what? Helen asks angrily.

– When I went further in, he says: right in, because she showed me the way.

Helen takes a step away from him, as though he has struck her.

– Why did you kiss me then? she cries.

– Because I wanted to, he retorts, outraged at her stupidity: that's got nothing to do with it.

George standing crossly under the street lamp is golden, a sunburnt man with a solid body and with short curly hair tipped with gold light and springing in all directions like a halo. He has a pink pullover, and brown wrists and hands, and is all sun-shone-upon, and burnt brown and fresh. She is the woman who is left behind, quite forgetting that she has chosen not to go. One of those Greek heroines, Queen Clytemnestra, stuck an axe in her husband on his return. He had murdered their daughter as an offering to the gods. Like him, George has murdered. She rises up to protect her female self, she can feel the blade of the axe against her palm, touching it secretly, long, sharp, wicked.

George chatters on, not knowing what else to do, nervous, not wanting her to make a scene.

– She told me, Germaine did, that there used to be monsters, sort of mammoths, in those caves, in pre-historic times. Moufflons, she called them. Nice word, don't you think?

– Carry your own bloody bags home, Helen yells at him: go on, don't wait for me, I don't care, I won't wait for you.

– Helen, George grumbles: don't spoil everything. I told you, ages ago, not to expect me to be monogamous.

He did. She remembers it clearly. And the light of battle rising in her own eyes.

– You're so possessive, George goes on: you seem to think you can treat me as your own property.

– Here's the bus, she snaps.

She moves in front of him, so that he will not see the tears that fall from her eyes as thickly as flowers, like wreaths, flower garlands dropping on to the body of someone once dearly loved, now gone. She can see the axe sticking out of his back, and is shocked. She must have stuck it there herself. She turns round hastily and bumps into George. The contact with his heavy body fills her with despair. She knows, even before he tells her, that the affair is over. He shoves his bags into the cubby-hole under the bus stairs and then follows her to the top deck, to the seat right at the back. They sit in silence, shoulders unwillingly touching. In her hatred, Helen is a mile away from him, cool, untouchable.

– So when are you going to see Germaine again? she asks at last.

– She's coming over in a fortnight, George says, pleased at her comprehension, yet puzzled by her willingness to talk about it: she's unemployed at the moment, so at least she can take time off.

That reminds him. He turns to her courteously.

– And how's your work going? How's the book?

Helen stares out of the window, clenching her teeth and willing her tears not to begin again.

– My publishers turned it down. They said who wants to read about an emotional retard. I suppose they didn't realise I'd drawn on my own experience or they might have phrased it differently. But they'd still have meant the same thing.

– I did some writing while I was away, George says complacently: I think it's going to be one of the best articles I've ever done.

– I felt terrible, Helen says: and I still do. I felt completely destroyed.

– You must see my article, George says: I'm going to rewrite it this week before I submit it. I'd like you to have a look at it.

Helen is floating near the ceiling of the bus, calm and detached. Looking down at the passengers, she can see George's curly hair, the head of the woman sitting next to him. Will the bus never stop? It chugs on and on through the darkness and flashing lights. It's much too hot in the bus. Helen flies out of the window into the frosty night and sails among the dark clouds high above Hampstead Heath in the company of owls and bats. Someone, the woman sitting next to George, is chatting in a high, bright voice about George's holiday in France. How boring she is.

– Helen, George says clearly and slowly: are you all right?

His voice swims towards her through icebergs. She peers through the darkness, but can't see him. She'll have to come down a bit lower. She rushes downwards through whistling layers of snow and lands on a rock next to his, tucking her wings neatly around her and cocking her head on one side, closing her beak.

Helen suddenly lays her head on George's serge shoulder.

– Fascist supermen wear greatcoats like this, she mumbles: you should be ashamed of yourself.

Awkwardly, he puts his arm around her. They sit in silence for the rest of the journey, safe as long as they do not speak, locked in a terrible parody of affection, Helen thinks before she escapes out of the window again.

Their formal declaration to each other of the end of the love affair comes a week later, in a tea-shop near the offices of the magazine where Helen works as a part-time temp. She looks down out of her fifth-floor window and sees the clock over the newsagent's reading four pm. Her stomach churns and she rushes to the Ladies. She looks critically into the mirror at the tight, worried lines of her face. If she applies mascara and kohl, then she won't be able to cry, because they'll run and smear. Her hands hesitates on the zip of her bag. Warpaint to make her feel brave and frighten George with a hissing, glistening Medusa face. Or naked skin worn as a mask of babyhood, vulnerability. She compromises by washing her face and brushing her hair. She is late. She runs down the back stairs, avoiding her friends in the office, and up the street towards Covent Garden tube.

It's just finished raining, and everything gleams: the shiny colours of cars that are brick red and orange and plum blue, and the black streets like coal. At the greengrocer on the corner of Long Acre, there is a press of people, and she halts, looking up over the buildings at the clear, pale blue sky, freshly washed. A hand plucks at her sleeve, and she sees George standing next to her. He's looking very tall and burly today in his dark blue serge workman's coat with leather patches on the shoulders. His face is creased with seriousness as he looks down at her.

– Hello there Helen, he says, resting his hand on her arm.

– Hello George, she replies.

She turns right round and looks him full in the face, while the greengrocer's assistant watches patiently.

– I'm buying oranges, he explains: you can have one too, if you like.

He turns back to the young man waiting behind the counter.

– Make that four oranges, George decides: not three.

He offers her the brown paper bag, and she helps herself to an orange and puts it in her pocket. This simple transaction fills her eyes with tears.

– I'll buy you tea, too, if you like, he says: come on.

She chooses the cafe with care. Not the cheap, cheerful place where they always used to go, with its kind Italian waitress and seething cauldrons of chips, not somewhere where they are both known, recognised as a couple, teased and fussed over. She leads the way instead to the Viennese-style restaurant in the shopping arcade, where the seats are covered in crimson plush, the little round tables rock on spindly legs, and the walls are covered with paintings of Alpine scenes. George lowers his large frame on to a chair opposite hers and catches her watching the delicate frame buckle slightly under his weight. He grips the menu.

– I'm on a diet, he explains, nodding at the bag of oranges in front of him.

– You look thinner to me, she exclaims: after your holiday, not fatter.

– No, he says, shocked, and patting his belly: I put on some weight while I was away. All that delicious French food.

– A bit rich and oily for you, wasn't it? she mocks him: bit of a change from what you usually eat.

Aware of his tactlessness now, he blushes, and looks away from her to address the waitress hovering at his elbow.

– Tea, please, and quiche lorraine, and a roll and butter. What about you, Helen?

– Tea, a pot of tea, and two eclairs, please.

– It's all right for you, he complains: you're as thin as a rake.

– I haven't been eating properly lately, she admits: I kept forgetting to. I'm starving.

She watches him tucking into his food, head down, all attention concentrated on clearing his plate as fast as possible. The way I was brought up, he once explained to her: you didn't linger over meals. The point was to finish eating before the food got cold.

It reminds her of their first date together, in a Greek restaurant. How he relished his dollop of moussaka, how he smacked his lips over chunks of raw onion in his salad, how he swigged back the yellow retsina that tasted of pines and lakes. He finished his dinner in five minutes flat, and then raised his head and looked at her. She wanted to lift her hand and stroke his face. How he reminded her of her father, another large man given to loud chewing and swallowing, gulps and burps in public, physical pleasure. She pushed that thought away, it made her uncomfortable.

– George, she says, laughing at him across the Viennese-style plastic lace tablecloth, loving him: if you're on a diet, what are you doing with all those rolls and butter?

– Oh but, he says earnestly: I've given up potatoes.

Affection and exasperation warm her stomach as much as the tea she is drinking. Why does it have to be like this, feeling easy with him because there's a distance now, because it's ending? It feels more like the beginning, before things became so angry, so confused, before she began to reproach him and he to back away. There is a lump in her throat. It's not the eclairs, which lie untouched on her plate. She swallows hard, and washes the lump down with hot tea. The moment of pleasure between them dies, and dries up like a stain on the glossy tablecloth.

George clears his throat, and begins the post mortem. The dirty table linen, once examined, will be washed, and then tidied away. No blame, the spill was just an accident. She drags her attention unwillingly towards what George is saying.

– We just didn't suit, he says heavily: you're so intense, you have such a strong reaction to things, you made me feel inadequate.

Helen clutches her napkin in both hands, and stares down at it.

– And then, he goes on: the thing I found most difficult was your sexuality. Somehow it seemed as if it wasn't just about sex. It must have meant something else, only I never understood what.

There is a terrible pain in the napkin Helen holds. It writhes and twists between her hands, and she has to wrestle with it, trying to wring the pain dry, trying to wring the napkin's neck so that the pain

50

will slump, felled, to the floor.

– There's no point talking about all that, she says in a shaking voice once she has noticed he is waiting for her reply: we both agree it's over. Let's leave it at that.

– Shall we have some more tea? he asks, concerned, seeing the trembling of her chin: we can be friends, surely.

Helen folds the dead pain of the napkin neatly beside her plate. The only thing she would be able to do with a fresh pot of tea would be to pour it over George's head, watch with pleasure as it brought him out in blisters, burnt him. She stands up hastily, pushing back her chair.

– I must go, she says: I'm all right, but I must go home. I'll be all right, don't worry, I'm sorry, it's just that I must go home.

She runs across the restaurant. Without noticing it, she has scalded herself. Burning tea pours out of her eyes, almost blinding her. At the plate-glass door, she turns and looks back. George's head is down, and he is eating her eclairs.

She runs up the street towards the tube, buys a ticket, and plunges into the packed lift. As they descend, she begins to calm down. She is on a journey, travelling from work to home. She knows where she is going. She always feels safe in the tube. She takes deep breaths, and when the lift stops and the iron gate creases open to let them out, she strides confidently forward, elbowing past people laden with shopping bags and attache cases.

How odd. There is a woman seated in the corridor leading towards the tube platform, sitting very still and quiet on a wooden box. She has a pretty face and a serious expression, and she is dressed in a white jumper and white ankle-length pleated skirt. Helen glances at her, idly wondering what she is doing there. Perhaps she is sitting waiting for someone. She has the resigned posture of a woman at a rendezvouz waiting with her hands neatly folded in her lap. But this woman's hands are elsewhere. She has no arms at all. Just tiny hands sprouting from her shoulders, like fins. Little fish flaps. Little wings. She has a calm, proud bearing, and no arms. As she meets Helen's gaze, she rises, and comes towards her. The rush-hour crowd files hastily past, flattening itself against the wall, looking away embarrassed from the two women standing together under the bright lights.

Helen stops, not knowing why, but arrested by the woman's imperious look. There is a tin box at her feet half full of coins, but she does not come to Helen as a beggar claiming payment for guilt. They gaze at one another with a deep recognition.

51

– Hail Mary, the woman says at last: the Lord is with thee.

She has a soft Irish accent that takes Helen straight back to convent school and fresh-faced Sister Imelda, energetic and wistful, homesick for the mountains of West Cork, telling Helen all about them.

– The Lord is with thee, the woman repeats: and blessed is the fruit of thy womb.

A man hurrying behind Helen cannons into her, and she stumbles. The crowd sweeps her onwards towards her train, and a moment later she hears the rails whistle at its approach, sees them shine far off in the tunnel. Sitting in the swaying, smoky compartment, she has a sudden vision of the train as a pregnant snake, long and silver grey, its swollen belly the armless woman's only home. And mine too, she thinks, wrapping her two long strong arms around herself: and mine too.

Two

The cat's fur is white, unevenly splashed with orange and black. It sits very upright on the hall table, still as a china figure, glossy in the sun. Behind it is a bronze blur, as the leaves in the garden ripple and quiver, turning over and over at the end of their thin stems, so that the entire mass of leaf is in a state of dance and of constantly changing shades of brown as the sun tears in and out of clouds. Behind the cat is a yellow blur, too, dahlias and marigolds against the olive privet hedge. Helen has left the hall door propped open, so that the cat sitting grave and unblinking on the wooden table the colour of buttermilk, the little balcony where the table has been set, and the brown and yellow blur behind, are all presented with the formal arranged air of a still-life to confront anyone entering the long narrow hall by the street door at the other end.

The two women come blinking into the coolness and the quiet from the warmth and bustle of the street between the bus stop and the house. Helen pulls the heavy front door to behind her and leans against it to click it shut, shifting Beth's bulky carryall from one hand to the other. Beth, already halfway up the hall, turns round at the crash of the massive latch, and is brought face to face with the hanging stretched on the wall opposite. It is of silk, the ground the colour of mushrooms and oysters crossed with bands woven in faded yellow and rose and sky. As Beth puts down her rucksack and lightly strokes the cool smooth silk with her palm the cat stands up, stretches, blinks, and with a flick of its tail is gone, leaping with casual grace from the balcony balustrade down to the garden below.

– It's beautiful, Beth exclaims: where did you get it?

– From Thailand, years ago.

– Did you buy it? Beth persists: I've never seen it before. Where have you been hiding it all these years?

– Steven gave it to me, Helen says: when we were together out there. But I've never lived anywhere in London with the space to hang it. Not till I came here.

Beth looks at her. Helen's face, pegged by her pointed ears, is as taut and shiny as the oyster-coloured silk, two spots of pink flaring on her thin cheeks and her eyes gleaming a fierce pale green like knobs tied in a weaving. Beth can see her, pinned out flat, two-dimensional and no creases, taking up just the minimum of space and no more.

– You're terribly thin, she exclaims: I've only just noticed.

– Don't nag, Helen says: I know I've lost a bit of weight. Don't go on about it.

Beth moves away from the hanging and picks up her rucksack.

– All right. I won't. Tell me where to put this.

– Oh, leave it there for the moment. Come and have some coffee.

– Show me the flat first, and then I will sit down. I'm shattered, I don't know why, just from sitting on a train.

The upper flats in the house are reached by a door and a closed-off staircase at the end of the hall next to the door leading out on to the balcony. Helen turns to a door on the left, near the front door, and opens it. The bedsitting-room is large, with graceful proportions, double doors on one side, and, on the other, a wide window reaching almost to the ground, its shutters, half-pulled, dimming the brightness of the street. The sun seeps in, one long golden splinter fallen on the floor. The mouldings of the ceiling, though blurred by layers of white paint, are intact, and the floor is of pink and grey marble scattered with shabby rugs.

– This used to be the ballroom of the house, I think, Helen explains: though it's unusual for it to be on the ground floor. Somebody's whim. The kitchen's through there, a sort of ante-chamber, and the bathroom's through that, in what must have been the conservatory. It's a funny sort of conversion, but I rather like it.

Beth crosses the room and throws open the big wooden doors. At the back of the kitchen is a wall of frosted glass and another door. Helen has hung plants everywhere, from the ceiling and from a plank suspended along the glass wall, so that it rains tradescantia and geraniums.

– I like all the plants, Beth says, touching a geranium leaf and releasing its lemony harshness.

– It saved me putting up curtains. Felix didn't have any. He didn't believe in furnishings. As soon as a room was full, he sold everything in it.

Balinese carpets. Mexican hangings. Chinese bamboo chairs. The rooms have sported them all, over the years. Felix, the travelling dealer, is always one step ahead of his customers' tastes, always able to supply whatever fantasy of life abroad is currently fashionable. Himself, he lives and dresses out of a suitcase, a guilty ascetic who never knows what to do with money except make more of it.

Beth peers through the cracks between the tendrils of green tumbling down the misty glass.

– Nice little bathroom too. But is this all there is? Where d'you sleep?

– Back in there, on the sofa. It's one of those that opens out to make a double bed. It's quite comfortable.

Beth sits down on it and bounces up and down experimentally.

– Not bad. Where's that coffee? And let's open the shutters and have a bit more light.

They sit at opposite ends of the sofa, eyeing one another, balancing their cups. Helen drinks hers from the French cup and saucer given to her by George, and Beth drinks hers from a mug in thick white china, patterned with deep blue swirls. The shape and feel of it pleases her, and she curls her hands around it.

– It's been five months not seeing each other this time, she says: tell me how you are. What's been happening? Oh, I know we've written a bit, but that's not the same.

– There's so much to say I don't know where to start.

Suddenly, Helen can feel her heart beating heavily in her throat with swift slams, deep irregular strokes. She gasps involuntarily, puts down her cup, and covers her face with her hands.

– I must have made the coffee too strong. I'll be all right in a minute.

She feels acutely embarrassed, as though she has stripped in front of a stranger. Beth, her oldest friend, now living in a northern city, is a stranger these days. Helen can feel a wave of crimson covering her face, and when she brings down her hands and unclenches them and clenches them in her lap, she sees red blotches springing up on them.

Beth, not a demonstrative person, hesitates, then takes her friend's hand and gently forces the fingers to uncurl.

– Don't worry. Lie back and relax. It'll pass. Lie back and close your eyes.

Helen is lying on the chintz sofa that has a pattern of birds. She swishes her thick tail from side to side, and she snarls, she rolls over from side to side, grimacing, tearing at beaks and wings and soft feathered breasts with her long sharp teeth. Her hands curve into claws, and her feet, tight little arched paws, velvet arches, beat at soft cushions of down.

She opens her eyes and looks at Beth.

– Sorry, she whispers: how idiotic. You must think I'm mad.

– You're not mad, Beth protests: you're one of the sanest, strongest people I know. If you'd only realise it.

– I haven't felt very strong recently. Not underneath. I keep getting these palpitations, and this rash. Every time I try to do anything.

– Have you been doing any writing?

– I don't dare. The last time I tried to sit down and get going, I came out in this rash. So I stopped. I just sat and stared at the wall.

Rarely, so rarely, spending time alone with her mother. Busy busy busy. There is little time. Helen remembers one occasion when she was seven, a memory laid carefully away, treasured in her mind's box. The whole family together, on a camping holiday in France. Running out of money sooner than expected, Catherine and Bill decide not to stop for sleep but to drive all night to catch the ferry home from Le Havre.

Midnight, somewhere in the middle of France. Bill hands over the driving to Catherine and settles himself to sleep in the back of the car with Felix on one side of him, his breathing coming first in gusts and then in silence as he falls into unconsciousness with his son huddled against him. Helen sits at front, wide awake, excited by the treat of the drive at night along the dark narrow roads irregularly sliced by the headlights of oncoming cars and besides and beyond that, nothing but blackness and utter peace. Helen and her mother are the only people awake in the whole of France. She feeds her mother sugar lumps to keep her going, and, at her mother's request, chats to her and tells her stories, almost choking with delight.

– Mmmm, her mother repeats at intervals as she puts her foot down hard on the accelerator and sends the car swinging into the fresh tunnel of gloom ahead: go on.

For five hours they travel on together, their heads illuminated in the green glow from the dashboard fittings.

– We'll pass through Chartres, her mother decides: so that you can see the cathedral.

And Helen does. Her mother is a huntress, Artemis who gives her the grey dawn like a pelt slashed with ribbons of blood; she gives her the vast plain, flower-strewn, before the city; and she gives her the cathedral, rising silently like a great silver snail with shining horns. Catherine pulls up and switches off the engine and they sit in silence and see it together. Her mother is the cathedral stooping over her, its vaults and arches her strong thighs and arms, its rosy windows her eyes and breasts. Helen prays to her inside herself: thank you. Then they turn off the main road and park outside a workmen's cafe, and the others in the back stumble irritably out of sleep and they all go into the cafe and breakfast on strong coffee and fresh bread.

– Is it about George? Beth prompts: you wrote and told me it wasn't going well.

– George. And just about everything else. My novel being rejected. And having to move again, as soon as Felix comes home. I can't bear the thought of being homeless again. I don't want to have to face it.

She looks at Beth, hardly daring to believe she is allowed to go on, take up this much time.

Another of those precious occasions was a couple of weeks ago. Helen, bolder now, stays up late on a visit to her parents, waiting for her father to go off to bed so that she can see her mother on her own. Mrs Home senses her daughter's need, and stays downstairs in the sitting-room after her husband, yawning, has turned off the television and gone upstairs. She puts down her knitting and gazes at her daughter.

– Your hair, she says with a sigh: what a mess.

Helen squints aside, into the mirror, sees her curls, tight and tangled, almost like dreadlocks. She's never had hair this long. Always, as a child, she was taken to the hairdresser to have it trimmed, with a swooping sideways fringe and short over the ears and at the back.

– D'you remember when I had it so short, years ago, that it was like having a shaved head?

56

– I do, her mother says tartly: thank heaven you've got through that stage. I can't imagine what possessed you to do it. Wearing jeans and boots all the time, you looked just like a boy.

– And when I came back from Thailand and you saw it just after I'd cut it all off, you said to me, I'll always remember, there must be something wrong with your hormones, and then you cast on your needles and knitted me a stripy hat because you said I was bound to catch cold.

Helen laughs, and tries to catch her mother's eye. Mrs Home doesn't care for displays of emotion; she carries on knitting.

– Well, she comments: you've calmed down a bit, that's something.

– I promised Nana I'd grow my hair, Helen says: we made a bargain. She said she'd write down her life story if I grew my hair. She was saying tonight it wasn't long enough yet.

She whoops with laughter.

– Sssh, her mother cautions her: you'll wake her up, and Bill too.

Helen sits quiet and still a moment, watching her mother's bent head, the blonde chignon streaked with grey, the hollows beneath the cheekbones, the deep-set eyes with the curved lids lowered over them. Her mother, nearing sixty, is a beautiful woman.

– Put my hair up for me, Helen suddenly suggests: go on, show me how to put it up like yours.

– You haven't got a hairbrush, her mother says, looking pleased, and a bit flustered: I'll need to give it a good brush first. You have to pull it sleek.

She puts down her knitting, rises, and fetches her handbag, extracting her own hairbrush and a couple of plastic combs. Helen crosses over to the sofa and sits at her mother's feet, resting her shoulders against her mother's knees. Mrs Home starts to brush.

– This may hurt a bit, she says: I'm sorry, I can't help it, it's so tangled I have to pull a bit.

– It's all right, Helen says: it doesn't hurt a bit.

It's hard to get the words out, with the pleasure rising so strongly in her throat. She can't remember her mother touching her as a child, except to kiss her goodnight. Perhaps Helen didn't let her. She ponders this.

– There, Mrs Home says: that's the best I can do. It's silly, really, you'll have to undo it all to go to bed.

She doesn't sound as though she really minds. Helen jumps up and hugs her, flinging her arms around her.

– It's terribly late, Mrs Home says: come on, we must go to bed.

- This is awful, Helen says: I haven't seen you for five months, and here I am talking about myself already.

- Helen, you loony, Beth exclaims: we've got to start somewhere. You rang me up and said you wanted to see me, so I came straight down. You give me your news and then I'll give you mine. We've got a whole week-end together, there's plenty of time. Go on, start with George.

It is raining, the first time that Helen meets George. May, just five short months ago. She is on her way to a Sunday lunch-time party on the other side of London, and is impractically dressed, as is often the case with her because of her unfailing optimism about the weather. No coat, and no umbrella. Walking up the hill to her friends' house from the little railway station she feels her skirt flatten and dampen against her bare legs under the first onslaught of the spring storm, and knows that quite soon the blue dye will begin to run and paint her flesh like woad. She begins to laugh, but at the same time to wonder whether to run the rest of the way or to look about her for a refuge. At this precise moment a battered Renault pulls up beside her.

- Which way is number nineteen? Up the street or down?

- Up. I'm going there too. D'you know Julia?

- Hop in, then, and I'll give you a lift. It's going to pour in a minute.

She peeps sideways at him as the car shoots forward with a roar of gears. Large man, with a creased face and thick curly brown hair combed into a rock and roll lick above his forehead. A tremor suddenly passes over her, her insides churning with sweetness. She drops through space, her mouth opening involuntarily. She puts out her hand to steady herself, and draws a deep breath, just as the car pulls up outside Julia's house.

- Watch it, Julia breathes into her ear two hours later: he's not right for you.

Helen takes no notice. She gets drunk fast on lust, risk and exhilaration. She spins and sparkles for him, showing off, and he likes it and calls for more.

- Don't go yet, he says to her: I'll drive you home.

Helen cannot drive. She sits and watches his confident hands on steering-wheel and gear-lever. When they pause at a traffic light he takes hold of her hand, and continues to hold it, reclaiming it after every change of gear. At the second red traffic light, he bends across and kisses her with great gentleness.

58

In Helen's street, the hush and rush of water is still everywhere, beneath car treads, on the runways of tree-trunks, gurgling along gutters and the kerb. Now, at evening, the trees are as dark and soft as spinach, and flowering creepers glimmer on front fences, grape-blue, golden, pink. The sky is a luminous peacock blue. For the moment, the spring storm has exhausted itself, and the night is still.

– You're just the sort of woman I like, he says happily, braking abruptly outside her flat: so strong and confident.

A warning bell clangs in her head, but she ignores it. She has, after a long period of sexual solitude, been claimed and named by a man. This will heal the wound of the recent trouble with Beth. She falls into his embrace like a suicide jumping off a cliff.

Helen sniffs, and blows her nose.

– Thanks for listening, she immediately begins to apologise: I feel so much better for talking about it.

– Don't thank me. You'd do the same for me. You have done, lots of times.

This is true. Beth is far more confident about asking to be listened to. At least, she was, until five months ago.

Helen yawns, to hide her embarrassment.

– It's lunch-time. Let's have something to eat. Oh God, I was going to clean the kitchen before you arrived. It's in a state of terminal squalor.

– I'll help you tidy it up, if you want, Beth offers: before we eat. Come on, I'll help.

– It's extraordinary, Helen muses, girding herself with an enormous navy-blue apron: not cleaning up before a guest comes. Anarchy. Breakdown of rules governing proper behaviour.

– I'm not a guest like that, Beth says sharply: we lived together once, remember?

Their flat was on the attic floor of a decaying gothic mansion in north Oxford, damp seeping through the walls and the hot water system always breaking down. They ended up using a tin bath on the open landing outside their sloping-ceilinged rooms. Some nights, pink and shiny after steam and soap, they'd sit on the stairs in their nightgowns talking to their landlady as she cracked her second gin bottle of the day. Mrs Aves's bosom curved and rolled just like her yellow pompadour hairdo, heaved like a sentimental sea as she told them tales of her first husband. Oh my dears, she repeated, telling them for the tenth time the story of her wedding day: I flew down the stairs like a bird, like a bird. Helen, sitting on the damp stair-carpet that stank of cats, would turn her head and smile at Beth. Yesterday with you and today and tomorrow: the happiest days of my life. Their friends mocked them: the old married couple. And then one evening Helen found Beth's cap and cream left carelessly on the kitchen shelf, and realised that she had a lover. No words for that particular jealousy.

She catches the springtime late, like a disease. It clutches and over-whelms her, like a fever.

George kisses her goodbye, and then closes his front door, and she wanders down the street towards the bus. It feels like summer, a summer night smelling of fruit and dust, and there are flower-sellers outside King's Cross station offering freesias and violets to the hurrying crowds.

They were much too quick. Shyness. It would have been better to wait, she thinks afterwards.

– That was nice, she says.

– Let me show you my article I was telling you about, he says, and leaps gratefully out of bed and crosses to his desk piled with fat red files.

Half an hour later, she gets off the tube in west London. Felix's flat is in Holland Park. Some of the big houses have their long front windows thrown open, rectangles of gold releasing the hot clatter of jazz around her ears as she passes under the little balconies. The sky is smoky blue, with creases of violet and mauve. The air is cooler now, laying itself along the backs of her hands like chilly satin gloves. A night for dancing, for strolling the streets under bars of neon light, the blocks beyond the houses and the trees glittering. A night for rapture, for warmth between cold sheets, the windows and the curtains open on the fragrant blue dark. The scent of fields drifts inexplicably along the street, blue smells in dusky blue air.

He was so quick, she confesses to Beth: and she wasn't bold enough to teach him how to be slow.

He has his article to be getting on with, and she has a novel to be playing with. They're both writers, aren't they? They've got some-thing in common, their work which they can discuss.

Beth squirts cleaning liquid into a yellow plastic bowl and tops it up with a stream of water from the tap. She opens the kitchen and bathroom windows wide, fumbling through the trails of plants for the dusty window catches, and lets in blue sky flapping like a teacloth, sunshine, cold air. There's the strong smell of the soapy water in her bowl, and, from one of the flats above, the smell of beans cooking.

– Those beans we used to get given for college lunch, she says inconsequentially: butter beans, dry and thick, with skins flaking off like paper and sticking in your throat. I've never been able to eat them since. Don't you dare tell me we're having them for lunch.

– Don't worry. One of the pleasures of living on my own is only eating my favourite things. When I remember to eat, that is. We're having prawns.

– You remembered I like them too, Beth says: you've got a good memory.

Some of the things I remember, Helen thinks: are not so pleasant. But there's plenty of time. Take it gently.

That's what Nana, her grandmother, says. One step at a time, duck. No good running before you can walk.

– I tell you, George says: I never want to have a child.

– For someone that determined not to be a father, Helen snaps: you don't seem too bothered about contraception. You've never once mentioned it.

– But, he asks anxiously: you use something, don't you?

– That's not the point, she says angrily: it's your responsibility as much as mine. You just take it for granted I'll use something.

– You've got a coil in, he says: I know.

– How do you know? she asks in surprise.

– I could feel it.

– What does it feel like?

– An obstruction.

Why has she got the damn thing in anyway? So that a man won't have to bother thinking about the consequences of sleeping with her. It's for his convenience, not hers. It makes her feel invaded, physically and emotionally. Perhaps she'll have it taken out. Then George would have to start thinking about a method that would suit them both. She looks hopefully at him, opening her mouth to speak, but his attention has wandered back to the television news.

Helen turns on the radio, then rolls up her sleeves, shivering slightly, but pleasurably, at the chill running over her forearms, and seizes a sponge. She begins to clean the tiles around the sink and the taps, watching with satisfaction as the dirt on them dissolves and they begin

61

to glitter. She's suddenly very happy, being with her friend and being helped to clean her kitchen. On the radio a Spanish seventeenth-century mass is being sung, five voices exquisitely embroidering the air, loops and cascades of silver notes. She remembers the nuns at school telling her: to work is to pray. Sister Immaculata in her blue gardening apron sitting at Mother Superior's feet, her face upturned and rapturous like a child's. She looks at Beth, who is now sweeping the floor with great energy.

– Thirteen years of knowing you, she says, and then, in surprise: look, my rash is gone.

She remembers George stating: I hate housework. I despise it. She marvels at him, she skates across the kitchen with a sponge for dancing partner, she sings along with the mass wanting to bellow like the golden-throated trumpet, she sniffs ammonia and sneezes, and the sun falls cleanly on the window-sill.

There are some things George and Helen cannot talk about, that she cannot and will not say, for fear of being thought heavy and difficult, for fear of having to face the truth.

They are both drifting off to sleep. Helen moves, and reaches out an arm to switch off the bedside lamp. George jolts upright out of her arms.

– I'll just finish that cigarette, he says crossly.

She lies beside him, troubled.

– You always have clean sheets, don't you? he comments.

– Yes, she says: I like the feel of them, cool, rather sensual, that's why I change them so often.

– Hmmm, he says.

– And, she adds: I always want to make a nice bed for you to come to.

She still desires him. He falls asleep in her arms after she has coaxed him to make love and he has come. He cries out and clutches her and then lies down in her arms, puts his head on her breast and falls asleep. She holds him lightly, not wanting to wake him with too fierce an embrace. His thick, curly brown hair brushes her nose and cheek and smells of sweat, faintly sour.

In the morning she accidentally sets alight a frying pan full of fat while intending to make a cup of tea for them both. The match also burns her fingers.

She wants to melt him down, like fat, in the frying pan. Render him free and runny, smoking and hot. He lies heavily on the unmade sofa bed, raising a joint to his lips.

She is unable to tell him what she wants. He goes on writing his articles and reading them to her, he goes on coming quickly and falling asleep, and she goes on pretending, playing the perfect mother.

Soon she will be a fully-fledged practising arsonist.

Beth and Helen sit at the kitchen table, eating their lunch. The table is made of wood, roughly stripped, and now scrubbed. At one end of it is a row of earthenware flowerpots containing begonias, the red and pink flowers blooming small and numerous amongst the rounded pinky-green leaves. On the table are thick slices of porous yellow bread, coarsely textured like the wooden table-top which serves as platter. They eat avocados filled with George's gift of strong green olive oil, and mop up the extra oil with the bread. This is a feast in itself, but there is more: the prawns. Helen piles a blue plate high with them, and dumps it in front of Beth.

– There's mayonnaise too. Here.

Beth dips a piece of bread into the mayonnaise and tastes it.

– Home-made. You are amazing. I wouldn't bother.

Her voice is slightly contemptuous. Helen winces, and begins to shell her helping of prawns. She grasps their whiskery scarlet legs, she crushes their pink carapaces between her fingernails, she smears their squishy bundles of orange eggs under her thumb.

– Oh God, she says, laughing, and tearing the head and legs off a prawn with fine sadistic fervour: this prawn's name is *George*. Oh how awful.

The prawn revealed, stripped of its armour, curls small and defenceless on the blue china plate. She pushes at it with her forefinger.

– Poor George.

Then she pops it into her mouth and chews it. It tastes of rubber and freshness and salt.

She has been waiting for him all afternoon. He turns up in the early evening, when she has given up all hope of his arrival and is typing furiously. He stands in front of her, filling up the doorway, a cowboy today, in tight scarlet jeans, broad leather belt and denim waistcoat. She starts teasing him and getting bearhugs in response.

– Oh, if you're not going away with your women's group till Sunday morning, he protests: we can go out tomorrow, not tonight. I needn't have come over, I could be doing some work instead.

– Why can't we go out tonight? she cries: I know you, you'll ring me up tomorrow and say you haven't finished working.

– Well, he temporises: we could go and have a quick drink, anyway.

They walk down the street to the pub, their bodies brushing. Hers tingles all over at each chance contact. It's light still, and seven o'clock, and the market has packed up leaving cabbages in the gutter, and she's with George. She wants to kiss him, but he's talking seriously about the television news.

When she comes back from her week-end away, he chatters anxiously, and, when they are in bed, will not let her touch him. Deliberately obtuse, she caresses him a couple of times, and each time he catches hold of her hand and restrains her. She understands at last, and lies unwillingly still.

– There's something you ought to know, he starts bravely: before we make love.

– What?

– I slept with Anna on Sunday night.

She leaps out of bed and goes over to the record player, and crouches over it, her back to him so that he can't see her face.

– You could have warned me, she bursts, her shaking hands busying themselves with turning over the record: you let me get all involved with you without letting me know you still slept with Anna and then you just spring it on me.

– I didn't know I was going to do it, he says, exasperated: it just happened, it was spontaneous.

She holds the record in both hands, in an effort to still them.

– Why did you choose to do it the first time I spend a week-end away? Were you jealous about me going away with my group?

– Of course not. You're the one who's jealous, not me.

– I am jealous of you and Anna, she says, full of pain: because I see so little of you anyway. She sees more of you than I do. Only I didn't know you still slept with her as well.

– She doesn't make such a performance about everything, George mutters: and she doesn't particularly want me all the time, like you do. Half the time she pushes me away.

– And that makes you feel safe, Helen says: I frighten you because I want you.

– You want me too much, George says: you're always wanting to talk or make love. I feel exhausted.

He rolls over in bed and faces the wall.

64

– You're so intense. You're always going on about feminism, for example.

– I thought you were so keen on strong women. Anna isn't a feminist, I suppose?

– She's different. She's a feminist, but she needs me. She needs me to help her. You don't. You go off with your women friends and your women's groups all the time.

She puts down the record and crosses the room and gets back into bed, lying quietly beside him. He turns over and casts himself into her arms.

– I can't make love, he whispers: you're too much for me.

– Let's go to the market, Beth says as they drink their coffee: I haven't been for ages.

– Good idea. Then I can do the vegetable shopping at the same time.

– You've changed, Beth remarks: you used to be a fanatic for having everything organised. D'you remember how you used to leap up in the middle of supper to do the washing-up?

– Till you stopped me.

Helen flicks her finger against her pretty French coffee cup, remembering the evenings in the Oxford flat. She and Beth fighting about how to make salad, whether to dress it with vinaigrette or blue cheese, whether to add tomatoes or keep it classically green. Sometimes they had to have two salads, the fight was so intense. Omelettes caused further battles, Helen favouring them pure and plain and Beth wanting to whip up the whites and add them in for a souffle effect. Their friends lounging in chairs and laughing at them.

– Not husband and wife, Beth quotes telepathically: just wives.

After supper, they would smoke dope, argue about politics, listen to rock music, invent games. Then there would be early morning outings, at three or four am, down to the end of the street where Jericho began and where the baker was just bringing out his first batch of bread. They would tap on the rotting blue wood of the window frame, leaning their bicycles against the Victorian blue and white tiles of the shop front, and the baker would hand them lardy cake through the window. Two and sixpence it cost, and it was heaven to eat, hot and stodgy under its sugary spicy crust.

– What shall we buy for supper? Helen asks: what would you like?

– I don't care, Beth says indifferently: anything. As long as I don't have to cook. It bores me stiff, nowadays.

65

Helen picks up a fat black grape and bites hard into it, feeling the juice squirt down her chin.

– How's Peter? she asks.

– Oh, Beth says, spreading her hands and almost dropping her cigarette: the same. Though he's started complaining I don't spend enough time with him.

She frowns, stubbing out her cigarette.

– He sticks to me like a burr. He makes me feel so guilty at not seeing more of him that I want to turn nasty. But however rude I am to him, he comes back for more.

– It's easy for you to criticise men, Helen says: when you've got one as tame as that.

Beth bursts out laughing.

– It's not the only thing in life, you know, being with a man. It's supposed to solve everything, but it doesn't. That's when your problems *start*. You don't need to be envious of me, really you don't.

Helen chews grape pips, pondering.

– I still dream, she fumbles: of the perfect lover. You know, the gentle, strong man who's a companion. Like a brother.

She stops suddenly, swallowing the pips. Bitter, they slide down. She has seen so little of Felix over the last five years. He's always leaving for some distant place, always living, stripped right down, in readiness for emergencies. She never meets his girlfriends. He keeps them separate from her, treasures in a crate to be taken out occasionally and fondled and then put back. Splitting up with a woman is the signal for his moving on, the emergency that sends him off to collect more rare and beautiful things. At the moment, she can't even remember his face. She knows that it's like hers, but that's all.

– How *is* Felix? Beth asks: you haven't mentioned him yet.

– Oh, he's fine, I think, Helen says, quoting his last postcard: he's moving around a lot, so it's hard for me to write to him. He's in Peru at the moment, buying handicrafts. He'll be back in a few months, I think.

She watches Beth's face register contempt. Then she leans over to pick up the coffee pot and pour herself another cup. She watches the sputtering liquid, the brown dregs. She sips her coffee, drinking down guilt. I shouldn't be living here, she thinks: I'm colluding in the way he makes a living. Living off the fact he wheels and deals and makes profits out of other people.

Even at school, Felix is a master of the art of swapping. Marbles, model cars, packets of sweets all blossom and multiply between his

66

hands and those of other children, and are briefly stashed in his bedroom at home. He loses interest as soon as he accumulates a certain amount of anything, needs to move on and prove himself with something more difficult. The point is always to persuade someone else to part with some prized possession. Once it belongs to Felix, he no longer cares for it. Lectures on ethics by his desperate mother have little effect. Well, Bill Home tries to console her: he'll make a good business man. Felix is deeply hurt by his mother's attitude. At first he lays his spoils at her feet. Then, after several rejections, he takes them elsewhere. At first, to Helen. They sit in their den, the cupboard under the stairs, and he plies her with gifts which dazzle her. For a brief time, she is his slave, awed, ready to do whatever he wants. Then, as he begins to need a wider audience that will be more difficult to impress, he begins buying his way into the boys' gang in the street. Helen sits behind the net curtains in the sitting-room, watching him.

– Anyway, Helen says hurriedly to Beth: I haven't had your news yet. How's the carpentry course? And the CP?

Beth lights a fresh cigarette, pushes her chair back a little, and brings her knees up against the table edge.

– You sound *so* polite. Why don't you say what you mean?

Her voice is sharp, but her eyes are teasing: come on, Helen, my old sparring companion, my old opponent for philosophical football, come on out into the open and challenge me like you used to do.

– You *know*, Helen says: I didn't think you should join the Party. You know I felt you should stick with the women's movement and be a socialist inside it. You know all that.

– You felt really betrayed, didn't you? Why didn't you say? Why did you lie?

– It wasn't a lie as such, Helen says, gripping the edge of the table with both hands: I couldn't face you with how I felt straight away, that's all. And anyway, you wouldn't let me talk to you.

– You keep things back, Beth protests: you keep people at a distance by not telling them things they ought to know. Look at George, the way you didn't tell him things. You said so yourself, before lunch, you lied to him. Not telling your friends how you really feel, that's dishonest.

Beth's words grip Helen by the shoulders and shake her, punch her in the belly. Taken aback, she stutters, wants to weep. It's like being a child in the school playground again: you beast, you hurt me, I'll tell on you. But there's no one to tell, no one except her oldest friend sitting opposite, suddenly grown implacable. Helen wants a cigarette to ward off this blow, but she's given up smoking. She digs her hands into her pockets and looks fiercely down at the heap of massacred prawns on her plate, willing herself not to cry.

– Sometimes, she defends herself: you just can't speak. I do feel now that I can discuss it with you, but I couldn't have before. I was too angry with you, so I couldn't write to you. I was too afraid.

– Of what?

– Of losing you. I hated you for five months, and I couldn't bear it. So eventually I asked you to come down. Anything's better than feeling hate like that.

How weak she is, she thinks, stunned. Love at any price, is that it? What kind of love is that?

George rings Helen up out of duty now, full of guilt. She is angry with him because he doesn't love her. He doesn't want her to love him, and even though she recognises this, she can't let go.

– We could go to the fair on Hampstead Heath, he says heavily down the telephone.

Her clammy hand sticks in the sun to his black leather jacket. They go on the big dipper, shooting round at breakneck speed and hurtling up and down. She enjoys shrieking with fear, her cries drowned by raucous fairground music, while her pink and purple skirt flies over her head.

– I've always wanted an airgun, he says, taking potshots at castles of crinkled Coca-Cola tins piled up in front of pink canvas: I could sit out the back of the house and shoot at dandelions.

– What d'you want to shoot flowers for? she asks.

But she's good on the space invader machines in the makeshift arcade, concentrating intently on firing her rockets: wham!

– I've always wanted a box kite, he says, as they walk away from the fairground and up to the hill where the kites are flying. There is one particularly splendid one, swooping and darting, silver fins hissing, made of pink and purple metallic paper stretched over ply-wood. There is one like a blue moth, with white spots. The sunlight is hot and clear, the far hills and the London skyline glistening and glittering, seeming so near and distinct that you could scoop them into the palm of your hand.

She glitters too, in her new clothes. He says nothing about her being all dressed up, except to remark, when they get off the big dipper, when her skirt has flown over her head exposing her tights to the populace, that she isn't really dressed for the fair. She swishes her long pink and gold spangled scarf angrily as they walk past the fortune teller's booth.

She and Beth visit the gypsy on the pier during a summer week-end away in Whitby. It's a cold, foggy morning in July, which they welcome with eggs and bacon and strong tea, before going down to the pier to have their fortunes told. The gypsy is eating her own breakfast when they arrive, a plateful of eggs and chips which she hastily shoves under an embroidered cushion. Her little concrete tent is hung with bright blankets. She is middle-aged, with shrewd little eyes, and she speaks very fast all in rhyming couplets. She sells Helen an expensive gold charm shaped like a boot, and then clutches her hand and peers at it.

– You're an egotistical young woman, she cackles: not to be married yet.

Above the concrete roof the gulls swoop and cry, and the thick grey fog closes in over the tea-shops and the souvenir stalls. Helen and Beth lie in bed that night, laughing about it, in the vast bed-and-breakfast double bed crammed between a mahogany wardrobe and the window draped in grey veiling like the fog outside.

I'm a hopeless egotist, she thinks sadly, looking at George: a baby. I want him to tell me I'm beautiful and good and don't frighten him. I want him to compliment me on my outfit bought specially for this outing with him, I want him to read my books and enjoy them and discuss them with me, I want him to desire me.

George looks back at her.

– I don't think, he remarks: that you're really dressed for the fairground.

She is a pink and purple kite flying high up and free. He reels her back in, and she's not at all grateful.

The two women finish the washing-up and then head out into the street. It may be September, but it feels as warm as summer ever was. A muggy heat has descended on the city, the sun close and moist behind clouds and then breaking out, a furry gold disc. The market in Portobello Road is crowded with tourists, local inhabitants shopping for the week-end, hippies left over from 1968, punks, Rastafarians, politicos selling newspapers, people of all sorts happily on the strut, all mixed up together. Cars rev and hoot, blocked in their progress by the crowds, who consider the street today their right of way, and stall-holders, made irritable by hard work in the heat, swear loud and fluent as they hurl carrots, onions and potatoes onto their brass and enamel scales.

Everywhere, people have let themselves slow down and simply sit and watch the day flow by. In one side alley just off the main market, an entire family has placed orange boxes on the cobbles and plonked itself down for the spectacle and the sun, feet planted among cabbage leaves and heads veiled in the damp washing strung between aged tenements. The street has a strong smell: of beer, wallflowers, coriander, refuse, coffee, talcum-powder, sweat. Helen and Beth float, carried along like the rest of the crowd between stalls selling silver, carpets, socks and medicines, turning their faces to sniff carnations and pinks on one side and kebabs and hot fat on the other, hair oil and incense, rubber and bread. Helen remembers the sweaty, fragrant markets she visited in Thailand years ago, and slackens her pace for a moment, remembering also a certain hotel room in Bangkok, the silent rage that hung quivering and heavy between her and Beth. This time, the cause, the dividing factor, is not a man. She's wordless again. Beth slows down too, catching her thoughts, and they turn their heads towards one another, sharing a grimace of irony.

Encouraged, Helen seizes Beth's hand.

– Just in case I lose you again, she explains: come on.

Touch will work magic, heal the political split. She hasn't held hands with Beth in the street for a long time. She beams at everyone that they pass, feeling energy flow up and down their arms and exchange in their palms.

– We'll sort it out, she begins to tell Beth, but Beth doesn't hear her, halting so abruptly that Helen bumps into her and gets her foot trodden on. Beth doesn't notice her yelp of pain and annoyance. She drops Helen's hand and gazes at a stall displaying a velvet-covered tray of earrings.

– Mmmm, she murmurs: these are nice.

The man behind the stall is charming and attentive. Smiling, easy, with not a care in the world. His long, hennaed hair curls about his ears and displays his own earrings, gold stems loaded with brilliant glass and china beads. He has a tiny hoop stuck through one nostril, and he fingers it as he watches Beth plunge her hands into the tray of jewellery and rummage happily. Helen stands awkwardly behind her, buffeted by the people surging past.

– I wonder, Beth says at last.

The vendor cocks his head on one side and watches with bright eyes, his hands on his hips. Beth flirts with him, exchanging roguish glances, showing him the earrings she has selected. They are very pretty, Helen has to admit that: deep blue glass flowers encircled by tiny green glass leaves, strung on to gold stalks ending in blue and gold beads. Beth dances around to face Helen.

– What d'you think? D'you like them?

– Very nice, Helen mumbles.

– I was going to buy them for you, Beth says, looking disappointed: you wear clip-on ones sometimes, don't you? I wanted to buy you a present.

– But I haven't got pierced ears, Helen says, shocked.

– Simple. Let's go and get them pierced.

– *You* haven't got pierced ears, Helen says: I suppose Communists think it too frivolous.

Beth's eyes snap.

– They'd suit you, but not me. All right?

Typical Beth, always knowing, clearly and without hesitation, what is best for her friend, praising her looks, admonishing her for lapses into self-hate. Helen doesn't want these qualities to be lavished exclusively on the members of Leeds CP.

– All right, she says: yes please.

They go together, Helen clutching her present, to the shop down the street from the market which is a jeweller, hairdresser and beauty salon all in one. Three cramped rooms lead off one from another, partitioned by hardboard. The beauty parlour is right at the back, and has a pink carpet, a sparkling chandelier, pink-lined walls, and a couch spread with a pink paper sheet. Helen tiptoes across the deep pink pile of the carpet, feeling suddenly large, grubby and clumsy, as though she might break or stain something merely with her presence. She perches on a flimsy gilt chair and flicks through a pile of leaflets advertising beauty aids: magic spells for getting rid of blackheads, flab, cellulite, wrinkles, old age and death.

– There's nothing here, she teases Beth: about how to deal with emotional scars. Face-lifts, yes. Moral uplift, no.

Beth sits down, facing her, on a pink plastic pouffe.

– I didn't join the Party, she explains patiently: to make myself feel better. It's about a commitment to other people, not just about me.

Helen frowns.

– You're fooling yourself somewhere. Why not start with yourself? Or at least try to connect the two?

– I've done all that. It's time to move on.

– Do you or don't you, the beautician demands: want your ears pierced?

They've forgotten the other woman standing there, assembling her equipment.

– Just tell me it won't hurt, Helen says nervously, getting up.

A flicker which might be a smile passes over the beautician's face, but she says nothing. She seats Helen on the couch, facing her and the mirror on the wall, then dabs at Helen's earlobes with surgical spirit and cottonwool. Next, she marks a blue dot with a felt-tip pen on each of Helen's ear lobes. Finally, she produces from the pocket of her pink intern's overall a sort of staple gun which she loads with something looking like cartridges.

– All right? she asks.

Helen looks into the mirror. She sees her own face, familiar and yet sharpened up, focused, by her expression of eagerness and anxiety. In a moment she will be utterly changed. She will have holes in her ears. She will have acted upon her own body, and altered it.

– All right, she says.

The pain is bearable, lasting only a second. Helen looks at herself in the mirror again. Same green eyes, same curly hair, same broad nose. But in one ear she has a gold stud, and in the other a diamante one. She begins to smile, and then to laugh, and jumps off the couch to parade for Beth, who smiles back at her and then begins to laugh at Helen's smug expression.

– It'll be tattoos next, she prophesies.

– I've never been asked to put in odd studs before, says the beautician, putting her gun away in her box: that *is* odd, if you ask me. Ten pounds, please.

Helen gulps, sobering up. That's a fifth of her weekly earnings.

– Let me pay, Beth says quickly: I earn far more than you do. It's part of your present.

– Thank you, thank you, Helen repeats: I'm so pleased, I can't tell you.

It is as though she were a member of a tribe living in a deep green forest, not at all like the environs of the Portobello Road. Just before her twelfth birthday, she is taken away into a clearing deep in the secret heart of the forest, along paths known only to the senior women of the tribe. They guide her steps. Strange birds and insects she has never seen before start up and whirr across her face, animals whose roar she does not recognise prowl deep in the bush.

Up until now a child, she has gone smooth and naked. But the time has come for her to be initiated into the mysteries, the hour has arrived for her body to be painted, her hips to be fringed with sweet-smelling waxy flowers, her head to be crowned with a garland of green leaves, and her ear lobes to be pierced and then laden with rings of coral, bone and shell. And at night, around the sacred fire, she dances for the first time in public, in the company of women, her ritual dance.

She walks down the street as proud as a queen, holding her head high, her hair tucked well behind her ears so that her new studs show, balancing her head delicately on her neck, her head with its two new weights, its decoration. She hears the rev of car engines, she looks at adverts for vodka and hair-spray, she wants to babble of red parrots screaming in a green shade. And all the time she buys ice-cream and chatters to Beth and laughs with her as they try on old clothes at the stalls, she catches glimpses, out of the corner of her eye, of decorated female bodies that flash like fish in blue and green pools, that float like birds under blue and green suns, and is rendered speechless.

– Let's go for a swim, Helen proposes over their candlelit dinner in a Greek cafe: up on the Heath. It's been so warm this week, the ponds won't be too cold.

They are naked except for the earrings. They have climbed over the wooden palisade surrounding the women's pond, because that is the most beautiful of the three, and the most secluded. No men are ever allowed in, just as no women are allowed into the men's pond. The mixed pond, they decide tacitly, does not fit their mood.

The moon glimmers on their pale bodies. This is a silvery place, the moon floating in the night sky reflected in the flat steely surface of the pond beneath it, and all the tree tops silver-tipped. They look curiously at one another like children do, comparing, wondering whether their bodies have changed since they last took their clothes off in front of one another. Helen is taller than Beth, lean, with broader shoulders, wider hips, longer feet. Beth has a smaller waist, sturdier arms and legs. Her hair is luxuriant and red, curling around the base of her stomach and across her calves, while Helen's is dark blonde. Beth scratches her armpits, and shivers as the wind ruffles the weeds.

A duck squawks. Their bare feet shift on white and silver gravel. They are standing by the edge of the pond, a dark stretch of water overlaid with silver, encircled by a dense growth of reeds, with trees and bushes coming right down to its edge at one end, and with a small diving-board set on a platform at the other. The grass slopes back as lawn a little way, and then there is a further thick belt of trees. At their feet, in the daytime, would be the scarlet silk rags of flowers. At night, despite the moonlight shining on the pool in the clearing, you cannot see in very far under the trees or decipher what the flowers might be. Trees and shrubs are just dark shapes, watching.

They lower themselves gingerly into the water from the little wooden platform where the diving board stands. Once in, the water strikes so sharp and cold that they utter muffled shrieks and have to swim frantically to warm their shocked limbs. They gasp, and laugh, and beat at the icy water with legs and arms.

As the rapid movement brings life and warmth back to her body, Helen lets herself slow down. She turns over and floats on her back, feeling the water creep through her hair spread out on its surface, her curls long enough to float like flowers. She can see her bush of hair sticking out above the water, like an island covered with forests. Below her is darkness and above her darkness too, as the moon skates behind a cloud and leaves no dividing line between dark and dark. Pool and sky and encircling reeds are one, a whole dark world in which she is free to float, swim, fly.

– Where are you? she calls softly to Beth: where are you?

Beth surfaces beside her, shaking her head in a whirl of drops, spluttering. They embrace each other, holding each other lightly, both treading water, bumping knees and chins, laughing, their breasts bobbing against one another. They duck their heads and kiss each other with wet mouths. Two minutes with their shoulders out of water and they are shuddering with cold.

– Oh, Helen gasps, releasing Beth: I'm going to have to go in.

They jump up and down on the diving platform to warm themselves before sawing briskly at their bodies with their shirts.

– Brrr, Beth whistles: that was good.

She shakes herself like a dog so that water flies in all directions.

– Beth, Helen cries: get off, you're soaking me.

Beth lumbers at her and catches her in wet arms and Helen screeches with laughter and pummels her with her fists. Both of them stop dead still and stiffen as twigs crack loudly behind them back in the trees.

– There's someone there, Helen whispers: watching us.

Do you remember the crazy man? How he was always waiting for you, like your own best friend? Ready to claim you, like a lover? The world is a dangerous place for girls alone. Better stay home.

– Let's go and see who it is, Beth says firmly, dropping her arm and releasing Helen.

They pad in the direction of the cracking twigs, going as quietly as possible over the crunching gravel that hurts the soles of their bare feet. Behind a tall laurel bush they find the man. He sits back on his knees as they burst into view and looks at them in alarm. His face is so pale, his body so puny, that Beth, in relief, begins to laugh derisively. She capers about in front of him, gibbering, scrabbling her hands in her armpits and rolling her eyes. Her shirt drops to the ground. Helen begins to laugh too, at this point, and the man to cower.

– You beasts, he whimpers: leave me alone.

He hunches forward and upwards, so that he is standing, stooped, in front of them, his eyes darting from side to side, calculating the best route of escape. Then he uncoils his body, dashes in between the two women and trots away up the path. He reminds Helen of a rabbit, terrorised, at bay, his silvery mac bobbing up and down like a white scut.

They scramble into their clothes again, which feel warm and glowing after the chilly water and the night air, rough after the silky water and the slimy reeds.

– I'm not enjoying this any more, Helen shivers: I want to go home. There might be another prowler in there.

Once they listen, they realise that the surrounding undergrowth is full of noises. All kinds of men in there for all kinds of purposes, some summoning each other for rendezvous, others waiting to nab foolish solitary passing girls. Doubtless plainclothes police too, hunting, picking them all up.

– I know what you mean, Beth agrees: let's go. Let's try and find a taxi and go home. I'm freezing, too, suddenly. I don't know why. It's a really warm night.

She gets up, and does a little dance to stop herself shivering. Helen comes across to her and starts to rub her back, and Beth stops dancing and stands still, feeling the energetic strokes spread warmth between her shoulder blades.

– Better? Helen asks: let's go, then. I'm scared.

The moon sails out from behind the clouds again, large and cold and pure. After the heat earlier in the day, the air is still humid. Beth and Helen are breathless, as though steaming towels have been pressed over their noses and mouths. Under the trees the air is fresher, and damp, smelling of earth and leaves. They walk through the moist blue woods where the moonlight spreads itself like the thinnest of veils and the shadows thicken at either side of the sandy path.

    — With a full moon, Helen is explaining: you mustn't look at it for the first time through glass. It's supposed to be unlucky.

    — Superstitious rubbish, Beth says.

    — And, Helen continues unperturbed: you must turn over silver in your pocket while you say your greeting.

    Beth grunts, but obediently rummages in her pocket for change.

    — Now what?

    — Now we have to curtsey, and say: I bow to thee, o lady moon, I expect a present before the month is out.

    — Huh, Beth scoffs: fat chance.

    But she repeats the invocation nonetheless. Then her eyes sparkle, and she turns to Helen.

    — You were telling me about the moon goddess this afternoon, about the way the moon's connected with the menstrual cycle, right? Well, the present that women ask for from the full moon must be their period. It's a prayer asking not to be pregnant. I bet you that's what it is.

    She's very pleased with herself, and later, when they clamber into the sofa-bed together she lays her head shyly on her friend's shoulder. It's an unusual action for Beth, and Helen does not turn her away.

Three

    — I'll go and buy some wine to have with supper, Helen says on the following evening: I shan't be long.

    A slut is a woman who goes out with her slippers on. Helen doesn't realise she's done it until she's well away from the flat and idling along towards the shops and the hard metalled surface of the road strikes up through her thin soles. She giggles nervously as she realises she is also stockingless and braless and is wearing a loose frock that is a cross between an overall and a nightdress. Her solecism, as she understands it, is to have brought the feminine boudoir, the mateyness of the harem, into the public domain, where it does not belong. Demi-toilette and no particular need to please. Being sloppy, the nuns at school called it: all this lying about on beds in the daytime. Such a pleasure, she wants to explain to passers-by: do you recognise it too?

To forget to wash my face sometimes, to forget all about my appearance. Because my friend is here.

On their first summer holiday hitchhiking together, when they are still students, Helen and Beth stop off in Paris on their way down to the South. The city of light swims, golden and tranquil, around them, making them drunk, and too happy to talk. They go to the North African mosque and buy tickets for the women's hammam that afternoon. Waiting for their number to be called, they drink peppermint tea in the cafe, drinking in also the carved wooden screens, the hexagonal tables inlaid with mother-of-pearl, the stained-glass windows, the fretted pattern that sun and shadows make shifting over the dark, massive walls.

Inside, the first room of the hammam is alive with the chatter of women relaxing after their steam bath on mattresses laid side by side around the walls, with the splash and tinkle of the fountain set, among green plants, in the centre of the marble floor. They strip, hang their clothes on wooden hooks high up on the blue and yellow walls, and pad through an archway into an antechamber where women lie on wooden planks being lathered, massaged and scraped. Through another archway, they pass into a room that is merely warm, where hoses lie coiled on the floor, and then into the hot room.

They stop, and catch their breath, for the steam stuffs itself into their throats like boiling rags. Then, accustomed a little to this new atmosphere, they move forward, very slowly, their bare feet caressing the stone floor. The room is dimmed by steam, which puffs lazily from vents under the tiny windows whose panes seem slices of ivory. Light comes in dull, a diffused amber that melts and runs down their skin. In the centre of the room is a large raised stone platform like a fourposter bed, and around the sides, open alcoves separated by arching pillars of stone curving above more stone beds. They find a space on the central shelf, and lie down, propping themselves on their elbows to look around.

Women everywhere, women of all ages, races and shapes, and every one different, and beautiful. Here, with no critical, classifying, dividing male eye upon their bodies, the women are relaxed, whole, belonging only to themselves. Helen feels pleasure surge up along with sweat and pour from all over her. She succumbs to wetness and heat, her skin a curtain between two hot seas, she lets go of language and thought and becomes all her senses, enriched, newly alive. Nothing to do except lie back and enjoy.

She and Beth massage each other as they see the North African women do, squatting over each other, firmly stroking skin and muscle and fat, finding out what is bony and hard and what soft, rubbing hard with a string glove to scrape off dead skin in limp, dark curls, and then making a body mousse with lathery soap. Water runs from their pores constantly, and streams along their relaxed contours, shaping them to even further gentleness. When they begin to scorch and gasp, they move like sleepwalkers into the next room and do a slow dance under the shower, a music of ice bullets. They spend five hours in the hammam that afternoon, they discover afterwards when they consult their watches, and yet, like a dream, the time passes in a single second that never stops. With a deep contentment inside them, they put on clothes that now seem restrictive and alien, and go back into the street, where the catcalls, whistles and sidling whispers of arrogant men begin again.

On Ladbroke Grove, Sunday evening strollers look at Helen askance, at her bare legs, mosquito-bitten ankles, flapping green canvas mules. Young men look at her loose breasts and whistle, to bring her to heel with their fantasies, and then look at her slippers and know her for a slut, one in whose domination they have little interest. She has joined the ranks of the women tramps simply by putting on her slippers in the house and leaving them on in the street. The slippers are her home, and so, now, by extension, is the street.

The homeless are found frightening and offensive by those who do have homes. They represent litter and mess, the blot on the shining white conscience. They are unable, the male tramps, the female vagabonds, to tidy themselves neatly away into glass, steel, concrete boxes. They will be swept away, if found lurking messily on street corners, by the police, the cleaners of the state. Keep off the streets, the police say sternly to women alone, the unemployed, homeless people, blacks: and you will be safe. Rot inside, and do not dare to possess the city as your own. Otherwise you will be flushed down side streets by hoses, sprayed with gas and rubber bullets as though you are cockroaches, punished by fascists with clubs, by rapists with knives.

Helen sees a policeman eyeing her, sees his Alsatian tugging at the end of its leash, and panics, running into the off-licence and stuttering out her request for a bottle of wine. When Felix comes home, she thinks, walking home to his flat: I shall have nowhere to live. A single woman, with a low income and no savings, throwing myself onto the street. There's a housing crisis. No homes, certainly not if you're single, unless you've got money. Yet I want one, for me.

So she does want a home of her own. She hasn't known that. Or rather, she has known that wish, but has kept pushing it down every time it popped its head above water and bobbed alongside her where she swam a neat breaststroke, back and forth, back and forth. This desire is monstrous. It does not belong in the clean white-tiled swimming-pool where she practises life, training for it earnestly: its home is the jungle, the forests and the deep lakes, where it can lash its huge scaly tail and create tidal waves. It wants Helen to join it there; it beckons to her, murmuring seductively about true independence and freedom, about hot sun and tearing through grass. In her dreams, the monster is benign, more of a child. It lives in a deep cave in the mountains, by a waterfall fringed with luxuriant green, and is covered in hair from head to toe, except where its little breasts and knobbly knees stick out of its fur. It waves to her, and then leaps up and down, a large sandwich clasped in one paw. She runs away from the monster, up the steps of her brother's home, and slams the front door in its face.

– But I've got nothing to wear for a party, Beth wails over supper: you didn't warn me we'd be going out anywhere special. I look so scruffy.

Helen contemplates her friend's long red curls and brilliant blue eyes, her little pointed chin, and can't help smiling.

– Rose only rang me yesterday, she defends herself: just before you were due to arrive, and anyway, you look beautiful whatever you wear.

Beth snorts.

– That's not the point. You and your glamorous friends all dressed up in trendy clothes. I shall look like some despised provincial. Which is what I am.

She pushes her plate away, lights a cigarette, and glares at Helen.

– I know, Helen exclaims: those dresses you gave me last year, those thirties evening frocks your mother was throwing away when she was packing. D'you remember? Just before she moved to Hertfordshire. We could wear those. There are three of them. You could choose.

– You've still got them?

– Of course I have. They're in my trunk. I thought you might change your mind and want them back some day.

– Oh no. They're not my style. That's why I gave them to you. I was sure you'd wear them whereas I knew I never would.

Beth sounds pleased, though.

– Let's get them out and have a look, anyway, Helen coaxes: I've got lots of other bits and pieces you might like.

She jumps up and waves a hand at the debris of their meal.

– Let's leave all this. We can clear it up later.

Beth follows her into the sitting-room. Helen bends over the trunk wedged under the window-sill and begins to clear it of ornaments preparatory to opening it.

– It's a shame you never wanted the dresses yourself. Your mother would have been so pleased.

– Too feminine for me, Beth says: but not for you. But let's have a look at them, anyway.

She peers at the little object Helen has just picked up.

– What's that?

Helen closes her fingers over it.

– You despise femininity, don't you? It's all right for me, fluffy little Helen, but not for great big strong Beth. Don't be so bloody patronising.

The words come out with effort. She's unused to criticising Beth aloud, to her face.

– No I don't, Beth says uncertainly: and I certainly don't despise *you*. You're so brave.

– Me? Brave?

Helen is astounded. All her memories of their joint past are of Beth taking the lead, Beth being brave. Beth a tiny Boadicea heading student demonstrations to prevent Enoch Powell speaking at Oxford Town Hall, Beth spending nights at the Clarendon building during the student occupation calling for greater democracy in university politics, Beth being arrested during a sit-down protest outside a racist shop that turned away West Indian customers, Beth organising coachloads of students to go to the Vietnam demonstration in Grosvenor Square.

– The last time I went on an anti-fascist demonstration, Helen exclaims: years ago, the Lewisham battle against the National Front, I was so scared I shat in my trousers. I thought I was going to be killed when those police horses charged us. And I was so frightened by the violence, the men's violence, our comrades yelling for police and fascist blood and hurling bricks, that I've not been on one anti-fascist demo since.

She talks rapidly, confessing, her head down, not daring to look at Beth.

80

– You see before you an anguished white liberal, swept aside by the tide of history and fear.

She's trying to laugh, but she can't.

– You're talking as though politics were simply a matter of going on demonstrations, Beth protests: you know it's not. And anyway, you went on the demonstration even though you were frightened. That takes courage.

Helen turns over the little figure in her hands, her head bent. The clay goddess doesn't speak to her. Other figures do: the outraged nun, the hurt relatives, the mocking male reviewer, the male militant, the correct feminist. A gang of them lining her up against a wall and firing injunctions at her: stop; you are boring, obscene, self-indulgent, peripheral, *wrong*.

– You *are* brave, Helen, Beth insists: look at the way you struggle on with your writing.

She has not said this for a long time, and Helen is surprised. Beth, practical Beth, so scornful of anything smacking of self-indulgence, so prone to criticise the elitist, individualistic nature of artists' style of work, suddenly affirming the value of novels.

– As a matter of fact, Beth adds: the last few months, I've been thinking of writing a novel myself. Of course I haven't got the time at the moment. Doing all this Party work doesn't leave me much time for anything else.

This comment, familiar to Helen from conversations with other people, has begun to irritate her. She has stopped producing the expected supportive, apologetic, humble response and now demands brutally instead: why don't you make the time then? I wrote my first novel at nights and at week-ends. If you really want to do it, you'll find a way. Get on and *do* it. This is one of her mother's brisk maxims, and Helen is amused to recognise her growing identification with Catherine's practical attitude, resisted for years. Just now, however, it's inappropriate, and her flare of irritation dies.

– I can't write, either, at the moment, she admits: I can't do anything. I can't think about anything but the horrors of international politics. It seems obscene to bother about writing. I ought to be finding somewhere to live, and I'm not doing that. All I manage to do is earn a living three days a week temping. I suppose that's something.

Beth perches on the arm of the sofa-bed and looks at her friend.

– I know you're feeling low just now, she says gently: I do understand that. I can't offer you any comfort. But I do see where you are.

Helen bursts into tears. Beth's words of recognition are the most unexpected and delicate of caresses. No exhortation to cheer up, no reminder of how privileged she is to be doing work she enjoys, simply a loving witnessing of how she feels. Beth, she knows, has plenty of experience of depression, bleak cold depression lasting for months at a time. Suddenly, she's meeting her there, and in that barren place is a most warm consolation. Blessed are they that mourn, and show their trouble to friends, for that shall comfort them. She is wounded, and Beth touches the place where it hurts, and she begins to heal. She sits in silence for a while, her body relaxing as the tears die and give way to peace, remembering, through this feeling, every time she and Beth have sat together over the years, usually at night, talking eagerly into the small hours, sharing their lives, taking care of each other. She yawns, and then begins to sniff.

– I need a handkerchief, she says, searching vainly in her sleeve: I'll go and use some loo paper.

She puts down the little object she has been clutching all this time and goes through the kitchen towards the bathroom. When she returns, Beth has picked it up and is examining it. The little figure is about four inches high, glazed in the bluey-green of ducks' eggs, except where the lower limbs have been chipped and broken off, revealing the red clay underneath, so that only a suggestion of the original squatting position remains. In its arms, resting on its lap, the little figure cradles a bird, a slender, elongated shape like a swallow.

– Where's it from? Beth asks, stroking the gleaming pale green shoulders with one fingertip: where did you get it? It's beautiful.

– Steven gave it to me, on my last trip out East, just before we broke up, in 1974.

A goddess with a sculpted, mask-like face, pointed ears, and slits for eyes. No hair, a flattened body like a boy's, and a green bird in her arms.

– It's supposed to be a fertility figure, Helen adds: that's what he said the man in the Thieves Market said it was.

One of Steven's fantasies is about making love to a boy. Helen plays with him, and it becomes one of their favourite games. She has lost a lot of weight, because it is too hot to eat, and she looks boyish once dressed in shirt and shorts. She waits until Steven has fallen asleep, felled by the heat, and then sits cross-legged on the hotel balcony looking out over the sea at Hua Hin, squinting into the mirror propped up against the white-wood railing, cutting off her hair. The thick, long curls drop one by one to the hot wooden planks. There is no breeze stirring the noon oven, but the back of her neck feels much cooler. She strokes it wonderingly, and then passes her hand over the silky bristles sticking up a quarter of an inch all over her skull.

She springs up, her whole body feeling lighter, and paces experimentally up and down the balcony, trying out a stride, and then a swagger. Then she folds her arms on the balcony rail and looks dreamily down at the garden below, where everything is still, hushed, sleeping in the white glare and dazzle of the sun.

A parrot screeching from the aviary at one side of the hotel wakes Steven and brings him stumbling out to find her. He gazes at her in astonishment. Then his smile begins.

– Vicars and choirboys, she says, lunging for him, giggling: my turn to begin.

– D'you know something? Helen asks as she comes back into the bed-sitting-room after her bath: I've changed my mind.

– What about?

Helen takes a deep breath.

– I'd far rather stay at home tonight and not go to this party. I'd rather spend the evening with you.

She is an acrobat edging across the tightrope towards her partner's hands, a whirl of darkness and white craned faces below, no safety net. She is out of practice at this, not having talked to Beth for months. Catch me, she prays: before I slip, and fall.

– I need to talk to you, she adds: I think we need to talk.

Her words hang in the air, a slow-motion somersault. This conversation, the discussion of their differences, will rip through all their tricks, cancel their past harmonious double act. Yet it's the only thing to do: risk it; fly through the air and find out whether they still connect. She wants to be the clown, the solo bareback rider in spangles, the freak lady in the sideshow, anything but this. She's not trained for it any longer, she's convinced, this delicate balancing against each other that is a combination of ballet and martial arts, so high up under the canvas that they are alone, able to take their time.

She watches Beth's face break into surprise, and then cautious pleasure.

– That would suit me, Beth says: I'm not really in a party mood. I only said I'd go because I thought you wanted to.

They sit side by side on the sofa-bed in their dressing-gowns, looking at each other. The evening is laid out in front of them, shimmering clear as the dance floor at Rose's house made ready for the party, empty. Up to them to step on to it together, work out what steps, what dance to perform. The silk frocks wilt over by the trunk, rejected by both of them.

– Bring in the rest of the wine from the kitchen, Beth commands: and then roll a joint.

Helen, lying face down on the hotel bed, has dressed herself, at Steven's request, in black: bra and suspender-belt in glossy black brocade, stockings in sheer black nylon, high-heeled shoes in black patent leather. She is inclined to giggle, and buries her face in the pillow to stifle the sound. Then she lifts her head and looks at Steven, who stands next to the wide double bed. He is still in his office clothes: cream linen suit, cotton open-necked shirt, loose tie.

– Now what? she asks him: what next?

He deliberates for a second.

– I know. I want to shave you. I want you to be nine years old as well. Is that all right?

She nods, and turns over. She sits up and arranges herself comfortably so that she can see what is going on, and takes a swig of whisky from the bottle standing on the bedside table.

Steven collects his shaving-gear and comes to sit next to her, prising her legs apart with one hand so that the fleshy lips open around the soft folds deeper in. He looks at the pink tissue, and bends over and kisses it. She lies there silently, but she cannot help flinching as she sees the razor approaching. He gathers up a handful of hair, tugging at it gently, and then watching her mouth drop open, his fingers entwined in the wiry curls pulling the flesh taut in readiness for the razor he holds in his other hand. He has covered her hair with a white wig of soap that smells of jasmine. The razor-blade rasping continuously across her skin is like a hand pressing down on her, pressing her deeper into the bed.

– I'm not hurting you, am I? Steven asks anxiously.

– No. Not at all. The opposite.

When he has finished his task, he sits still, full of wonder at what he has done, at the smooth meeting-place, delicate as a hair, of the two lips, exposed in the bare stubbly skin. He wipes off the remaining traces of lather with a warm wet flannel, and then fetches Helen's pot of face-cream, and begins to massage her, all the time intently watching her looking at him. The little bluey-green goddess perches next to the whisky bottle, looking on.

– Marry me, he begs her later: marry me.

Helen curls at one end of the sofa-bed, watching Beth at the other. Beth's hair, let down after her bath, tumbles around the blue shoulders of her dressing-gown. Her knees are drawn up to her chin, with her arms clasped around them, and she keeps her eyelids lowered, pondering how to begin. They have turned off the centre light and left burning just the lamp on the table, to create for themselves a cocoon of semi-darkness, shadows. When Beth lifts her head to look at Helen, the dull gold light of the lamp catches her hair and sets it on fire.

– It's complicated to explain, she starts: the decision was growing for a long time.

Helen meets Steven for the first time at an Embassy cocktail party in Bangkok, given for the seven Thai artists whose show opens the next day in Siam Square. She is working as a freelance journalist to finance her wanderings across south-east Asia, and has wangled her way into the party, sniffing a possible story, by bribing the doorman.

Steven is introduced to her as an engineer working on a British aid development project. She studies him. He is tallish and lean, moving gracefully like an animal on the balls of his feet. He has a hollowed-out face, a big, bony nose, brown eyes, and flopping brown hair. They talk about the political situation, the war in Vietnam, the work he is doing in Thailand for the British government aid programme. As they talk, Helen classifies him mentally: liberal, unwilling to take sides, upper-middle-class.

She's not sure how far this labelling is not pure self-defence. For she finds that she keeps wanting to touch him. Her hands will go on trying to put down her glass on the table next to her and lift themselves of their own accord, as though divorced from her will, and she has to restrain them, push them down again to her sides. They cling to her sides when they would far rather touch him. She wants to dance with him, to let her hands rise up and float in the air, to lay her hands along the air as though she were borne in a clear green sea. Now, standing opposite him, lifting her eyes to his and meeting them, she is surprised at the tenderness welling up in her for this stranger, a mere foot away, who looks back at her and listens to her as she speaks to him. As though they are two great birds settled by mutual consent upon a rock in the sun of a blue and green landscape, shimmering with heat and the passage of endless, tranquil time. She wants to lift her hand and touch his face, follow the line of his jaw, trace the scroll-work of his ears. She is shipwrecked, has splintered like decks and hatches to let the sea come in, and she is content to have it so, floating in sea-water, talking to him, gentle pirate, careless of drowning.

She finds with shock that they are already talking about sex, and that she can't remember when the subject of their conversation changed.

– Most Englishmen, she hears her voice pronounce: are frightened of women and haven't a clue about sensuality.

– Oh, not all of them, surely? Steven teases her.

He touches her bare arm, and she feels electricity shoot up it from his fingers.

– I've got to go up country for a few days on business. When I come back, will you have dinner with me?

He comes to collect her from her dingy hotel room where cock-roaches lodge in the cracked plaster walls and where the propellor fan whirrs noisily above the white drift of the mosquito net. She pours them both a glassful of ferocious Thai whisky, and sits nervously opposite him on the hard rattan sofa.

He puts his drink down, comes and kneels in front of her, and picks up her foot in its high-heeled green sandal. He looks at her questioningly, smiling. She smiles slowly back, remembering their conversation, and he begins to stroke first her ankle above the apple-green strap, lingeringly, and then her calf. When eventually they fall into each other on the dusty floor, part of her backs off, afraid.

– Let's take it slowly, Steven whispers, his breath warm in her ear: nice and slow.

He is curious about her body, explores it, wants to match his rhythms to hers. So she opens for him as for no man before him, she vibrates strongly as she embraces him, lying on her side and grasping him between strong knees, their mouths locked together, their bodies dancing steady and slow, her arms and lips enclosing him, and his hand stroking her clitoris. He waits for her, he enjoys taking a long time, moving gently with her until she feels the deep ache, the almost intolerable sweetness in her bones and gut, mounting up from her toes in long, slow waves that are stronger every time until they crash over her head and she comes with him, crying out and then losing consciousness until her body arches and kicks and brings her back to life and they lie exhausted on the wet floor as though dropped from a great height.

– I love you, Steven says into her neck: I love you.

86

– Well, go on then, Beth says: list all the things you disagree with about my decision, why don't you?

Her voice puts a sea of coldness between them. Helen gulps, and then plunges in. She's such a weak swimmer, buffeted by these currents, by these glassy waves which slop salt floods down her throat and threaten to choke and drown her. She's making for her best friend, but may never reach her, may need rescuing.

– You rejected Christianity, she begins her list: but you've simply entered another established church. Don't tell me Marxism recognises women's reality because I don't believe it. The CP has a masculine theory, a masculine view of the world, organises through a male model of the enlightened patriarch-party leading the masses and dealing out punishment for disagreement and transgression. Tell me where that's so different from the Protestantism you grew up in.

– Whereas you simply substitute a female goddess for a male god. What's so liberated about that? *You're* still religious, still believing all that mystifying rubbish about gods and souls and the after-life.

Trembling with rage, Beth leans back against the arm of the sofa-bed.

– But do go on. I'm fascinated.

Helen pours herself another glass of wine. Fortification against the cold.

– I think you're driven by guilt, she continues: the same old Protestant guilt. You want a secure belief. You want to believe not simply that the CP is pure, right and good, because you always want to believe that anything you do is pure, right and good, you need to believe that like we all do, but also that the CP is actually effective, that it will make the world a better place, remove all oppression and suffering, stop you feeling so guilty about being relatively privileged vis a vis people starving and dying everywhere.

– Are you so guilt-free? Beth shoots at her: look at you, dressing in second-hand clothes, apologising for who you are all the time, it drives me mad I tell you.

– But I'm poor, Helen says.

– Only relatively. You'd be better off if you made more demands as a working writer, if you *organised*, like other working people do. Instead of which you've bought the whole myth about writers starving in garrets. It suits you better, doesn't it? It means you're still a nice person, someone who doesn't complain. People *should* complain, people *should* go on strike. All right, don't tell me, I know that mothers can't, that lots of women can't, that the unemployed can't.

They are silent, glaring at one another.

– We're talking about you at the moment, Helen reminds Beth: I'm trying to tell you all the things I disagree with about your politics. Let me finish. Then it's your turn.

Beth laughs suddenly.

– Is this how you do it in your women's group? Each have a turn? Life's not like that. Democracy's not like that.

– It works though, Helen says: the principle is that each woman is given time that is absolutely hers, to do whatever she likes with, to be listened to. Something it's hard to get anywhere else. I never found, amongst right-wing men, nor on the left, that men were willing to listen to what I said. They always bloody translated it, into their own terms. Oh, they'd say: the concept of alienation. Or the Freudian ones would say: pathological. They never stopped reproving me for using my own language and ideas. *Incorrect*, that was what they always told me I was. So I rejected the CP, yes, for that selfish reason, because it didn't include the whole of me. I'm still some sort of a socialist, I suppose, but I'm much less clear what it means.

– I thought, Beth says mildly: you were supposed to be talking about me.

– People have to work things out, Helen starts again: from wherever they are, from the place they're in. Political parties seem always to me to dictate: what's wrong, how people feel about it, what should be done.

– You'd never want to join a party, Beth jokes: that would have you as a member. Elitist.

– I reap the benefits, Helen rushes on: of other people's struggles. All the time. I'm aware of that. But I'm more aware of women's fight, that's where I started from, that's what I come back to, all the time. That's what links me to other people. Our lives as women, how they link to other women's lives, and to men's lives. I don't see why it helps to join the CP to put that into practice. I think the CP stops you thinking deeply about your own life. I bet you still get depressed, don't you? Has the CP stopped that?

– How could it? Beth returns sharply: how can there be solutions to my own problems when the world's in the state it is?

– Unless you start taking your own personal problems seriously, you'll never be any good as a political person. You'll be lying, pretending that you're fine, being some sort of lady bountiful dishing out tracts to the working class. Jesus, Beth. Can't you see how patronising that is?

– We're going round in circles, Beth complains: talk about feminine logic. Are you criticising left-wing politics in general or the CP in particular or my personality?

– All three. They connect. All right, I'm being very muddled, not very rational. I've just got a feeling, a strong feeling, that being an upper-middle-class member of the CP is not the same as being a working-class member of it. How can you be so sure you share their struggles? Isn't that arrogant? Doesn't that involve denying whole parts of yourself?

– I'm not upper-middle-class any longer. I rejected all that.

– Concealed it, you mean. Your life style, your past, how you talk, you don't fool anybody, even if you do wear dungarees all the time.

Beth starts to roll another joint. With great care, she empties a cigarette, crumbles dope, licks paper, lights a match.

– People starving and dying everywhere, she repeats: capitalism overthrowing socialist experiments with great savagery, dissidents being tortured all over the world, apartheid in South Africa and the most appalling racism here, the war in Ireland, a government attacking just about every gain that working people have made over the last hundred years. Am I supposed just to sit by and watch it happen and not protest?

When Steven and Helen pursue the paths, overhung by creepers and drooping thickets, into the heart of the wild-life park, their legs quickly become covered by leeches, waggling like black commas on the white page of their skin. They prise them off each other, grimacing at the rivulets of blood left behind, and then Steven mixes chewed tobacco with spittle and smears it over their legs and ankles to deter any more leeches lying in wait. One or two lodge determinedly, and have to be burned off with a cigarette.

They go on over the muddy ground slippery from the monsoon rain, forcing their way along the track overgrown with bamboo and barred by fallen tree-trunks, until they arrive at the steep waterfall that flows between the rocks down to where the green river splashes and foams. Clothes off, they jump into the lowest, deepest pool, washing away sweat and blood and tobacco and spit. When they come out, the white glare of the sun scorches their shoulders, and they huddle under a flame of the forest for shade, reclining behind a curtain of dazzling spiders' webs. They smear each other with whisky and grapes, and then lick each other all over, the tender sunburned skin.

89

– My beast, Steven names her: my beautiful beast. My lord.

She stretches, arching her back, closing her eyes, purring and smiling, her outflung foot searching for his.

– My beast too. My lady. My beast.

– It started with student politics, sure, Beth goes on: and yes, even before that, perhaps, with guilt at recognising how privileged I was coming from an upper-middle-class family, trying for Oxford. It all got much worse there. Oxford seemed to me an insane place. I had to get into politics or go crazy.

She pauses, listening to what she has just said.

– I wanted a structure, I suppose, something coherent. I never wanted just to be a student rebel, going over the top for a few years and then settling down into some cosy well paid profession. You know all that. And then all those years in the women's movement, as an unaffiliated socialist. In the end I got impatient with the way our campaigns worked. I wanted more formal contact with the organised left, with the male-dominated left, if you like. I still believe that's where the power for change lies, especially if women become more involved. Of course it's crucial, women's involvement.

She pauses, lighting another cigarette. The empty wine bottle lolls on the cushions between them, and Beth caresses it absently with her foot.

– The problem was probably the same for both of us, but we reached different conclusions about it, different solutions. D'you remember when you came back from Thailand, after splitting up with Steven, in such a state? That was when you started writing seriously. You *needed* to write. That was your way of becoming involved in the world. Well, I *needed* to be political, to make the links with other people that way. It was one way that offered itself. I couldn't see any other. Then it seemed logical to move on from there and get involved in the CP.

– But what *was* the original problem? Helen asks: what was its name?

It's three am. The ashtray next to Beth overflowing with crushed stubs, empty tea-cups on the floor, smudges of tiredness under their eyes, all witnesses of the long vigil, the careful listening, the pain-staking selection of words, words that fail over and over again, Helen thinks, to convey one hundredth of what each of us means. Especially theoretical words, so dry, so over-simple, so rigorously placed in connection with one another, allowing only single and therefore

90

inadequate meanings. She is suddenly exhausted, her throat aching.

– You were saying earlier you wanted to write a novel, weren't you? she asks sleepily: where does that fit in?

– I'm not sure, Beth says: but anyway, I can't talk about it yet. I just know there's *something* there that wants to come out. I know I'm looking for *something*. I don't know exactly what it is.

She stretches.

– At the moment, the unknown it begins to take on the shape of sleep. Let's go to bed.

– It's as though there's a block, Helen muses, as she begins to untie the cord of her dressing-gown: which I can't see through. I'm beginning to think it's inside me. I've got to deal with it, before I can go on to whatever the next stage is.

She has reached the rock on which Beth sits, and, gasping with the effort, and with fatigue, pulls herself up and on to it. They are twin mermaids, the sea slapping at their tails which dangle into the water. Only now, when they are together again after such a long separation, when they hold their mirrors up to one another and gaze therein, they have to recognise their difference. The old enchantment, relied upon for years, no longer works.

– I'm really confused about everything, Helen admits: whether all the parts of me have to fit neatly together or not.

Beth starts to comb her hair. It crackles and jumps, an electric tangle of red.

– That's probably as good a place as any to start. That seems to be your way, anyway. Making a pattern out of a muddle.

She tugs at a tangle.

– You seem to believe that really radical, profound change is extremely slow, like evolution is, and happens inside people. A sort of evolution of consciousness, isn't it, what you mean? Or of unconsciousness, or of the soul as well as the body. I don't understand what you mean, really, with all those words. You seem to be talking about some sort of progress, some sort of conscious interaction with the environment. Fine. But I suppose I want to speed up that evolutionary process, and I still see the route there as being through political and economic change. Some sort of mighty push possible, yes, I do believe that.

– How does the push happen? Helen starts: by force? What sort of force?

They're back where they started. Evolution. Revolution. They grimace wearily at each other, yawning, tacitly deciding to leave it there for the time being, to repair their strength in preparation for the next round, to abandon words as they abandon dressing-gowns, to join one another through darkness, simple and similar in sleep. They say goodnight awkwardly.

Helen goes on sitting on the rock, the night laying damp, salty hands on her bare shoulders. She is weary of mirror-gazing, of hair-combing. On a sudden impulse, she reaches down and hauls her tail, slippery and shining, out of the sea. Fish-woman. Fish-woman from the waist down. Seductive and cold. She starts to cry as she recognises herself, her fish nature, and her tears are indistinguishable in their taste from the sea surrounding her.

Then she's back in her parents' house, sitting in front of the dolls house they've given her for Christmas. She opens the door. The interior is bare, except for a twig lying on the floor of one of the rooms. As she watches, the twig begins to blossom, breaking out into a bluey-green double-petalled flower that quivers and shimmers like a pair of wings clapping very slowly, that stretches and grows. And now it's a butterfly dragging veils of turquoise gauze, blundering between the cardboard walls, searching for a way out into the light, the heat of the sun.

Second Visitation: Winter

One

The first thing that she remembers is the pram. It is enormous, deep and dark, like a coffin, and the twins look up from their pillows and see a slit of grey sky between the two hoods. Helen has been swallowed up, her brother Felix too, and they journey over the uneven pavements, not yet mended after the war, in the belly of the whale. At night they sleep in twin carrycots placed across the bath in their grandparents' house: Bill and Catherine are homeless, and the grandparents take them in and give them a home. Helen doesn't remember sleeping over the bath, but she does remember the pram, like a pair of dark lips closing over their heads.

Now, after years of poverty and living in other people's homes, she is still poor, but she has borrowed her brother's flat and has a room of her own, of sorts, in which to write. She prowls about it as though for the first time, like a cat with a new cardboard box to examine, testing herself within it, measuring. The December sun falls on the floor in precise bright oblongs of gold. The middle of the room, where she has set up her table near the sofa-bed, is comfortably dim and shadowed, and at the back, the sunlight is fragmented and shifting as it dazzles through the leaves of the plants obscuring the kitchen and bathroom windows. Shrouded from the garden and the street by this pattern of green leaves and light, the room is tranquil.

Helen has a wooden chair, a trunk, a dresser, a typewriter, a bed. She has bought herself an extravagant bunch of roses and put them in a jug on the table, she has made herself a cup of coffee, she has stacked fresh white paper on the table, she has inserted a sheet of paper into the typewriter and sits in front of it.

The day stretches ahead of her, long and inviting, like the room. Her only task is to begin, to fill the day with meaning, to impress herself upon it, to cover the white paper with words damp and black from the new typewriter ribbon. A sheet of paper all to herself. A day on her own in which to please herself. Cars rev in the distance. She is alone.

Helen's first orgasm was on her own. She was eighteen. The first that she remembers, that is, for presumably there were others, long before, that she has forgotten about. The feelings aroused by masturbation, tentatively practised during the first long separation from Felix when he has departed on his trip to North America do recall certain sensations from childhood. A dampness and itchiness between her legs when she ran or climbed trees; the pleasing rough-ness of the sheets when she lay in bed; the hot water lapping her body when she climbed into the bath and prickling between her thighs; the churning of her guts when at ten years old she read *Lolita*. Later, parted from Felix for the first time, she feels them surge back as definite and joyful terms: sexuality; orgasm. She is overwhelmed by this event, lying in the dark in her room, panting and wet, clutching her hot and throbbing secret. When her own hands sweep her body into darkness, violence, sobbing relief, she is amazed to be flying, pouring, dissolving. She immediately does it again, to make sure she is not dreaming.

Her father is her king in a tweed cap, god of the allotment, so handsome she catches her breath. He is tall and not at all fat, with muscles standing out on his arms when he rolls up his shirt sleeves to do the gardening. He wears old cord trousers, and, to keep him warm, a sleeveless knitted pullover. Enormous wellingtons with a wet black gleam. Curly hair cut very short, and a twinkle in his eyes. He lets her take worms for rides in the wheelbarrow, up and down the narrow cement path between the dark earth of the flower-beds tidied up for winter's approach. He rakes up the leaves into crackling heaps and lets her help him. She bends over, puffing, and scoops up bunches which she clasps loosely in her short fat arms. She doesn't know how to throw yet, can't transfer the leaves through the air onto the big pile her father has made, so she drops them.

She goes back to the worms, and cuts them in half with the edge of her father's spade which is as tall as herself. The last leaves come drifting down out of the blank sky, and the wind is cold. She has killed the worms, when all she meant to do was see whether they kept on moving once chopped in two. She bursts into tears. Her father is a long way off, bending over the brick edge of the compost heap. He pulls off his battered leather gardening gloves, stretches, and grins. He rolls a cigarette and lights it, shielding the flame from the wind in cupped calloused hands. She is desperate, overwhelmed by guilt and grief, and at that distance he looks pin-sized. She cries louder. Too late, he comes, throwing the cigarette away and looming as big as a bear, squatting down beside her and putting his arm around her, hugging her, tickling her to make her smile again. He picks her up, and carries her inside to tea, proud as a queen.

There is a fly buzzing around the room, summoned by the heat of the sun, bumping noisily against the window-pane as it searches for an exit into the light. Helen jumps up from the typewriter, leaving her blank sheet gratefully for an easier task, that of lifting the heavy window-sash, clogged with paint and dust. She pushes it up, gasping with effort, and the fly zooms out. Immediately, the noises of the outside fly in: the next door neighbour's son whistling; an aeroplane crossing the heavens; a voice blaring through a loudhailer on the main road; a dog barking; a radio playing. Helen hastily pulls down the sash again, then sees that there are now three fresh flies diving at it with forlorn buzzes. She swears, shrugs, sits down at the typewriter again.

The main thing is just to get started. She knows that. But her wrists and forearms itch. She scratches them impatiently, and settles herself more comfortably on the hard chair. The itching, however, continues, and when she pushes back the sleeves of her shirt and inspects her skin, she sees the large red blotches again, straggling across her skin like red bites. The irritation is enormous. She can practically see the red bumps pulsate. Her entire body throbs. Work is impossible. She gets up and paces the room, willing herself not to scratch, clutching her arms to her body, nearly in tears with misery.

Helen's father is a hero. He fought in the war. He tells her tales of his exploits, mostly late at night, when she is too anxious to sleep, or wakes, terrified, from nightmares. Sometimes he comes to sit by her bed and tell her stories to coax her back to sleep. She fights sleep, holding on to his hand so that he won't be able to leave, and begs for just one more account of how he woke up in the morning in a barn in Belgium with a freshly slaughtered pig bleeding all over him, how he larked about in the barracks playing tricks on his mates, how he was caught one day by the sergeant with his trousers down.

She closes her eyes and sees again the photographs in the family album: her father in uniform, his young face bright between peaked cap and stiff shoulders, his hair shaven to invisibility and a moustache pencilled smartly above his lips; her father, in serge trousers pleated from the waistband and a fair-isle slipover, standing on his head on the lawn and waving his legs for the children's delight; her father, with rolled-up shirt sleeves and trousers tucked into wellingtons, leaning on the gate of the newly-built house in the new suburb and grinning with pride.

Her father not only tells stories; he writes them down, too. When Helen is old enough to have started writing essays for English class at primary school, he pulls a creased manila file out of the bureau in the corner of the sitting-room and shows it to her. The bureau is sacred, its rows of pigeon-holes containing the tools and vessels used in the worship of the household gods: here are cheque books, diaries, address-books, her father's business visiting cards. The little drawer underneath yields further magic for an exploring child: stumps of scarlet sealing-wax and a gold seal ring; paper clips and drawing pins; a little box of steel nibs used by her grandfather and passed on by him to his son; brass buttons cut from old army uniforms; military badges and studs. The child fingers these totems with fascination, murmuring over them more compelling than a rosary.

The lid of the bureau, unlocked with a little gilt key, opens out to make a writing shelf. Here stand the serious machines: the stapler that bites with steel teeth in a single pounce; the massive hole-puncher in black metal decorated with gold arabesques, stately as a lion; the wire letter rack that is a mouth chewing on correspondence. The airmail envelopes received from abroad, striped in red and yellow and green on blue, franked with scarlet and black and navy exotic place names, and stamped with miniature pictures of plants and birds, are mysterious packets, carrying people's thoughts expressed in black hieroglyphs on delicate paper that rustles and is so thin you can see through it, thoughts made transparent. Here too is the blotter, bound in green half-calf, the tub of pencils and fountain-pens splayed out like a rainbow, and the row of bottles of ink, dumpy, wide-shouldered containers of forbidden liquids glowing red, black, purple and navy blue like the great flasks, full of ancient potions, in the chemist's shop.

Her father closes the bureau lid and pulls open the top drawer underneath. He rummages through a stack of files marked mortgage, insurance, Masonic Lodge, bills, and pulls out a manila folder marked: me.

– Here, he says to Helen: you can read them if you like.

– Real stories? she says excitedly: you've written real stories?

– Never published, though, he says, flicking the type-written sheets: still, no harm in your having a look.

She holds the folder tightly in both hands, feeling raised to adult status by this honour.

– Nobody would publish them, her father goes on: I sent them to all the magazines after the war.

He laughs, and ruffles her hair.

– When I was your age, I wanted to write. I was convinced I'd make it, too. Burning with ambition, I was.

Instead, he has become, as far as the child can understand, another sort of magician. A wizard absent all day and present at week-ends, who sits at a big glossy desk and passes pieces of paper from one tray to another and makes money which he brings home in his leather briefcase.

– I'm going to be a writer, Helen tells him, and blushes. She looks at him in misgiving, fearing his mockery, but he is smiling.

– You should try and get to university, he says, and sighs: that's another thing I was never able to do.

This is one of his stories that she knows. How he had to leave school at fourteen because the family could afford to support only the eldest son in an education and needed the other two to go out to work. I'll make it up to you, nine-year-old Helen promises her father silently: I'll go to university and be a writer and you'll be proud of me. I'll make it up to you. She squares her shoulders. She is Sir Galahad, whose story has leapt from a library book and gripped her; she has a mission in life now, a Holy Grail.

Helen sits down at her table again, holding her stinging hands in front of her, hearing her mind clatter with thoughts as briskly as a typewriter. Perhaps she should give up. Perhaps she should have a bath and a sleep. Perhaps she should scribble some graffiti on the bed-sitter's walls. She lifts her head, listening to words that float back to her from a Sunday newspaper. The groans and howls of the new feminist fiction, one woman reviewer called it, the kind of book that she writes: humourless, whining, strident. Language laid on like whips, words with the hiss and punch of arrows, the armoury of the new witches.

W is certainly for Woman and Witch. She picked up a nineteenth-century reprint of an old herbal in a bookshop once, cheap because second-hand and slightly damaged, the thick laid paper spotted and foxed, the headband rubbed. She cradled it between her hands, and then opened it, leafing idly through the index. The male author's entries for W rivet her: warts; weevils; whites, women's whites, how to control; witches, how to guard against; wolfbane; womb: women's weeping therefrom; women in childbed; women's complaints, how to soothe; women's courses, how to stop, how to bring on; women's diseases; women's longings; women's pains; worms in the ears. When she turns the leaves of the index back to M, she finds no corresponding entry for Man.

Too much white space on the page, too much white space in the room, filling rapidly with suppressed cries. She looks at the red blotches on her hands and arms.

Why ever did she think she wanted to live on her own?

None of the women in Helen's family has a room of her own. The houses in the suburb, of whatever size, are divided up by function: dining-room, sitting-room, bathroom, bedroom. The kitchen is a particular domain of Helen's mother, certainly. She guards the larder with its shelves of home-made chutney, jam and marmalade; she stocks the big old fridge smoothly curved like a fifties automobile; she gets down on hands and knees to scrub grease and dirt out of the oven.

On Monday, the kitchen is a temple of steam and wet, dedicated to the wash. The washing-machine churns and thumps, filling the little room with clouds of warm, moist air, the smell of soap. Catherine prods and pulls at the washing with a pair of wooden tongs, and swishes a rag, with her foot, over the puddles leaking from the old machine across the brown lino floor. For lunch on Mondays they always have cold meat left over from the day before: a picnic of mutton, mashed potato, pickles.

On Tuesdays, if the washing hung out in the garden has dried, there is the lengthy task of folding and sorting the sheets and clothes in preparation for doing the ironing. Catherine tackles this whenever she has a spare moment throughout the rest of the week. Helen helps her, learning how to iron her father's shirts, handkerchiefs, underwear. She serves him gladly, running to bring him tea when he returns from work in the evening, adoring his slippers, little leather shrines. By Saturday, it is as though the life force in the kitchen has exhausted itself from so much labour; last Sunday's joint has turned itself into shepherd's pie, rissoles and spaghetti sauce throughout the week and is now extinguished; the family eats toad-in-the-hole before Catherine starts the housework.

Bill uses the kitchen in the early mornings. He stands dreamily in front of the window, shaving, a sturdy man in vest and trousers, his eyes on the blackbirds pecking for crumbs on the window-sill, his mind roaming meditatively and his hand dipping the razor into the chipped enamel jug of hot water curling with steam and then drawing it steadily down his cheek to scrape away the curds of soap and reveal long neat swathes of skin. On Sunday night he uses the kitchen, too. He collects the family's shoes, ranging them on a sheet of newspaper laid on the draining-board, and cleans them, humming to himself.

All the rest of the week, the kitchen is his wife's domain; she keeps the cooker company. She is the spirit of the house and is everywhere in it, wherever the demands of her family define her temporary place. Her husband and children are lazy; they shout for her from whichever room they happen to be in, and she erupts from the kitchen, shouting at them not to shout at her. Or she comes in from a Townswomen's Guild meeting or her teaching job and is instantly met by her family's needs.

Sometimes, on a Sunday afternoon, in her brief resting space between the washing-up and the preparation of tea, she sits in a chair beside the fire, puts on her glasses and reads the papers, and has peace. Then she picks up her knitting and creates her family's clothes, or darns their socks and jumpers, or mends worn sheets. She creates endlessly, she weaves the fabric of the home out of her very self, like a silkworm producing the gold thread from its marrow before it dies.

Helen gets up and checks her appearance in the mirror over the mantelpiece. Her eyes are anxious, her shoulders hunched. Her body hides itself within a vast old boilersuit. To write, Helen always feels she has to cancel her body out, become pure mind. Genderless, transcendent, like a man. She stares at the reflection of her face. It's a game, to see how long she can look deeply into her own eyes before she begins to feel frightened. Today, she can only look at herself for a few moments at a time, constantly repeated. To and fro between the typewriter and the mirror opposite.

Her pacing reveals to her that the room is too large for just one person. There are aching spaces on the sofa, and the rugs cry out for someone to be lounging there. Helen doesn't want the furniture to start talking to her. She must fill up all these gaps herself. One way to do it would be to go out to the off-licence and buy a bottle of wine, ease herself into sweet red oblivion. Another way is to summon Felix back, piece together all the occasions on which they have met since leaving home, re-member him. She tugs the invisible cord she has tied around his ankle, waits for the warmth to start flooding her limbs as his voice faintly calls her name. Nothing.

She finds herself squatting in front of the trunk where she keeps her things. The rusty hinges squeak as the lid, thrown back, touches the floor. The lid is lined with blue cotton, and the insides of the trunk with blue checked paper. She lifts out piles of fat brown envelopes and exercise books. She always loved exercise books, loved stationers and found every possible excuse for visiting them. These exercise books have stiff cardboard covers crumbling a bit at the edges, marbled fly-leaves and checked pages. They are just like her trunk, and are packed to the brim with words, blue ink, blue words on blue checked paper.

These are her diaries. Six volumes that chart her from aged ten onwards. For all these years her diary has been her most intimate companion. This shocks her, for she insisted to herself that Felix always has been. In fact, the diaries tell her as she flicks hurriedly through them, she has been betraying him steadily, compulsively, all this time, by talking not to him at all but to herself. She has lain curled up inside this trunk, flattened between these blue and white pages. She has been a word struggling to be spoken, to be heard and understood. Only she still doesn't know what that word is.

As she turns over the faded blue boards and the checked pages of her history and forces herself to dwell on the cries scrawled in blue ink, she is gripped in turn by nausea, panic, nostalgia, bewilderment. It appears to her now that a diary is not at all like a mirror at the time of writing it: it can pretend as much as she wishes, and without her having to be conscious of that. She made sure she wasn't. It is only much later, as she re-reads, that a picture becomes clear, swimming up for the first time, it seems, like prints laid in their bath and slowly revealing themselves. Lies, lies, lies, fictions, harmonious stories invented to create tolerable memories for later on, to gloss over and deny the pain and confusion, at the time so terrible and so over-whelming, of the transition from childhood to adolescence.

For ten years she allowed herself just five lines a day. Underneath these blue words lurk rage, unhappiness and hunger, which is utterly clear to her now, reading the large ink characters. She wants to burn all these diaries and never write new ones. She forces herself not to do that, to stay squatting on the floor looking at herself, to skim through the diaries one by one, slowly piling them up on the floor at the side of the trunk.

She was so hungry and lonely in those days. She still is. She wants to let herself write more than five lines of lies a day. She wants a companion. The diaries hardly mention Felix at all.

Helen closes her eyes and imagines she is sitting with her grandmother, that longed-for beach on to whose breast she crashes like an angry sea. Put down that broom, put away those saucepans, drop that darning needle, and sit down here and open your arms and listen. Be wise for me.

Old Mrs Home obeys. She changes herself into a witch. She is young and beautiful, her red hair cut in a silky Cleopatra bob around her high cheekbones and swinging forward over her sea-green eyes. She curls in the depths of a crimson armchair, one foot tucked beneath her, one slender ankle dangling. The witch is full of mystery, and tremendously old, despite her look of youth. Her wisdom goes back years, beyond the day of Helen's birth, beyond the nine months in the womb, to the generations and the centuries beyond. Her ears can hear the echo of old voices, ancient griefs, and far-off battle cries; her eyes can pierce the soul, see ghosts, glimpse distant lands that Helen has not yet visited.

Helen is visiting her grandmother in the late afternoon, when outside it is dark and cold. The witch's cave is dark too, but warm, a fire burning in a large brazier, a cauldron slung above it, and a lamp glowing in the corner where Helen lies on orange velvet cushions watching her. The walls are hung with crimson silk and the floor is spread with richly coloured rugs. The witch has an owl, perched on a stand, and flowers in jugs: anemones in scarlet and purple and deep blue, hyacinths in white, their thick waxy blooms suffusing the cave with a heady scent, pinks standing frilly and stiff and smelling of cloves and pears.

– What do you want? the witch asks Helen gently: why have you come to me? Tell me.

– I want to be healed, Helen whispers, and holds out her arms.

The witch peers at the rash. It flowers rosily across Helen's skin, each bump a dense red at its centre and fading to pink at the edges where it merges into the skin colour before the next bump begins. The witch nods, but says nothing. She listens.

– I try to write, Helen begins: calmly, as though I were sticking photographs of happy holidays into my album. It should be that simple, I feel, purely a question of order, a pleasing design. My toenails are carefully painted the colour of blood. They perch on the end of high-heeled espadrilles. Those monsters I trample in my nightmares have smeared themselves across my feet, and by day they return to torment me in their own fashion, in their own turn. They press themselves against me, imprinting themselves on my body in the form of a rose-coloured rash, bloody lips pressed to my skin leaving their mark. They turn into serpents and crawl down my throat when I am not looking, and I gag on them, and spew them up. They claw at my soft tissues, and I have a sore throat as a result. I try to write words on the blank page, but the monsters have already won the battle; they inscribe themselves on my body in their rosy ink.

The witch has been sitting very still, lost in concentration. Now she stirs, and looks at Helen.

– There's something you're hiding, she remarks in her usual brisk tones: from yourself and me. It's the same thing you hid in that novel of yours, the one your publishers turned down. Something left out of your account. What is it?

Her grandmother's uncanny ability to go straight to the point.

– I'm scared, Helen whimpers: and I don't know why.

– Try again, her grandmother says gently: you needn't be scared. There are only the two of us here.

– Red bumps, Helen starts: red marks. To mark, to notice, to inscribe. Traces of red on my skin trying to tell me something. Marks, school marks. I must be top of the class every term, do well, please you. I must write a good novel. Only I am frightened, because what I need to write about will tear the seamless garment of goodness and sexlessness I have worn so long. To mark. To brand and to burn. To burn at the stake. Sexual women, independent women, are witches, and will be burnt at the stake. It is dangerous, what we are doing, practising witchcraft, and we will be punished for it. Marks on my skin. The Word is made flesh. Each red bump a little red mouth shrieking with longing and rage, each red bump a little female hill, swollen, pulsating and hot with desire.

– Desire for whom, Helen? her grandmother presses her: desire for whom?

Helen is silent. She glares. She bears her secret on and in her hands and will not relinquish it.

– Can't you give me medicine? she pleads: mix me a potion from your secret store of drugs?

She can see the glass vessels, ranged on a high shelf, containing liquids that glow like ink.

– That nice Steven Gressing, her grandmother says thoughtfully: I never did understand why you didn't marry him. You wouldn't tell me, and I kept asking you.

Helen wakes from a deep, dream-filled sleep, to find that she is slumped over the trunk. She jerks up, her head fuzzy and heavy, and finds that her eyes are wet. The light is different now, slanting long and low across the floor. She has a headache, presumably because she has been lying in the sun for hours. What she needs, she decides, is a bath. It will be evening soon.

She sits on the edge of her bath, her heart pounding strongly. She has given up cigarettes and she is trying to write. Writing means being alone, and feeling terrified at how much there is inside her, wanting to come out. Sounds from her mouth which won't be strangled but which ricochet around the bathroom like bullets and leaves.

She bends down and takes off her shoes, stands up and begins to remove her clothes, turns on the taps. She lowers herself into a deep hot bath, only her head sticking out at one end. She is a root plugged into the earth. She must travel down inside herself, pull the earth over her head, explore her twisting passages, her narrow tunnels, her connecting caverns underground. No idea what she will find. Alone, she is so big, so light, so airy, she could drift up and off, cut free, cut loose, never come back. But her body-root holds her safely down, the earth grips her. Let go, then, and go down deep. Creatures from her buried mind will creep back into her, surge along her veins, burst from her mouth. She will give birth to a rain of lizards and snakes. She will speak, and there will pour forth a stream of serpents and monkeys.

Smiling, she dries between her monster toes, the bath draining. One of the bathroom windows, a square casement, is open. Through it comes the sound of the tenant upstairs playing the piano, golden late afternoon light, the last burst before the sunset and then the dark, a large bee awakened from its winter sleep. Automatically she swishes at the bee with her towel to direct it outside again.

Then, standing on the floor covered in dusty linoleum, smelling the scent of talcum powder and listening to the piano in need of tuning that falters through a sonata by Beethoven, she is overcome by a sense of the uniqueness of this moment that can never be repeated. The fat, honey-coloured bee, the flowery talcum that smells so sweet, the patches of December sun falling warmly across her feet and the floor, and herself standing there naked and completely still, all these things make a pattern which she must become part of, not separate from, a pattern which shifts and changes from second to second, as the bee moves, furry and stumbling, towards the window, as the sonata's notes drop through a veil of tradescantia, as her feet curl and then spread with delight in the warm sun. She only has this day once; it will not recur, and not a drop of it must be wasted; all must be let in.

Her rash has completely disappeared. She yawns, and stretches, and then wraps her towel around her and potters through the kitchen back into the bedsitting-room, mindless, easy. She plonks herself happily down on the sofa-bed and picks up her notebook, bought for the new novel and so far unused. She chews her pen, gazing idly out of the window at the darkening sky. The first thing of which she is aware, she writes: is the dark.

The telephone shrilling at her side makes her jump. She puts down her pen and notebook and leans across to pick up the receiver. At the sound of her mother's voice, so unexpected, she smiles with pleasure, and then the smile drops off her face as she hears her mother's troubled tones.

– Helen, Catherine says in a hesitating voice very unlike her usual firm one: I don't want to worry you, but I knew you'd want to know. Nana fell over, a really bad fall, this morning, and we only found her a couple of hours later, when we came in. She's broken her hip. She's in hospital now, Bill went with her in the ambulance. I'm just about to go down there too, only I wanted to ring all the family first and let everybody know.

Her voice deepens.

– They're going to operate. They say there's a certain chance. But she's hardly conscious.

Two

– The world as we know it, Helen says: is going to end in two years' time. There's going to be a nuclear war.

Beth looks at her dreamily, then turns her attention back to the late afternoon. The late January sky just above the roof tops is flushed gold. The air is chilly, but has a hint of wetness, of warmth, that makes you inspect the earth and flower-beds for a hint of green tips pushing through. Hyde Park is pure, silent, cold. One bird sings: chink, chink, chink. The air is as fresh as in the country, reminding Helen of the landscape around her parents' current home: the narrow West Country lanes like tunnels, steep banks lacy in summer with green weeds, damp tree trunks, dawn floating coldly above sleeping cattle, a wood etched sharply against khaki fields, the smell of manure. At this time of year the land huddles under a coat of snow, the roads sheeted in black ice. Unwelcoming, turned in on itself, and night falling at four o'clock.

Her grandmother hated the winter, which eventually possessed her for its own, entering her silently and involving itself with her very bones, as she sat, wrapped in a fleecy shawl, by the electric fire, writing to her grand-daughter. She could no longer get out, she wrote to Helen, to visit all her friends in the village; even with her stick as prop, she was too scared of falling on the ice and breaking her leg. She fell indoors, on the carpet, enough as it was. Her son drove her to the Protestant church at the end of the village every Sunday, and helped her up the long path under the beech trees; her only outing. Don't tell Bill and Catherine, she added, about my falls. They would only worry so. Ever your loving Nana.

Winter and darkness win. Nell Home dies, aged ninety-nine, in December, the long night of the year. I shan't make it to Christmas, she prophesied to Helen, holding her hand: the cold's got me, and I'm too old. Death of a grandmother: light snuffed out.

Beth yawns, then glances at Helen apologetically. She has been up since the early morning, busy with her CND conference in north London, and did not sleep well the night before with Helen tossing restlessly at her side.

– So what, she enquires: is to be done? Surely the point is that we must refuse to accept the possibility.

Helen does not reply, but fishes out her cigarettes. Her grand-mother has died, and she has started smoking again. She offers one to her friend. On their right, the branches of a tree knot themselves sideways and spread, knobbled with tiny black buds. Their bark is like plaited hair.

– You're not taking me seriously, Helen says at last: you think I'm crazy.

She looks crossly at Beth, who is peering up at the sky, which has begun to turn cold lemon, greenish.

– All this, Beth says with a sweep of the hand to indicate the park: will go? *No.* It's unthinkable. You mustn't let yourself imagine it. That's giving in. That just makes it more likely.

Helen looks around. If this were the last breath. If these pink and brown leaves sticking to the damp ground like curled shreds of suede were scraps of human skin.

– All this will go, she echoes.

Beth looks at her. Today, Helen is hidden under an old serge greatcoat, stiff as a tent, while Beth, making an effort to cheer up her friend, has adorned herself with a blue tweed jacket, blue scarf and blue leather boots. She makes another effort, and grips Helen's hand in her own. Their fingers, hard and rigid at first, relax, and then intertwine.

– There's a bench over there, Beth says with a nod of her head: let's sit down for a bit.

On their right now is the Serpentine, its grey surface ruffled and pitted by the wind. Ducks huddle in the clumps of reeds nearest the path. The little wooden boathouse looks neglected, the paint peeling from its dark timbers. On their left are the trees and the criss-crossing pathways between wet, muddy stretches of grass. The topmost part of the sky is ice-blue now, pearled as darkness creeps further up.

They sit down on a bench of wrought-iron painted green, with a plank seat and curly legs. They hold their cigarettes in their woollen hands, and blow smoke towards the Serpentine and the hotels beyond it on the far horizon of the park.

– The prophecies of Nostradamus, Helen explains: have been reinterpreted. I've been reading about it in the paper. There will be a new anti-Christ, another world war. Nuclear bombs exploded by the super powers will wipe out whole parts of the world.

Beth throws away her cigarette.

– Helen, she says abruptly: I need to talk to you. I'm pregnant. What shall I do?

– So I, Catherine Home says, her mouth turning down at the corners: am the eldest now. It feels so strange.

In her black dress, she does look older, as well as beautiful. The nights of strain and worry have scored new lines on her forehead and around her mouth. She sits very upright, as always, her shapely legs tucked to one side and her hands, beginning to be marked by arthritis, clasped together in her lap. She has not cried a lot for her mother-in-law, she tells Helen, deeply as she loved her, for crying is not her way. She tries to keep all her grief inside, stilling it with clenched muscles, rocking it to sleep through wide awake nights. Helen has been crying for three days, ever since the morning at eight o'clock when her father rang her to say that his mother was dead. Helen could only reach out towards him with her voice, and he began to cry in response to her sympathy, and then hastily put the receiver down.

Helen sits alone, trying to comprehend the news and finding she does not want to. It hurts too much, ripping her flesh, tearing her apart with sobs. She splashes cold water on her face, her eyes swollen so much they will hardly open, and staggers off to her typing job. That night, she sits at home again, her eyes shut and her arms tightly wrapped around herself, trying to comprehend nothingness, trying to draw back from the insistent pain. When, eventually, she lets go of her control and lets in the pain, she becomes all mouth, gaping, wanting, crying out, the earliest and most terrible of hungers reawakened, loss coming at her from all sides and threatening to overwhelm her. There is nothing but darkness, and herself in the middle of it shouting no no no. She can't sit still.

To the whisky bottle for false relief, the sour yellow alcohol plugging down the cries in her throat, burning them away, cauterizing the wound. Up and down the room, near demented with pain sharpened by the drink, swinging the bottle by one hand, useless companion. Tears corroding her eyes, a sizzle of tears and whisky etching new lines on her face, she can feel them being scored in. Up and down the bedsitter in her nightgown, willing the pain to stop and her grandmother not to be dead, and then giving way to it again and trying to go with it, like labour pains, her body swept by an ache that recurs with ever-deepening force.

– I can hear the others arriving, Catherine says, turning her face towards the front door: will you go and let them in?

The funeral is in an hour's time.

On the rare occasions when their parents snatch the chance to go out together for the evening, Mrs Home comes to babysit. The two children frisk in the bath, slithering all over each other, while their grandmother chases them with flannel and soap.

– You big babies, she scolds them: needing me to wash you. At your age. Well, I declare.

She knows perfectly well she is spoiling them. It is a favourite game: the eluding of soap, the snorting of bubbles, and then being captured in large towels and hugged dry, talcum powder sifted between their toes. Then into their pyjamas, rough and woolly, and their dressing-gowns, and downstairs again for supper: apples, cocoa, baked beans on toast.

Mrs Home pokes the sitting-room fire and gets a good blaze going. Then she settles herself in the big winged armchair on one side of the fireplace and looks at her expectant audience opposite.

– A story, they clamour, piled together in the other armchair: tell us a story, Nana.

Mrs Home is in the middle of an epic, which she makes up as she goes along. It is all in rhyming couplets, and very rude, featuring respectable friends of the family embroiled with chamber-pots. Helen and Felix, brought up to be excused, to spend a penny and to wash their hands, are enchanted by this saga of adults caught on the hop; they stuff their sleeves into their mouths to repress their giggles in their eagerness to hear more, they jab each other with their elbows as punctuation, they squirm in rhythm with their grandmother's happy London vowels.

– That'll do for now, Mrs Home decides after half an hour of the adventures of Jack and Drusilla and a brimming pot: enough is as good as a feast.

She cocks an ear as the grandfather clock in the hall chimes out a sonorous ten.

– Ten o'clock struck at the castle gate. Off to bed with you now.

In the bedroom upstairs, the excited children run from one end of the room to the other, shrieking with delight, racing each other to complete laps. Their grandmother stands in the doorway watching them, smiling as Felix leaps over Helen's bed and charges back towards the big wardrobe that stands against the far wall. His slippered feet skid on the highly-polished lino and shoot from under him. He falls heavily forward, his face meeting the iron key in the wardrobe door with great force.

Blood everywhere. On Felix's face, obscuring his eyes, nose, and mouth, and on Mrs Home's blouse as she holds the unconscious Felix in her arms.

– Not his eyes, she sobs as she wipes the blood away with her handkerchief: don't let it be his eyes.

Helen does not remember what happened after this: she pieces the subsequent events of the night together years later, when she asks her grandmother what happened next.

– Felix was all right, Mrs Home says, surprised that Helen has forgotten: it was just a bad cut to his forehead. I put you to bed and I sat waiting for your parents to come back from the hospital after they'd been fetched from the cinema. I've never seen Catherine in such a state of weeping, though she never said a word to me about it, she was so good. Then, all of a sudden, the sitting-room door opened, and there was this little figure all in white. My heart nearly stopped.

And then I saw it was you, in your nightdress, I'd changed you out of your pyjamas which had blood on them, and you were sleepwalking. You came right up to me, very slowly, and you said in a queer voice: there was a little boy, and now he's gone. I didn't wake you up, I took you upstairs again and put you back to bed, and in the morning you were as right as rain. You were a funny child, always walking in your sleep.

– I thought I'd killed him, Helen remembers for the first time years later: I thought I'd killed Felix.

Felix comes out first, the son so much desired, and Helen followed him. Who wants girls? In some countries they do the amniocentesis test and then make abortion available to the mothers of girls. In some countries, Helen read, twins were considered an aberration, a freak of nature, and left on the mountainside to die. All through her childhood convinced he was the favourite. The real baby because firstborn and male. Eve is made from the spare rib in Adam's side. Adam is wild and unruly, such a trouble to his parents, who therefore need to concentrate on him, put time and energy into chastising and retraining him. It is possible to be envious of punishments; these demonstrate the sinner's importance. Eve's sin is secret; on the surface she is hardworking, submissive, polite, nice, good. Only at night does a different Eve emerge, a different face, hissing through nightmares, wetting the bed, sleepwalking, armed with a knife, over to where her brother lies.

The gold line of a jet pushes like a needle, weaving between the black branches of the bare trees and the cold turquoise sky, stitching rents together.

– Of course, Beth says thoughtfully: Pete would like it a lot.

She sounds very smug, Helen thinks, kicking her boot against the iron leg of the bench: pregnant women always do.

So many of her friends either getting pregnant or thinking of doing so, pleased as punch with themselves for putting it off till their thirties, pleased as punch for deciding eventually to do it. Helen gets to her feet.

– Let's walk a bit. It's too cold sitting down for long.

Helen is striding up and down the park, watched by Beth who has paused under a tree and is leaning against it dreamily. Under their feet is the brown, pink and gold mash of dead leaves. Helen tramples them, she packs down the leaf mould, enriching the earth. If her life could only be like that, if the dead parts of her would strip themselves off, if the past and all its memories could all just rot down together and fertilise her soul. She digs her hands deep into her greatcoat pockets as though that will keep her from crying, but tears fill her eyes anyway. The wind is cold and drives at her face, scattering her tears. They splash out warm onto her cheeks, and then the wind takes them.

She would like to be pregnant. She hasn't known this. She wants a baby so much. It shocks her. Images of a daughter named Lilith, Lily for short, with tufts of black hair and a greedy mouth open for milk, tiny red fists curled up and the red mouth bawling, tiny red feet with exquisite toes and nails. Her own arms are empty. That's why she stuffs her hands into her coat pockets, to let them contact something beyond air and nothingness. She aches with wanting.

Beth falls into step beside her and they walk on towards Notting Hill through the black park.

– Why did you ask me what you should do? Helen asks: you sound, really, as though you want it.

– Tonight I do, Beth says: tomorrow I probably won't. I go up and down like a seesaw. Can you see me as a mother? I shouldn't have thought I'm the type.

– As much as any woman ever is, Helen replies shortly: there's no such thing as a born mother, you've been telling me that for years.

It's hard for her to speak, with so much crowding and jostling inside. Hard to know what to say first. Beth doesn't seem to want to talk much, either. They pad on in silence.

The day of the funeral is the day of the winter solstice, the shortest day of the year. The snow has melted, and it is raining. The path up to the church is a river of mud. The hearse creeps up it, its wheels occasionally spinning in the soft ruts obscured by the deep puddles. A black limousine behind carries Helen and her parents and the other close relatives. Other family members and friends follow in a long line of cars that park under the dripping beeches. All the village, for Mrs Home made many friends, has turned out; people walk up, soberly dressed, from their houses and cottages. Old Mr Home died long ago. After his death, Mrs Home comes to live with her son and daughter-in-law. They insist on taking her in, just as she took them in when they were newly married and had no home. She shocks Catherine by burning all her marriage photographs. Nearly every night, she tells Helen years later, she dreams of him, love long lost, and she

110

complains to him: where are you, lover, where have you gone?

She has been dying for some time. On every visit, looking a little thinner, more fragile, her energy for life poured now into a description of how it feels to age, a catalogue of the new frailties.

– I don't believe in heaven, you know, she tells Helen on the last occasion they are together: I told the vicar, too. I said to him, where's heaven, then?

– What did he say?

– He said it's a place of green fields. Up there.

Mrs Home waves her hand in the air.

– And I said to him, she goes on, sounding pleased with herself: how can there be green fields up there?

She looks at Helen, who sits on a stool at her side.

– Heaven is us together here now.

Helen wants to revive her grandmother from death, be the Christ, believe in Him. Watching the loved face, hearing the loved voice, she wants to preserve her grandmother with her love. If I'd loved her more, if I'd shown it more, she mightn't have died so soon, she thinks, standing outside the village church and waiting for her parents to come over and join her so that they can go in together. She knows it's selfish and wrong to think like this. She knows that her grandmother acquiesced in her own death, with some struggle, that she decided to go. She was dismayed, but she consented to death. She closed her eyes and slipped off (and Helen wasn't with her); she tunnelled down through the bedclothes, prisoner of pain she dug an alley down, and then she cut loose, and left Helen alone.

Her grandmother is better than any priest for an anguished child. Helen confesses her misdemeanours to her. She tells her that she lied about the man making her go with him on the day when she was late for tea after the hockey match. Mrs Home puts her knitting down and stares at her grand-daughter in perplexity.

– Oh, you fibber, she exclaims: you story-teller. What ever did you do it for?

Helen can't explain, but she feels forgiven. Absolved by love. And when she steals three plastic ducks from a friend's toybox and hides them behind her mother's chest of drawers where they are certain to be found, she confesses that too.

– Stealing's wrong, Mrs Home says firmly: you go on and give them back right away.

Such a relief, to be scolded. Mrs Home is stern about right and wrong. A detached arbiter on whom to rely. Then it blows over and is forgotten, the sin, and the child is comfortable again.

Years later, when Helen has left home, the two of them keep in touch by letter. Helen keeps every one that her grandmother writes, treasuring the bits of wisdom, the prose style, the humour, the large rounded script that fills the notelet page and then curls irrepressibly all around the margins and usually ends at the top.

Her grandmother sends her advice. Why can't you fall in love and marry and settle down comfortably? You never know anybody until you have lived with them. There is always give and take, in everybody's lives. Another thing, my dear Helen, you smoke and drink too much. No doubt it is the custom to do so, for the people with whom you mix. But you will ruin your health. Please dear, do not take umbrage at all I say, but I am your grandmother, and have watched you grow up, I grieve to see you on the wrong path. I know you have to live your own life, but you are getting on now, and should know, to where you are leading. I have always been so proud of you. You were such a loving little girl, and so clever. So forgive me for being so outspoken. Do you know my parents would have flung me out of the house if I had talked about men like you did last week. I think I am broad-minded for a ninety-six year old, but really, Helen. You know whatever happens, your parents would forgive. Well, I have had my say, and relieved my mind, but I had to get it off my chest. I hope you will have a good time in Rome and see the Pope and all the sights. A very happy Easter, it will soon be here. We are all going away for a few days, that is, if I last as long. Despite all the snow, the snowdrops are standing up well, and daffodils shewing fat buds. Soon the primroses will be blowing. Well dear, I must close now, as Bill is going up to the post. Ever your affectionate Nana. PS More snow! the landscape all blotted out, blow it.

Helen weeps when she receives this letter. She weeps again, remembering it, recognising how she never allowed her mother to address her with similar words, how she kept her at bay, ran to her grandmother instead, used the older woman as buffer, as refuge. She stands at the churchyard gate, watching her parents greet relatives and friends, and sees that the time has come for her to ask for forgiveness, to cross the distance, to move back. They look old, she thinks, watching Bill and Catherine: they've become *old*.

When Helen is six, she has an adventure. She creeps into the kitchen, opens the larder door and stands tiptoe to reach up for the biscuit tin.

112

She steals six, closes the door again, and goes out the back way so that she won't be seen. No one, meaning her mother, knows where she is. She is free and she is alone. She runs through the back streets of the suburb to the park, and roams there all by herself, speaking to no one, sitting on a park bench and consuming her tea out of its brown paper bag. It is a cold spring day, the sunlight sharp as lemon juice spilling on to the big playing field.

Here she is in a park twenty-five years later, feeling the same loneliness, excitement, fear.

If she ever does have a daughter, just say it's a daughter so that she can use the pronoun she, then she'll have to accept that Lily also will need to run away from home, to hide from her mother, to have her own secret life full of thoughts and especially doubts. Helen who prides herself on her imagination and her memory, who is propelled by the particular feeling of the air one evening across time into a similar occasion twenty-five years ago, who can summon up the past like a magician drawing the ace of spades from the pack at will, Helen has reached the age of becoming a mother. No longer a proud, unreachable child, but a mother.

So that's, partly, what she's crying about. Goodbye, childhood, goodbye. We all move up one. There's her grandmother dead, there's her mother Catherine pulling down her mouth as though from a sour taste and remarking: so I am the eldest now. You have to weep for what you're leaving behind. That's what lets you go.

Helen's grandmother tows Helen after her. She makes her grow on up. And now Helen is one step nearer to death, and that deep sea where Mrs Home rocks through the year's long night. And there's Lily, running out from under the dark masses of the trees, in a stained frock with a ripped hem. Fruit stains, all over her hands, and when she sees Helen and Beth, she turns, and comes straight at them, arrow from a bow quivering straight to Helen's heart.

Seeing the coffin is the worst thing. Such a little, specific box. Made of light pine, it sits on the wooden uprights placed there earlier that morning, one large bunch of red and yellow tulips set on top. Bill Home sings in the choir. Despite the bronchitis that afflicts him every winter and makes him short of breath, he wants to take part. His face is red above his white surplice. He has been so angry with his mother for preparing to leave him, snapping at her sometimes, then frightened at himself, at his own violent emotion that hurts the one he loves, and needing reassurance and comfort from Catherine. Once, when he was little, he fell off his bicycle and broke his head open. His mother nursed him, and hushed the doorknocker with rags. Now, she who had cradled his cracked head, is busy dying, fitting pain to her like a stiff new boot, ignoring him. Rage swells him, a hectic red balloon. How he bawls, an old baby.

Today, in church, he is red again with grief, and he sings loudly the words of consolation, the anthems promising green fields where they all shall meet again. Once the service is over, and the congregation is milling in the porch shaking hands with each other, he looks around, lost and unhappy: where's Catherine? where's Catherine?

– She's here, Dad, Helen says quickly: she's here.

She's so touched by the way they need each other, take care of each other, two passionate people who have spent years arguing long and ferociously. It breaks her open. She leans against the low wall of the churchyard outside, desolate, rain and tears pouring down her face, watching her parents shake hands with every one of the mourners and thank them for attending. She looks, hollow from wanting, at the cool mud, the stalks of grass, and thinks of nothing, of nothingness. She can't grasp it. It makes her feel despair. But the resurrection, the incorruptible flesh, how she doubts that, the consolation of patriarchs wishing to deny the female bodies that create by giving birth. Perhaps there are only bodies rotting as they must, to enrich the earth, complete the cycle, enable seeds to grow, her grandmother sailing off now to the crematorium to huddle in a wooden coracle and disembark in flames.

No woman may help carry a coffin. If only we were allowed to help perform that last service. If only we were allowed to be priestesses, to chant the laments when a woman dies, to sing of a woman's life, to praise her movement through her life, to throw the flowers, to dig the grave. Man that is born of a woman, the vicar intones over Mrs Home's body: hath but a short time to live, and is full of misery. He cometh up, and is cut down, like a flower; he fleeth as it were a shadow, and never continueth in one stay.

– I'm sorry, Helen says eventually, awkwardly, her face burning: I wasn't more generous. I am pleased for you really. Only I know I'm envious as well.

– Don't worry, Beth says briskly: I understand.

Helen kicks at the dead leaves under her feet.

– You always do. You're so tolerant, I can't stand it. Whatever I say, whatever I feel, you say it's perfectly all right. There's one rule

114

for you, and another for me.

– What are you trying to say? Beth asks patiently.

– It's the way you're talking about the pregnancy, Helen bursts out: you sound so cool about it. It's an accident, you say. You haven't told Pete yet, you say. Why not have a baby, you say, now is as good a time as any other. Pregnancy's such a big thing for a woman, and you talk about it as though you're going shopping.

Beth continues pacing along, frowning. They are descending Portobello Road. On their way up it earlier, at five o'clock, the market was going on in the dark, wooden carts rumbling along the street, electric lights slung across the stalls, bare yellow bulbs hanging like strange vegetables and swaying as the wind moved them. Now, the street is hushed, littered with fish and chip papers, prowled by scavenging dogs.

– It's because of you, she says at last: I wasn't sure how you'd take it. I don't want to have to cope with your envy. I just want you to be pleased for me and not make a fuss.

– Oh, Helen says, feeling instantly ashamed of her egotism: oh.

– I value your intensity, Beth hurries on: there's no one else in my life who confronts me like you do. I love it. But right now, I need a bit of peace. I'm sorry. I need to work out whether I'm going to have this baby or not –

– You've already decided, Helen breaks in: you'll have it. I know you will.

Beth stops, and clutches Helen's hand. They stand under a gas-lamp, their faces a garish yellow.

– Really?

– I can hear you saying it. I can hear you wanting it. That's why I'm envious.

How could I possibly have a baby? Helen thinks. To have a baby you're supposed to be married and have a home of your own, preferably a mortgage, and a wicker crib and an account at Mothercare. It's the doctor who makes you pregnant really. You know nothing about it of course, because he's the expert, you lie on the plastic-leatherette couch in his office and he tells you you're going to have a baby. He's God, he's the angel Gabriel. It all has little to do with you. Unless you're the Virgin Mary, better not be a single mother. No father for the child! No-one to tell the baby whence she came: what class, creed, family, race. Just the mother, opening her own legs wide and seeing her own child poke her own head out. Her body is the baby's house, and her name is hers, and she gives her life, and a soul, and milk.

115

Helen's not fit to be a mother, chorus the social workers, doctors, lawyers and priests who stand under her window at night and wake her with their derision. Some nights, some mornings, she agrees with them, and cowers, whimpering, under the blankets. Other times, she fights back, leaping out of bed and striding angrily up and down the room, calling to them to leave her alone.

She might be infertile, anyway. And the world, she remembers suddenly, is going to be blown up.

– All right, darling? Catherine asks.

– More or less.

Helen takes the tray of teacups from her mother.

– Here, I'll do it.

She's grateful for an excuse to escape from the sober party, or gathering, she doesn't know what to call it, after the funeral. She doesn't want to chat to relatives and old family friends; she wants to bawl. She leaves to her mother the responsibility of greeting the guests, introducing those who haven't met before, offering around tea and cakes. She's behaving like a child to skulk like this, she knows it, and she doesn't care. She still has some mourning to do.

She stands at the kitchen sink, alone, sliding hot water and green bubbles over the cups which swim in the plastic bowl, and then transfers them one at a time to the stainless steel draining board. She notes mechanically that her mother's begonias, on the window-sill, look healthier than her own.

She stares through the big square of the window, searching through glass for meaning, at the garden and the field beyond, and at the blue rise of the Mendips behind. Small hills at this point, comfortable rounded shapes patchworked in olive and blue made misty and deep by the rain. The view from the window soothes her, as it always does, pulling her towards itself, telling her to lie down on the hill's shoulder, for consolation and sleep.

Her grandmother is now in the earth. They have surrounded a rose tree with her ashes; between turf lips she lies compressed, a word in a green tongue. An older burial site swells in the fields beyond the garden, a grassy mound nibbled at by cows. Only scholars can talk to that dead goddess in her tumulus. Helen's own mouth is locked up. She wishes for words of incantation; she wishes to summon the female dead, to speak to them, to learn. Where are you now, my grand-mother, white-haired warrior, indefatigable voyager? Your pine coffin was the boat you chose to launch, and death the great water it furthered you to cross. My fists thunder on your breast, the bony gate to Hades and the ribbed boat that takes your spirit there; I harrow Hell, calling out for you lost in the dark. Does the soul exist? Where are you now?

Her father's white surplice glimmers in the hall. It is beginning to grow dark, at not yet four o'clock. Helen tiptoes past the shut sitting-room door, behind which trembles the serious, muted conversation of the other mourners, and up the thickly carpeted stairs. Her grandmother fell over at the bottom of these stairs, lay on the carpet, her penultimate bed, in agony, her hip broken, fragile bone enduring whole for almost a hundred years.

Her bedroom door is closed. Helen opens it and goes in, closing the door behind her. She sits down on the single bed under the window, smoothing the white coverlet with one hand, looking at the embossed cream wallpaper bare of pictures, the four sides of a pale tomb. The room is so small that there is little space for more furniture than the bed, an easy chair, a bureau and a wardrobe, all packed tightly in.

The room is full of peace, tangibly so. It reminds Helen of the Quaker graveyard she stumbled upon one day as a child, exploring Harrow-on-the-Hill for the first time. She found what seemed to be a garden, a small enclosed place thick with flowering bushes sprawling on to sweet-smelling grass and laced with honeysuckle. It was still, and quiet except for the drone of bees and the chirp of blackbirds. Helen crept in, and sat down on the grass by a redcurrant bush, and was silent, and it seemed to her as though God was in the garden, and touched her face very gently, and said: be healed. Her grandmother's bedroom feels just the same.

And then she hears her grandmother's voice, brisk and distinct, whether inside or outside herself it is impossible to say. The voice is simply quite real, and inside the room.

– Well, dear, Mrs Home says, as though continuing a broken-off conversation: look after yourself. Have a basin of onion gruel at night sometimes, that's what I'd do. Or some rum. Those lodgings of yours must be full of draughts. Make sure you wrap up warm.

Helen doesn't move, for fear of disturbing the voice and making it go away.

– Nana, she whispers: hello Nana.

– You rewrite that book, her grandmother continues: and get a bit of the sorrow from your soul. And take care of Felix when he comes home. You can give him some comfort. You have had a few affairs yourself, you know how it feels to lose people, so perhaps you can console him.

A pause. Helen holds her breath and listens harder, for the voice, when it begins again, is fainter, as though Mrs Home is moving away.

– My husband's ashes were scattered under the sweet peas in our old garden in Edgware. My sister-in-law asked me to leave a will for my ashes to be buried under the rose tree with my brother's. I said: what, all that expense? Mad, I think. My ashes will be blown to the winds.

– We've taken care of that, Nana, Helen says timidly to the spirit hovering near her somewhere in the room: and Dad's collecting money for a memorial to go in the church.

– Green fields, her grandmother jokes: green fields.

And then she vanishes.

The withdrawal is complete. The room is still peaceful, but it is empty. Just four cream walls, and Helen sitting on the white counterpane of the little bed, shivering slightly because the radiator is off. She stretches, and yawns very deeply, as you do after weeping when the crisis is past. Then she gets up, and goes downstairs to offer her mother some belated help with their guests.

You've withdrawn from me, Helen thinks, looking at Beth: and I can't bear it. But I'll have to. I'll have to get used to it.

Some sort of law, enunciated by families. A woman must leave her mother, and cleave to her chosen man. A woman lives with her man, and her women friends, however dearly loved, are at a distance.

I don't want to leave my women friends, the tribe of us, and I don't want them to leave me.

– More coffee? she asks Beth.

– No thanks. I'll never get to sleep. My God, I'm tired. It's time for bed.

Probably for the last time, Helen is drearily sure, she lies down beside Beth under the Indian duvet cover patterned in blue and green. Beth is instantly asleep, healthily tired out by their long night walk through the silent city and the dark green park, curled up, hugging a pillow, into a comfortable hump. She can sleep anywhere, undisturbed by phantoms, the proximity of a friend. Helen lies rigidly next to her, eyes open upon the dark, and one word hammering insistently inside her head: gone; gone; gone.

– How big is your bag? Catherine asks: have you got room for anything more?

It is the day after the funeral, and Helen is preparing to return to London. Her mother has loaded her up with fresh eggs from the farm next door, Cheddar cheese from up the road, a trout caught in the local lake, a pot of home-made marmalade. Catherine has ransacked her larder and kitchen, now that her daughter proves willing to accept her gifts; they are suddenly pleased with one another, the items of food expressing all that remains unsaid.

– You mustn't give me any more, Helen protests: I'll clean you out of house and home at this rate.

But she's secretly still open-mouthed, nonetheless, at her mother's heaped bounty, and won't need much persuasion to accept even more.

– I don't mean food, Catherine goes on: I was thinking that perhaps you'd like one or two of Nana's little things. She didn't leave a will, as you know, and she didn't have anything of any value, but I thought perhaps you'd like a keepsake or two.

Helen follows her mother upstairs. They stand together in front of the old-fashioned wardrobe of dark wood. The double doors swing open, revealing dresses and skirts hung on one side, and a stack of drawers and trays on the other.

– I *must* get all this stuff cleared away, her mother says urgently: I want everyone in the family to have what they'd like. Is there anything here you could use?

They lift out the trays and dispose them on the bed. Christmas presents bought for all the family and not yet wrapped up; scarves and handkerchiefs; bath salts and talcum and soap. Jewellery: artificial pearls in thick milky ropes, bright glass jewels set in gilt claws to make brooches and pendants and rings. A leather wallet, rubbed purple morocco tooled in dim gold; a cardboard box containing curls cut from her children's hair; a stack of notelets with matching envelopes; a little Victorian pocket brandy flask.

Relics both pitiful and dignified, attesting to a life of semi-poverty and ferocious independence, of generosity managed even on an old-age pension. Nothing that can be classed as valuable, as an antique, to be fought over; simply these small domestic and toilet items arranged with exquisite neatness on the battered wooden trays.

– Nana gave me quite a few things already, Helen says, hesitating: before she died. She brought me up here and told me to choose.

She already possesses, therefore, a lace blouse, a garnet ring, a cut-glass ashtray, a paisley scarf, precious souvenirs from which she will never part.

119

– Didn't you give her the brandy flask? her mother prompts: why don't you have that back?

– The wallet would be nice, Helen says: it's an old one, it's really beautiful, and I haven't got one.

Her mother insists on adding a flowered cylinder of talcum powder and a mauve chiffon scarf to the flask and wallet. She looks pleased. Helen has a sudden memory of her weeping on the telephone after old Mr Home died, telling the woman doctor who lived next door about how awful it was clearing out Mr Home's clothes after his death: the polished shoes worn into the shape of his feet, and the pyjamas and vests. What could she do with them? It was the pyjamas and vests and shoes which hurt the most. Helen rarely saw her mother cry, saw her mother only in relation to herself, as provider or with-holder of love to a child. Seeing her mother cry down the telephone about her father-in-law, she comprehended for the first time, it seemed, that adults could love one another, and felt deeply ashamed.

– There's something else, Catherine says: that I'd like you to see. Nana started writing her life story, at long last. She got as far as four pages. It's in the bureau downstairs.

She turns to look at Helen.

– We all went on at her to do it, and at last she made a start. It's such a shame there isn't more. That's a whole piece of history gone. She was going to do a family tree, you know how huge her family was, but she never got around to it.

– My hair's grown quite long now, Helen says, feeling tears rise in her throat, she promised me she'd do it if I grew my hair.

Rapunzel, Rapunzel, let down your hair. The wise old witch climbs up the long, swinging plait that her granddaughter dangles down the side of the tower, and the two of them sit together in the little turret room at the top. Are you sitting comfortably? Then I'll begin.

Third Visitation: Spring

One

– Lunch with George and Anna? It sounds too civilised for words. Are you sure you're going to be able to cope with it? Beth asks: and since when was George ever in a couple? I thought you said he felt it was his duty to set the example of non-monogamy to the rest of us?

Helen laughs.

– People change. George certainly has. Anna's the woman he wants, anyway. It's quite extraordinary what a difference she's made to him. He's talking about living with her. And he's started buying cases of wine to offer the comrades when they come around. Nescafé simply won't do any more.

– So you've been seeing him?

– Not really. We bumped into each other in the market the other day and had a bit of a chat, and then he rang me this week and asked me round to lunch at Anna's house today. So I explained you'd be down for the week-end and he said to bring you. He said he'd like to meet you.

– Mmmm, Beth says doubtfully: well, as long as you're sure you've got over him.

– I have. Really. A merciful escape for both of us. He's too big for me, anyway. I prefer men a bit more my own size.

Beth refills her coffee-cup, sceptical, polite.

– It's a lovely day for a lunch party, I suppose.

They fall silent, curled up at either end of the sofa-bed, and contemplate the view through the window of the houses opposite. In the spring sun these are so bright, so pretty, so clean, that they look as though they have been carved from sugar and then dipped in colouring: almond, banana, coffee and rose. Overnight, it seems, the street has burst into bloom. All along its elegant, gentle curve, trees are planted, and this morning they are newly, boldly, turned into clouds of deep pink, as though invaded by a huge and delicate army of butterflies.

Beth lounges with one hand holding her cup of coffee set on the fat rounded edge of the sofa, the other flung up behind her head. She looks at the red slipper on her foot swinging to and fro, and then at her friend.

– I'll tell you something, she says: it's nice to see you smile again.

– Oh God, have I been such a misery for so long?

Helen leans forwards and takes Beth's hand.

– It's so lovely that you're here. I wish you didn't have to go back tonight.

Beth smiles and says nothing, and Helen moves their joined hands down to Beth's gently swollen belly.

– Can you feel it yet? Does it kick?

– It's not an it. It's called The Beast. And yes, she, he, does kick, mostly at night as I am falling asleep. That's when I get cramps, too. My GP suggested I ward them off with a glass of whisky, so I bought a quarter bottle and left it on the bedside table in case, and of course slept better than I've done for ages. And in the morning, what do I find but that Pete has drunk all of it during the night. I was *so* furious.

– It moved, Helen says excitedly: I felt it. I mean The Beast.

She is awed. Under the palm of her hand, the flutter of a hidden life.

Beth laughs.

– You can sit and feel it all the way down to Lewisham if you like. We should be going, surely. It's nearly half-past twelve.

She stands up. She is dressed in baggy scarlet trousers gathered over the hump of her pregnancy into her waist and engirdled with a gold sash; a red cotton shirt; a gold waistcoat; and red slippers. She catches Helen's admiring eye, and smirks.

– A present from my sister. Nice, huh?

– Well, frankly, it does make a change from the ubiquitous dungarees. I see that pregnancy is allowing your true femininity to emerge at long last.

– Shut up. And let's get going. We're going to be late.

– You'll look so beautiful when you're pregnant, Steven mumbles, his face between Helen's breasts: you'll be so *big*.

This conversation returns to Helen three days later, when she stands with Beth in front of the Shwedagong pagoda, their backs to the city of Rangoon and their eyes transfixed by the gold-plated, bowl-shaped dome of the central stupa. Glittering at sunset, it rears serenely against the green and peacock sky.

122

– We made it, Helen breathes: we made it.

Wrenching herself away from Steven, she flung herself into the arms of Beth, the white, freckling arms of a traveller newly arrived from London and sagging in the wet heat muffling her as she stepped off the plane in Bangkok.

– Only just, her companion returns.

Beth is not referring simply to the negotiation of entry visas, the purchase and smuggling of black market currency other travellers have told them is necessary given the exchange rate inside Burma, the persuading of immigration officials that they are bona fide tourists who will stay no more than the maximum permitted eight days. She is pointing to her friend's long dreamy silences, her sudden flushes and guilty starts, the unspoken word *Steven* that floats constantly in the air between them, the secret litany of love that Helen repeats to herself. Beth is angry, but, being Beth, is determined to cope with it. Not for her the tears and reproaches that Helen, on another occasion, might use. So she sightsees alone in Bangkok for two days, and runs to the Burmese embassy and back, and waits patiently for her friend to emerge from her cocoon of sleepless nights and join her in deciding which plane they will catch.

– I'm so thirsty, she says now: let's just have a quick look round and come back later when we've had something to drink. Or tomorrow. We've got plenty of time.

– Let's stay awhile, Helen argues: it's a shame to go away too quickly after we've just got here. Let's get a drink later. They all taste of scented hair oil, anyway.

Beth smiles, pleased. Helen is joining in, at last willing to make a decision, awoken from her drifting, memory-ridden state that roots her in Bangkok in Steven's bed by the vivid, lush green of this city, the shock of seeing the suburbs of Rangoon repeat the design of those in London: the roads flanked with green lawns, the stucco villas, the ornamental railings, all this transposed Englishness peopled by men wearing sarongs topped by knitted pullovers and carrying rolled-up umbrellas like city gents.

On arrival, they walk, shy, curious pilgrims, from the centre of town straight to the Shwedagong pagoda, which lifts itself up on a hill and blossoms like a small city. The central stupa is fringed by a thick ring of smaller shrines, and then encircled by a cool, wide marble pavement on which men and women kneel and pray. Outside this there is another ring of pagodas, and from here four covered stairways fall down the hill. The effect of the whole, to their dazzled eyes, is that of a fantastic fairground ablaze with silver cake-doiley roofs, mosaics of fractured glass and glittering stones, bright pink and blue tiles, gold leaf splashed on everywhere, striped gaudy plaster and stucco like liquorice allsorts, and garlands of jasmine, the white petals rotting amid coloured ribbons, looped along the railings of shrines and piled on the shining floor. They reel around the shrine like puppets on a roundabout set in motion by a giant hand, and lose all sense of where the circle starts and stops, sucked into a whirligig of prayer.

The eastern stairway, which they finally descend, stumbling and drunk on sensation, is dark, and tawdrily magnificent, a canopy of mouldy wood hung with cobwebs and gold tents, its sides pierced by lances of light from the gardens of the hillside viewed in a second's tantalising Zen flash through slits in the stone walls. The steps are broad, and choked with people: old women smoking fat black cigars, monks in flame robes holding out silver begging bowls in which they can drop offerings and make merit, men and women selling lanterns and inlaid boxes and papier-mache toys, girls plucking one another's hair above the ears. Hot, and richly smelling of incense and spices and tobacco, the tunnel unrolls itself like a carpet down the hill, spilling them at the bottom, doped merchandise, adrift in time, so that they have to shake themselves to collect scattered senses and brains, but remain enchanted, and have to laugh, and accede to being drugged, and shrug.

– A drink, Helen says cautiously: OK, that's the next thing.

Anna's house, in its little alley-like street, is set on the brow of one of the hilly parts of Lewisham. When George opens the front door to Helen and Beth and leads them through the hall and out of the back door onto the steps, the view bursts on them as a surprise.

They are standing on a green and flowery precipice. The whole of London, it feels like, drops far below their feet and away to the blue hills of the horizon. They exclaim with delight, and behind them George makes a small satisfied sound like a snort.

On one side is a cemetery, wild and straggling, a jumble of stone monuments and natural growth, and on the other side the neighbours' back gardens, long and narrow, packed tightly together, stretching away in vistas of blossoming bushes and trees. At the bottom of Anna's garden are pollarded limes in a row, their leaves uncurled into glistening green where the sun strikes them, and, at their foot, a little wilderness which will be bluebells. In front of this, the vegetable patch, set with rows of bean poles strung with black cotton to keep the birds off and crossed by a path constructed from red and brown bricks pressed into the earth. At the sides, along the fences, there are apple trees, redcurrant bushes, herbs, lilies of the valley. In the foreground, between the pear trees and the beginning of the vegetable patch, there is a small lawn, and reclining here on a blanket is Anna, laughing at them gawping at the view.

Anna's black curls are heavy with light, like the mass of trees in the dip between hills; her face and arms are already going brown. She is a big woman, a match for George, Helen decides, watching her. She wears the skimpiest of vests and tatty shorts, and her long legs, their strong muscles furred with hair golden in the sunshine, are stretched voluptuously right across the rug.

She smiles at Helen, whom she has already met several times at parties, and at Beth, who introduces herself. Then she motions with a sturdy toe towards the bottle of white wine keeping cool in the flower-bed under the pear trees.

– Bring the wine over, Helen. I'm too lazy to move.

– Where's George gone? Helen asks, looking around.

– He's gone to finish cooking. He'll be out in a minute.

George *cooking*, Helen thinks, stunned: he certainly has turned over a new leaf. She catches Beth's eye and winks, and Beth winks back.

– You got a cigarette? Anna asks: I left mine indoors.

– Sure, Helen says, hauling out a squashed packet: have one of these.

– I've never seen that brand before. What are they?

– They're from Indonesia. Felix brought them back from his trip there, and I discovered a packet when I moved into his flat. I should warn you, they're at least a year old.

The packet is bright red, with navy-blue ends. It has a little inset picture of a railway line and a row of gabled houses with verandahs, printed in red, navy and white, and a long yellow paper seal with the same picture printed in red, green and yellow.

– Felix, that's your brother who travels, isn't it? Anna asks politely: does he live abroad, or is he coming back?

– I think he's coming back tomorrow or the day after. I had a telegram a few days ago.

Helen falls silent, drawing on her cigarette, which is rolled in brownish paper and tastes strongly of cloves and cooily of mint. She inhales hot smoke which hits the back of her throat, while at the same time wet sweetness lingers in her mouth.

– You didn't tell me, Beth exclaims: I had no idea.

– Oh, Helen says: I forgot, that's all.

She is remembering one of the letters Felix wrote her from Indonesia a year ago, the page clear in her mind: rough brown paper torn from an exercise book, scrawled over with the fluid blue felt-tip pen. Her twin describes an incident he sees while being transported across Jakarta in a motor samlor: a crowd gathered on the pavement outside a shack watching a man beating a naked woman who sprawls screaming on the ground. Felix wants to jump out and go to the woman's rescue, but the samlor driver, a university professor purged from his job on suspicion of being a communist, warns him against interfering. It is, he says, most likely a brother beating his sister for immorality. And Felix adds: the man's face was exalted, confident and serene. Blue swims before Helen's eyes as she reads this sentence, and one hot tear drops onto the page, puddling the words in blue ink and rendering them henceforth indecipherable.

– Let's have a drink, Anna says, faintly bored: Helen, the wine, look, it's over there.

Helen is glad to drop the subject. She gets up and goes over to the pear trees, and bends to pick up the bottle of white wine. It leans against the blurred head and shoulders of a stone angel, which has travelled in, presumably, from the cemetery over the wall. She stands still, examining the angel, and the angel looks gravely back. She has a peaceful, but a mysterious face. Sphinx-like, she looks beyond the human, the material world, beyond all that which can be apprehended through the intellect or through the senses. She dreams in a different landscape, one remote and not easily entered, whose language halts and shifts, pitched in a low key that has to be listened for with patience and lack of pride, no guarantee of easy understanding. Her face, neck and shoulders rear above the earth, and her hands are folded across her breasts, warm shadows on her stone flesh.

From the waist down, she is invisible. She has shot up through the earth and come to rest in a flurry of flower bed, her shoulders dappled with the blossom falling on her from the fruit tree above. She looks as though she is waiting. The rest of her body is secret, and this makes her ancient underneath her nineteenth-century form. Her face hints at sisterhood, at something shared not only with the laughing thirteenth-century angel on the north facade of the cathedral at Rheims, but also with the smiling shut-eyed Artemis in the sixth-century BC temple at Ephesus, the smiling catlike guardian sphinx on

126

the tomb at Xanthos in Lycia. This angel, come to earth in London, does not smile with her face, but the corners of her mouth hint at olive groves in moonlight; her arms suggest she understands the movement of ritual dance. Her composure, her mystery; one moment of stillness between others of intense vibration.

– Helen, Helen, Beth cries: hurry up with the wine.

She stands up from where she has squatted to meet the angel eye to eye, and shakes off her attention, her attempts to connect and understand. She comes back with a sigh and a creak of the knees from the smell of lemons and wool, the sound of trumpets, flutes and cymbals, to the crowded garden bright with flowers and the faces of her friends. But Beth, she is suddenly convinced, has borne a lute and pointed her toe gravely under falls of pleated linen; she has lain, graven and heavy, on desert sands; and, a silver quiver at her back, she has put to flight both animals and men.

– Come on Helen, Beth mocks her: stop hanging about.

They settle to the business of arranging themselves in a comfortable group on the rug, sharing out the wine, drinking down the hope of a long hot summer to come, chatting idly, and then finding it simpler just to be with one another and say nothing. They loll, pleasure and the heat of sunshine putting a hand on their mouths and relaxing their limbs. Helen takes off first her red espadrilles, then her red and blue ankle socks, then her blue footless tights. She wriggles her toes and plucks idly at the golden hairs which grow there, stretches out her arms above her head, and then surrenders herself to enjoyment and lies back with the other two.

Their room in the Sabai guesthouse in Mandalay is like a deep narrow shoebox, with pale green sides, two wooden fourposters draped with mosquito nets, wooden pegs for their clothes, and a marble-toppped washstand. The communal bathroom is next door, with open colonnades giving a view over the little town, and a throne-like lavatory reached by three stone steps.

– Here is tea, says the Chinese hotelier: and the market is just over there.

At four o'clock the next morning they are woken by the gong resounding from the roof of the mosque. Downstairs, the hotelier waits with the driver of the trishaw he has ordered for them so that they will be able to catch the boat for Pagan. They perch back to back, clutching their bags on their knees, and the driver wobbles off with them. We must be so heavy for him, Helen thinks guiltily, looking at his delicate body's dark silhouette against the flushed sky. It is still night. The ride through the darkness is strange and magical, cocks crowing and a chant echoing up from the mosque, horses and goats asleep along the track, a light in a wooden house here and there, the stars still bright. Steven in Bangkok will be asleep in his air-conditioned bedroom still, though his maid will soon be up, to clean her concrete cell at the bottom of the flats, to make herself a breakfast of rice, to set off for the early morning market to buy food. Thinking about him, allowing herself to do so, opens up a hungry gap inside, which clenches and contracts. She swallows hard, and holds more tightly on to her bag.

– All right? Beth whispers.

– Yes, Helen whispers back.

Being white travellers who can pay, they are shown into the fore cabin of the boat; all the local people travelling on board squat and lie on the open deck. They dump their bags, and then, their guts lurching from lack of sleep and their throats already dry, they line up at the little bar aft for a cup of tea. They sit on wooden stools in front of a blue-painted rack hung with china cups stencilled with roses, and buy tea, a bag of buns, and two cigars. The tea comes, bright orange, with all the froth skimmed off the vat of hot milk poured into it, very sweet, and the buns turned out to be rather gritty sponge cakes. They beam at one another, and toast the enterprise.

– Hola, says George, coming out of the back door and down the wooden steps with a loaded tray balanced on one hand: here's lunch.

He deposits the tray in the centre of the rug, then bends down and kisses Helen on the mouth, putting his arm round her and flirting with her as she introduces Beth and pours him wine. Then, as a shadow falls across her lap, she squints upwards at the man who has followed George silently across the grass.

– Oh yes, George says apologetically: this is Robert. I forgot you don't know each other. Robert, this is Helen and Beth.

The three of them nod at one another, and then the man called Robert sits down next to Anna and helps himself to wine. Helen can't stop looking at him; he radiates energy even while tipping a long stream of cold wine down his throat. He is not particularly tall, and has a compact muscular frame, small hips tightly encased in faded blue jeans, and long, graceful arms, his rolled-up sleeves revealing his forearms, wrists and the backs of his hands thatched with fine black hairs. His black hair is cropped short, and has silver threads, and his face is a collection of jutting surfaces: brow, nose, chin, look as though they have been carved out of skin and bone rather than grown that way. Feeling Helen's eyes on him, he looks up and stares back at her. She goes red, and then he smiles, and his face is suddenly radiant like a child's, all its harsh lines broken up into intelligence and kindness, creases radiating from his mouth and eyes.

– The food's delicious, Helen says hurriedly.

– I made it all, George says proudly: from my new cookery book.

Helen looks down at her plate, willing Robert to speak, wanting to hear what sort of a voice he has.

– You liar, George, he says dispassionately: I had to chop up all the vegetables and make the mayonnaise.

His deep growl makes them all laugh.

– Not enough salt, though, Anna says with her mouth full.

– You'll have to fetch it, then, George remarks: I left it in the kitchen.

– Bloody hell, Anna grumbles, but she lumbers to her feet and back over to the house.

Helen is amused. But George doesn't mind being sworn at. He sits back amiably, his large hands cheerfully throwing food and gulps of wine into his mouth. Helen watches Anna coming back with the salt, watches the movements of her strong body, her legs. She has donned a man's shirt, big and white and floppy, the sleeves rolled up and the front carelessly buttoned, so that when she leans forward to plonk down the salt and pull George's ear you can see the lovely lines of shoulder bones and breasts. She is rather beautiful, Helen admits that, as well as being a revolutionary and an intellectual and very independent, thereby fulfilling all George's criteria for womanhood. She sighs.

Robert stands up in one swift uncoiling movement. She wonders fleetingly whether he practises this animal grace of his. Then he comes to sit next to her and she is flattered by his attention, his turning his back to George and Anna, shutting them out.

– How d'you know George? he enquires in his rasping voice.

– We met at a party, over a year, no, about a year ago or so.

– And Beth, he catechises her: who's she?

– She's my oldest friend, Helen says happily: we've known each other for years and years, ever since university days. Only she lives in Leeds now, so we don't see that much of each other any more.

She stops, and considers, and he waits.

– No, that's not completely true. We went through a stage of not spending enough time with one another, but now we see each other regularly. But she's leaving later this afternoon. She's got to get back to Leeds tonight. It's been a short visit this time. She was at her mother's yesterday and she only came to my place this morning.

She stops again, surprised at the amount of information she is volunteering to a stranger. This close to him, she can see the lines around his eyes and mouth, the beginnings of sagging flesh under the jaw, of a little pot belly. His clothes, with their carefully chosen shapes and subtle colours, their pleasing shabbiness, show that he cares a lot what he looks like. He's like a woman in some ways, she thinks. She judges him to be about her own age. Thirty-one or so.

– When's her baby due? he asks, sounding genuinely interested, surprising her.

– Mid-August, I think. Near the Feast of the Assumption of the Virgin.

He doesn't get the joke.

– She married? You?

– Neither of us, Helen says, amused at this inquisition: though Beth lives with her man. They've been together for years.

– You're feminists, like Anna, aren't you? he asks: how come she's living with a man, then? I thought feminists didn't approve of men?

She laughs out loud.

– Oh, we do sometimes. Though not on principle.

Without realising what she's doing, she lifts her hand and briefly touches the side of his face. It's warm, and softer than she expects.

– Though there are times, she adds, suddenly remembering: when it isn't easy.

– This trip's not working for you, is it? Beth asks: you might as well admit it.

She avoids Helen's eyes while she says this. They are sitting at the very top of one of the many white temples of Pagan. Below them far away in the hot, clear air of early afternoon, the green and brown landscape goes on flat to the horizon, ribbed with plantations and fields, and is studded everywhere, for this is a holy place of temples dedicated to the Buddha, with white stupas sparkling in the sun. They have climbed up the outside of this temple built like a four-sided staircase, have paused in the shadows cast by the buttresses of rose-coloured laterite, have peered in, with the sunlight, through arched openings in the stone, at the vast, peaceful figure of the Buddha seated within, his black marble forehead patched with gold leaf.

130

Helen doesn't know in what language to address him, whether language is appropriate at all. She feels wretched. She has a problem: an unquiet heart. She is nowhere near being able to rise above the yearnings and longings that attach her to flesh, earth, time. She gazes at the Buddha, puzzled and supplicating, and he gazes past her, over her. She is not in a fit state to learn from him. She is lost in the corridors and arcades that wreathe themselves around the severe white geometry of the huge domed shrine; she runs for the outside, peering through windows carved in stone lace and receiving not escape but glimpses of ruined interior courtyards overgrown with tangles of green.

– I miss Steven so much, she says desperately: I can't bear it. I didn't know I'd feel like this. I thought it was just a light-hearted affair I could end in order to come travelling with you.

Why did she think this? Why must a love affair, to be manageable, safe, have its ending built in, far from home? She doesn't know, doesn't want to think about that.

– But it's not like that, is it? Beth says, sitting with her knees drawn up to her chin and her eyes surveying a distant glittering lotus bud crowning a temple across the plain: it's more serious.

Her tone is final. She's better than Helen at recognising things, voicing what's going on. Helen recognises that the dome of the stupa they are both staring at represents the inverted bowl of the Buddha. She knows this because the guidebook tells her so. She wishes she had other books, scrolls of wisdom telling her how to behave in matters of the heart. She is forced to disown the Buddha and he her. They cannot speak to one another. She switches her attention to Beth. The sunlight, hot and harsh, picks out the glistening red in Beth's hair, the blueness of her eyes, the burnt skin on her shoulders and knees, the white dust between her toes resting on the soles of her cracked leather sandals. Beth does not look back at her friend. She frowns slightly.

– So what do you want to do?

Helen gulps. She has thought about this, long and often, in a series of anguished conversations with herself, ever since they left Bangkok several days ago.

– I think, she says, feeling her words chime out very loud in the drowsy silence up here at the top of the world: that when we get back to Bangkok, I'd like to stay there, with Steven, and –

Beth says nothing. Helen has got to say it.

– I'd rather not finish the trip with you down to Malaysia and Bali, Helen says in a forced, desperate rush: I want to be in Bangkok with

Steven for a while and see what happens.

– *Right*, Beth says: so you've decided. Good.

Helen winces as though from blows. Coward.

– Let's go back to the guesthouse, Beth continues: and find some tea. It's far too hot to be sitting out in the sun up here.

She repacks her shoulder-bag with great speed. Camera, sunglasses, guidebook, tin pot of tiger balm, bag of grass, notebook and purse are all flung back into the embroided black linen bag bought in Bangkok just five days ago, and then Beth is off, jumping with agile feet down the side of the temple's slanting side stepped with big white blocks of stone sparkling like sugar lumps under the sky's lid of heat, to where, far below, the driver of their hired horse and trap waits patiently under a skinny tree.

Helen follows more slowly, sweat pouring from her flesh and dampening her tee-shirt and flimsy cotton skirt to make them cling to her limbs and slow her movements as she clambers down, dazzled by sun, half-blinded by guilty tears of which she is ashamed.

I'm sorry, she wants to say to Beth, as they lie on their hard bamboo beds in the little bamboo guesthouse and rest from the fierce afternoon heat: really I am. But Beth won't permit her this indulgence, won't forgive her easily; she is not an ideal child with a grazed knee to be kissed and made better fast. She is brisk, and organising, and cool, twitching her checked sarong over mosquito-bitten legs with one impatient hand and reaching for the plane schedule with the other.

– We've got to fly back to Rangoon tomorrow, anyway, she declares: to be out of the country within the week. This doesn't make any difference. And I shan't mind travelling down to Malaysia on my own. I'll be fine, I can always join up with other travellers if I need to. There are enough of us on the same route.

Her tone is contemptuous, and Helen flinches, biting her tongue.

– *So*, Beth concludes: that's all sorted out. No problem.

Their eyes lock for a moment, and then Beth turns hers away.

– But you don't live here too, do you? Helen asks Robert: with Anna?

– No, he says, sounding faintly amused: Trotskyism's never been my scene. Not even this new sophisticated sort. I'm not interested in politics. I live north. North-west.

Near her part of town. She is secretly pleased.

– So how do you know George and Anna? she persists: are they old friends?

– Not really, he replies in the deep voice that sounds as though it is gouged out of his guts: but Anna and I are both teachers. We met up at a conference on nuclear war and education, you know, what and how we put across in schools. My kids, the kids I teach, are worried sick. So several of us got the conference together as some sort of a start.

– So you are interested in politics, she protests: you must be, to be thinking about the bomb.

He rolls over on to his back and closes his eyes against the sun. Look, his exposed belly says: see how vulnerable I am. Don't attack me.

– No. Kids, he mumbles through the piece of grass he is chewing: they're what matter. I just really like them. So they've made me start thinking about the bomb. You know what I mean?

She is silent, digesting all this. She wants to ask him more questions, but his eyes are still closed, and he looks as though, sated with food and wine and sun, he is falling asleep. She spins around at a touch on her shoulder. It is Beth, waiting for a lull in the conversation to attract her attention.

– Look, Helen. Have you seen the swings? Let's have a go.

She takes Helen by the hand and pulls her to her feet and over to the iron frame of the swings, set at the far side of the lawn. George and Anna watch them indulgently, like a couple of parents.

– They got them through a mail-order firm, Beth explains gaily: Anna was telling me, as a present for each other.

She lowers her voice.

– So George can't be that bad, can he? Though what you saw in him beats me. He's not your type at all.

Helen glances back at George, who is sitting with his legs splayed out in front of him and one large hand placed on Anna's thigh. His belly bulges out over the waistband of his jeans, and his shirt strains across his broad fleshy shoulders. He looks replete, and thoroughly content, sitting there with Anna, who is laughing at him. At his feet, Robert dozes. Jealousy flares in Helen's gut, jealousy of whom she has no time to ascertain, for Beth is tugging at her arm.

– Come on, Helen. The swings. Let's have a go.

Helen perches stiffly on the wooden seat, then settles herself more relaxedly and grasps the metal chains on to which the seat is slung. In no time at all she is swinging high, her feet stretched out in front of her, her arms tightly gripping the chains.

Beth seats herself on the other swing and dangles next to Helen, kicks out, pulls hard, and takes off. She soars with Helen high in the sky, their swings crossing each other in flight, and they smile, suddenly easier in each other's company than they have been for a long time, ever since Beth's announcement of the baby, rocking, flying, together, apart. As they come back to earth and let their feet drag the swings to stillness again, George and Anna clamour like children to have their turn.

Beth and Helen sit down on the rug again, next to Robert's recumbent body, and he opens one eye and grins at them. For the second time, Helen is surprised and delighted by his smile, the total change in his serious face, and wants to say something, tell him a joke or tease him, do anything that will make that sudden beauty sweep across his face again. She squashes down this desire, and turns her face to watch George and Anna on the swings.

She imagines them there at night, the moon shining on the shapes of trees and plants, the ground invisible. There is the swing, very tall, waiting for them. George and Anna are naked. She shivers, looking at George, seeing every part of him, the generous design of his body, rippling with smooth soft skin, muscles and curves. He seats himself on the swing and beckons to Anna. She sits on top of him, facing him, her arms clasped loosely round his neck and her legs slung over his thighs, where he fits snugly, invisibly, into her. She lays her cheek against his, to smell his smell, and to let him smell hers. Then they are off, at first gently skimming the ground and then swooping in long arcs, bold forward flights.

– Well, Beth grumbles: I suppose I'd better meet this Steven of yours.

So they sit, the three of them, in Helen and Beth's shabby hotel room in the Atlanta hotel in Bangkok, passing around a fat joint rolled from Buddha grass, sipping the local Mekong whisky that is gold and brown like coca-cola. The ice melts rapidly in their glasses. The wooden casement is wide open, but there is no breeze, the air as wet and thick as porridge, the smallest movement making their skins break out in a rash of drops. The propellor fan whirring overhead does little more than to stir the cocktail of heat and sweat.

Steven is enchanted by the little hotel room, so different from his glossy white flat, and by the close friendship of the two women. He wants to be a hippy this afternoon, and so he dons a pink sarong and sits cross-legged on the floor, admiring Beth's long fingers deftly rolling a nine-paper joint. They like each other, Helen thinks,

134

relieved: my two best-beloveds are getting on well. Steven is being charming to Beth, offering her comments and half-spoken questions in his most delicate, teasing manner, drawing her out, smiling, playing the rueful schoolboy, spreading his hands wide. And Beth is unbending rapidly from her rigid pose of suspicion and dislike, won over by his frank liking, his warm eyes, his genuine interest in her life.

– I'll go and see if I can get hold of some more ice, Helen says happily, and rises from her squatted position on the teak floor.

Neither Steven nor Beth takes any notice of her. She leaves the room and goes, humming, down the rickety stairs.

Helen remembers night times. She sits on the rough wool of the garden rug, her knees drawn up to her chin, her eyes darting out through her fingers to watch the two figures on the swing, the couple interlocked, their wild arms and legs a counterpoint to the sonorous music of the swing intoning up and down. Felix in his bedroom next to hers is doubtless fast asleep, one hand flung up above his head on the pillow. Her own bedroom is dark, the curtains swelling and fluttering at the window. She can't bear to watch them any more, doubts her capacity to control whatever fiend lurks behind the merry print of Peter Pan.

She tiptoes out, and down the corridor towards her parents' room. Her pyjama trousers are loose, their cord trailing behind her. She clutches a fold of winceyette in one hand, and keeps close to the wall, trailing her other hand over the cool distemper as she goes along. She is afraid of the dark, and frequently wets her bed because she is also afraid of going to the lavatory along the corridor that seems to bend and twist like the paths inside a labyrinth. Most nights, she wakes up exploding in her bed with wetness, she lets go with a welcome, relieving rush, and then lies in her wet smelly sheets weeping and calling out for help. But this night, she creeps to her parents' bedroom door, which is opposite the lavatory. The door is painted cream, and, made of wooden panels, it seems to a child very solid indeed. And firmly shut.

Helen's hand reaches out, grasps the little golden handle and pulls it down to open the door.

George and Anna have perfected a long, slow, swooping rhythm that takes them up high. George begins to sing, choosing a song that fits the beautifully simple motion of the flying bed that he lies in with Anna: one-two; one-two.

– Havana moo–oon, he carols: Havana moo–oon.

Helen can only hear the monster with two backs, that groans and laughs and shrieks. And all the time Anna and George keep on flying. Her arms around his body, her head on his shoulder one moment and bumping against his rough unshaven cheek the next, Anna can feel the sky jumbled up with the trees, her feet rollicking with clouds. As they swing forwards and up, she lies parallel with blueness and could go further and stand on her head all day in the blue sky, and then as they drop abruptly backwards and down she is floating on top of George, skimming with him over green grass and gravel. They are the original hermaphrodite, these two lovers formed back into one again; they have found, each of them, their other half that has been lacking for so long, and they hug one another gladly, determined never to part again, wanting nobody else.

Steven and Beth don't appear to notice Helen coming back into the room with a pitcher of ice, slopping and clinking, which she sets down on the floor before seating herself, folding her legs underneath her in the ratten chair.

They have been tightly bound together by the meshes of their flirtatious talks and laughter. Now they are bound together by a passionate embrace. Helen sits stiffly, her arms clenched around her knees, watching them, a part of her mind registering that this is Beth's revenge on her. Look, I could take your man away if I wanted to. Easy.

She begins to feel faint. She can't speak. She has no sensation of rage and jealousy at all, only a pit opening up inside her stomach, of fizzing feelings mounting from her feet and threatening to engulf her. She is very cold. She doubles over, doubles up, and falls in what feels like slow motion to the floor. She has blacked out, therefore can no longer sit upright in her chair but topples over. And yet at the same time she is fully awake and knows what's happening.

Steven and Beth, interrupted, kneel by her side, full of concern, holding her hands, guilty. She hears her own voice speaking to them, or to someone else she's not sure whom: you only touch me when I'm ill. Then she is sitting up, weeping furiously with shame, a noisy grief that makes them back off, puzzled but listening. She has never hated anybody as much as she hates them. She could win prizes for it, Olympic gold medals, awards in torture. And yet at the same time she is ice-cold, and feels nothing.

Robert offers them cigarettes. Beth refuses, but Helen takes one. The match flares in his cupped palm, and she takes a deep draught of nicotine. It goes to her head, making her dizzy.

– D'you know, she tells them both in a rush: I used to dream I could fly.

She nods towards the swings.

– This is just how it was.

In her dream it is always dark. She is away from her home where she should be asleep, and is standing on the top of a hill that rears up, like this one in Lewisham, in the middle of a great city. Far below her are trees and houses, huddled in dark clumps, pinpoints of yellow light here and there. She begins to fly through a simple effort of concentration, willing herself to rise into the air, directing all the energy of which she is capable into that one act. And she manages it, she rises through desiring it so strongly; desire and its expression know no dislocation. She whirrs through deep grey masses of clouds, she hangs in the heavens' vault, teasing herself, playing games, experimenting with how long she can hover, totally motionless, before she drops down again. Then she kicks her heels together and is off once more, her hair streaming out behind her, the night air wrapping her body like a robe. In this dream, she is trying to catch up with her parents, who fly always just beyond her reach. And always, in her dream, she wakes just before she touches them, only to find that her bed is soaking wet, or that she is standing outside the closed door of her parents' room.

– Come on, Steven says softly, wiping her eyes with his white linen handkerchief: cheer up. A cup of coffee, that's what you need. That'll make you feel better. I'll go and see if I can find you one.

He leaves her alone with Beth, and they hear his feet clumping rapidly down the bare wooden stairs. Beth keeps to herself, for the moment, what she feels. She touches Helen's hand again, and the much-desired contact brings on fresh tears.

– I'm so sorry, Helen gulps, blowing her nose on the large, soft, comforting handkerchief: I don't know what came over me.

She doesn't want to know. Not yet. She can't face it. Beth understands this.

– You fainted from the heat. You'll feel better in a minute.

Helen gets up clumsily from the floor and crosses to the washstand. She splashes her face with the tepid water from the tin jug and then sits down again, exhausted. Her cheekbones ache and her eyes still smart. She leans back against her chair, and lets her body flop anyhow, as limp as a puppet whose strings are dropped.

She remembers once cutting up vegetables, years ago, to make soup for the family's supper. She picked up a carrot that was deformed. It was really two carrots, but they had grown twined around each other so tightly that they were inseparable. Monstrous, she silently shrieked, and whacked at the coupled carrots, and chopped them to bits.

She yawns hugely.

– Better? Beth asks.

– Yes, thanks.

She gropes for words among the vegetable peelings.

– Sorry.

– I'm sorry too, Beth says: it'll be all right.

They both know that it's not all right yet. They'll have to sort it out later, when there's time, when the right time comes.

Two

– I'll drive you to King's Cross to catch your train, Robert offers: far quicker by car.

Beth looks annoyed at this suggestion, but can't think of any good reason for opposing it, particularly as she is going to be late otherwise. Farewells said to Anna and George, the three of them clamber into the beaten-up Ford Escort parked outside the house, and with a roar of exhaust they are away, heading towards the Elephant.

– I'll give you a lift home afterwards, Robert says to Helen, not turning to look at her where she sits beside him in the front seat: you said you lived over my way.

Helen's guts leap.

– Thank you, she says primly: that would be nice.

At King's Cross, he waits in the car while Helen accompanies Beth to the platform. The long tail of passengers is already flicking past the guard towards the train. Beth swings herself aboard, dumps her bag in a seat and returns to the open door where Helen waits for her, to say goodbye.

They look at one another in some amusement. Then they hear the guard's whistle blow, and Beth's expression changes.

– For heaven's sake, she hisses: take care. I'm not too sure I like the look of him. Too confident by half.

Take care, Catherine Home repeats anxiously, every time Helen reports, somewhat aggressively, that she's met a man she likes: you might get hurt. Her mother's solicitude, based on archetypal knowledge, annoys her, and Beth's, based on actual experience, even more. Perhaps, the thought strikes her, Beth is jealous? Of her? She is astonished, and, she has to admit it, faintly complacent. Let Beth whirl back to the arms of her enviable, faithful Pete, then.

– Don't worry, she admonishes her friend: I've learned from past mistakes, I'll be all right.

– Hmmm, Beth starts to mutter, when the train begins to move. She touches Helen's hands.

– I love you a lot. You know that. Till death us do part.

– You shouldn't say that, Helen mocks her: ideologically unsound.

Beth slams shut the door, and Helen steps back, waving and blowing kisses as Beth is borne away from her, sliding rapidly down the gleaming tracks, around the curving end of the platform, diminishing to a dot, and then lost from view. Then she turns round and strides back through the barrier, humming a song, and out across the main station concourse, and so back to Robert's car.

The brothel is on the edge of town, where the dusty highway stops, past the prefabricated suburbs where wives, almost fully clothed, receive their husbands briefly between their legs, past the canning factory and its attendant sprawl of shanty town accommodation, on the battered edge of town where the scrub and the jungle begin.

The night hums and drips, thick blue broken up with stars and the howling of stray dogs and moisture pouring every time you move. Felix's hands are damp; he plunges them into the pockets of his grubby linen suit, turning over loose change. He whistles snatches of the sixties pop song that he has heard in every bar in the city and then takes his hands out of his pockets and reaches up to twiddle a stray lock of hair. Warm, greasy coins, and warm, greasy hair; his fingers alternate between the two.

His companion, a plump Norwegian journalist whom Felix has met in his third bar of the evening, has been to this brothel before. He knows how much to tip the taxi driver, and the way into the large dingy room with a bar at one end and small tables around the walls. They sit at one of these, tossing back rum and coke, wiping the perspiration from their foreheads. It is the latter half of the brothel evening, the time when, according to a strict ritual, the girls begin to reappear in ones and twos after the early clients have departed. They look unwilling and sulky, most of them, as though doubtful of this open space, as though insecure once away from the long narrow hallway, dimly lit, with rooms opening off it on each side with the precision of nuns' cells, where they work during certain parts of the night.

Felix sits forward in his plastic chair, relighting his cigarette, jiggling his drink. The Norwegian is more at ease, eyeing the girls up and down, keeping up a flow of witty, disparaging remarks on their appearance, taking his time. Once he realises there is no hurry, Felix too relaxes, leaning back again, ceasing to fiddle with his change and the stray lock of hair. He peers at the girls, who lean against the bar, or move with an awkward, resentful grace, up and down the centre of the room.

The lights burn low, pink and green bulbs clustering at intervals along the brocade-covered walls under curly gilt fitments. In their dingy light, the girls are now green, witchy and sick, with long fingernails to scratch a man's eyes out and glistening greedy lips; now pink-cheeked, soft and blushing, with breasts like satin pillows and with tender eyes. Felix stares with disappointment at their silhouettes, so short, so dumpy, their hair back-combed into impossible shapes, their heels too high.

– You got time for a drink? Robert asks gruffly, turning the car into Portobello Road: before you go home?

She assents with a nod, and he pulls up with a jerk.

They settle, with pints of bitter, at a table in the corner of the public bar. Helen likes the pub, one she's never visited before. It sparkles with bottles of bright liquid, mirrors with gilt lettering, a wreath of fairy lights around a tank of tropical fish, shiny aluminium strips edging the shelves of glasses and the counter of the bar, a haze of cigarette smoke somehow adding to the atmosphere of intimacy and warmth. Such pleasure, sitting talking to this man, won over fast by the beams of affection and interest he directs at her.

Never talk to anyone you don't know. Never accept sweets from a stranger. Men are either Prince Charmings or rapists.

– I'll get these, he says, gathering up their empty glasses: the same again?

– It's my round, she protests: you bought the first one.

– I've got more money than you, from what you've been telling

140

me. I'll get them.

She watches him as he stands patiently at the bar, waiting to catch the barman's attention. She learns him: the set of his shoulders under his second-hand linen jacket, the length of his arms, the way he lopes forward with his head slightly bent, the way his hands dangle, awkward but graceful, as he waits for his change, the way he turns round and walks carefully towards her with their brimming gold pints, his shoulders hunched and his face splitting like a turnip into a smile.

Felix's girl is called Helena, she says in answer to his query in halting Spanish, smiling coyly at him and speaking with a soft voice. She tries to make him feel at home, pointing to the photographs of her family framed in plastic gold and lace, on the little dressing-table. She is a very pretty girl: honey-coloured skin, large dark eyes, high cheek-bones, and a mass of curly dark hair scraped back with glittering clips.

Her room is small. Besides the double bed, it is crammed to bursting with a large veneer wardrobe, two steel and plastic chairs, a trunk covered with frilly cretonne. Pictures torn out of magazines and framed with passepartout are pinned to the walls; the window sill bears a row of catering tins still gaily adorned with their bright labels and now containing plants; a pale blue glass rosary hangs from the mirror.

Felix recoils from so much femininity, from the smell of stale scent and candlewax, from the stockings and petticoat flung over a chair, from the fluff he can glimpse spilling out from under the bed, from the sweat staining Helena's sweater under the arms. In a business-like sort of way she has turned out the light by the door, leaving the room lit by a pink bulb swinging over the bed. She sits down on its grubby pink quilt, smoking a cigarette, her eyes hard, her mouth murmuring little endearments in broken American. Felix leans against the closed door of her room, hands exploring the torn lining of his trouser pockets, clinking his change through his fingers. She stubs out her cigarette, rises, and crosses the room towards him, smiling. She rubs herself against him, fondling him, touching her lips to his neck as she moves her hips expertly against his.

Helen and Robert come out of the pub, still talking, and wander along Portobello to the car. The street is deserted, and it's begun to rain a little. Helen realises with shock that it's night, and yet it feels as though they've only been together for a little while, rather than several hours. Being with him is very easy, like perching on a sledge

141

together and going downhill fast, their arms clasped around one another, shouting with pleasure at the speed and the view. The way he talks to her, asking her questions and listening and also telling her about himself, encourages her to open up, suddenly convinced that for once she's met a man not hostile to her as a woman, but, on the contrary, pleased at who she is. She's forgotten the deep pleasure of this, and feels it grow inside her, an intimacy suddenly discovered that's so simple it's as though she must have known him in some previous life.

He notices that her attention has wandered away from what he is telling her about his teaching job, and stops speaking. He doesn't seem to mind. They smile at one another, both more than a little drunk on beer and the attraction burgeoning between them, and halt as they reach the car. It is raining gently. Helen, unsure what will happen next, feels shy, and rummages in the depths of her bag for the fresh packet of cigarettes she remembers buying on the way down to Lewisham. Her fingers make contact with a squishy brown paper bag, and she squeaks.

– The strawberries. I forgot all about them. I bought them for lunch and completely forgot to bring them out.

Didn't want to, more like. Didn't want to share them with the others. Wanted to keep them, greedy woman, all for herself. She starts laughing, fishes out the soggy bag, and offers it to Robert.

– Have one. Madly extravagant and out of season, but I felt like having a treat.

– First strawberries I've had this year, he says, helping himself.

– Then you have to make a wish, she says, smiling with her mouth full, flirting.

They stand in the empty, quiet street which is both dark and shiny, eating strawberries. Helen concentrates, making her own wish. Then she starts seeing all the colours around her as though she's never seen them before, intensified by the strange light behind the rain. The blue sleeve of her sweatshirt, her scarlet espadrilles. Robert's olive tee-shirt. A mustard hoarding with purple lettering, and the pavements tinted red and green. The lavender and yellow tints on the shabby facade of the cinema, the tiny sparkling lights that run around its name like a necklace swung in the air. Everything that can, draws light into itself, and glows, loaded with it, and the strawberry that she holds in her fingers grows bigger and more luscious second by second, plump as a heart.

– We'll go home, Robert decides: shall we?

She assents gladly, for he has voiced what she also desires.

Helena, lying face down on the bed, has dressed herself, at Felix's paid request, in black: shoes, bra and suspender-belt in glossy black brocade, sheer black stockings. The swinging pink light bulb scatters pink shadows on her flesh. Felix, standing at the foot of the bed, is still in his street clothes, and his hands are still in his pockets. His voice, when he speaks, is low.

– I'm going to shave you first.

Helena starts up, releasing a flood of angry Spanish words. Felix guesses that she is demanding to be paid extra for this unusual request. She appears to be deeply embarrassed about his being interested in anything except the missionary position. Sighing at her prudery, her stinginess, Felix agrees to her new terms and pushes her down again on the bed. He sits next to her, prising her legs apart, and peers at the jumble of soft tissue exposed, and shrugs.

Obedient to his instructions, she lies there silently, but she whimpers as she sees the razor approach. Her eyes follow it as far as they can until it passes out of her sight. The blade rasping continuously across a small area of her skin is like a hand pressing down on her, pressing her deeper into the bed. Felix, who is angry with her for her haggling over the money, is not particularly gentle. When he has finished his task, he looks at his handiwork and almost chokes with pleasure. Then he stands up, stretches, and begins to take off his clothes, slowly, whistling under his breath, looking triumphantly at the half-naked girl sprawled on the bed.

Robert and Helen sprawl on the shabby rugs of her room, listening to music and smoking dope, their hands curved around glass flowers full of wine, white clear raindrops, drunkenly at ease with one another in a friendly silence broken by bursts of talk. The bottle of wine between them slightly obscures their view of each other, a window of thick green glass, and so Robert gets up to move it aside. Stumbling from the effects of the dope, he accidentally kicks Helen's leg. He murmurs in apology, and then squats down beside her and strokes her leg for what feels, to her dissolving insides, like several minutes.

– Come on, he says to her unspoken response: let's go to bed.

Two hours later, he falls asleep, and she props herself cautiously on one elbow to consider him, his back curled into her. She feels his buttocks against her belly, his hair against her mouth, and reaches one hand over him briefly to pat his soft and sleeping penis, curving herself around him nestled against her. Then she kisses the soft place between his neck and shoulder, and he shifts and turns round, sighing in his sleep, and pushes his head under her chin and flings one arm across her body. She holds him, and goes on waking, watching this person so separate, so different from herself, who yet has the courage to speak and to come close, asking for friendship with hands outstretched.

Warmth floods right through her. He wants to give to her: his body and his thoughts. She has been parched, and he gives her to drink. She is hungry, and he feeds her. She is lonely, and he embraces her. He nourishes her with his wants, with his leaping towards her, he regenerates her with his body, he fertilises her with his mind. This is alchemy, this is a true meeting, a true exchange. Something more than exchange, even: a creation. She holds something fragile and precious, a globe of green glass, a fruit, between her hands. They have made it together, between themselves, and, while he sleeps, she guards and watches over it, suddenly breathless with care that it does not drop or smash.

Drifting off towards sleep herself, to join him there, she becomes aware of her grandmother's presence in the room.

– Helen, Helen, Mrs Home admonishes her granddaughter: take it easy. Go slowly. You don't know what will happen. Isn't this what you young people call a one-night stand?

– I just want, Helen murmurs: to love him in the way a woman loves a man.

The sound of her own voice calls her back from sleep. Now she is eye to eye with the moon reeling towards her like a strip of film, a long dazzle of waxy white, of clear brilliance. She blinks, and Robert, in her arms, his face laid on her breasts, shivers and shifts as though the moon has dropped cold chunks of silver on to his bare shoulders. Holding him, and lying in the soft darkness of her bed facing the window, she has the sensation of being whirled backwards, over and over, in the enormous night, as the moon grips her and cuts her down to size. As though the reel has ended, and she is the film in the projector flicking and snapping round and round, just a loose end; as though she is one of the heavenly bodies, fixed in an eternal, lonely dance.

Then, very slowly, the moon's brilliance diminishes, and she hears the early simmering of birds, that gradually spills over, first into odd notes and single chirps, then into consecutive twitterings, and finally into long flights of whistling, the chink and squeak of song. And at the same time, the sky is changing, from absolute blackness into a deep inky blue.

Her own shoulders are cold now. She lifts an arm and pulls the duvet higher up, covering Robert carefully, and herself too, so that just their two heads poke out, and then she is warm again, cradling him, and floating towards sleep in her bed, her eyes closing on the maple tree that darkens like a blue fern against the window and the paling sky. And every time she stirs, or turns over, he quietens her, in his sleep, with his hands, stroking her, sliding his hands over her back as though, she thinks with sleepy amusement, she were a cat deeply curled into his lap. Eventually she lies in his arms in a way that feels just right, her head on his shoulder, one arm and one leg curved over his body, her right hand holding his left one, and is instantly, deeply asleep.

– You can't be, Felix whispers, his hands clenched over fistfulls of loose change: you can't be.

Helena appears not to hear him, but continues calmly putting on her skirt, pulling the fastening around to the front so that she can zip it up. His Spanish is not good enough for him to explain. He stands stiffly by the door, seeing little black devils dance in her dark eyes. How unattractive she is, now the bright light has been switched on again and he can see clearly her sallow, open-pored skin, her coarse lipsticked mouth, her thick ankles and legs. She smoulders with sex, she reeks of it, as the room does with female smells, a sweetish, sick odour. All the sex in the world has leaked out from between her legs and is flooding the room, has come from this woman, who tempts him, who lures him in, whose smell will suffocate him, whose fluids drown him, whose gaping hole will close over his head.

Her words still ring in the stuffy little room. He shudders, leaning back against the door well away from her grasping hands, desperate for her to finish dressing so that he can escape into the fresh air. She needn't worry, he'll pay her, the bitch. He digs into his pocket, pulls out his wallet, carefully counts out a dozen notes, thrusts them into her hands. As he closes the door, he has a last glimpse of her face. It shocks and bewilders him, so naked is her expression of rage, of humiliation.

Helen wakes up to the delicious feeling of a man's naked back against her breasts. She raises her head slowly, so as not to wake him, and contemplates him as he sleeps, lit by the sun of early morning. She feels so greedy: she can't look at him enough. His dark, lively eyes are closed, the lashes swept down, and his bony features are relaxed in sleep, his mouth gentle. Black hairs, very fine, grow thickly on his chest, as satiny as grass, tapering, beneath his collar-bone, to the flick of a paintbrush loaded with one full, heavy drop of black.

Once he had wings, this man. Terrible as the angel with the flaming sword outside the gates of paradise, he has caused the old Helen to die and the new one to be born. He is a bird, too, an eagle temporarily at rest, his great wings disposed around him in black and golden folds. And he is a leopard, long and lithe, loping out from under the trees at the edge of the forest into the waving grass of the clearing, stretching himself, his skin rippling over muscles, raising his head to smell the early morning air, and then settling himself, to lie, full length, in the sun.

She trembles all over, watching him; she is Eve, debating how to name him: animal, or man. Desire makes her knees shake, her heart knock, her belly leap. And so she names him: man, my brother and companion, and guardian with me of the plants and animals. She lies down beside him again, the sleeping man that she has found, and touches his bones, his skin's fur.

He wakes up out of a dream conversation, saying: you really should learn to drive. You need a car.

– I shall take lessons, Helen assures him: you're right, I should learn to drive.

– A Morris or a Ford Escort, he says sleepily: that's what you need. He stops, realising that he is awake.

– Hullo, he says to her: you're still here, then.

She beams at him.

– Hullo.

They settle comfortably into each other's arms for a long conversation about second-hand cars and the best place to buy one. Helen can hardly believe the happiness of this skin on skin: it's like being with an old friend, lying there discussing gear-boxes and carburettors and suspension. After they have made love again, they lie smoking cigarettes and touching one another and contentedly not saying anything, until Robert catches sight of the alarm clock next to the bed.

– Half-past seven. I must go. Got to be at school in an hour or so.

He sits up abruptly, pushing her away, and stubs out his cigarette.

– Wouldn't you like a cup of tea? Helen asks him: and some breakfast?

– I'll have a cup of tea at home, he says indifferently: I'll have to go

146

home first to have a bath and change my clothes.

He pats her stomach, leaps out of bed, dresses, and lopes over to the door, all in the space of a minute. He has removed himself from her with rapidity and efficiency, and she sits up in bed, watching him, her knees drawn up to her chin, her arms shocked at their sudden emptiness. At the door he turns round.

– I'll leave you my phone number, shall I? he says uncertainly: and I'll write yours down.

Two minutes later, she hears the front door of the house slam behind him, and then the roar of his car. She sits on, hugging her knees, her body remembering his, and then rolls over into the space he has left, burying her face in the sheets, smelling him on them. Then she yawns, and stretches, and throws back the covers and leaps out of bed. Breakfast. That's the next thing. She hasn't eaten since yesterday lunch-time.

She washes her face in cold water, to drive away her tiredness. Her soap is scented with jasmine. For some reason, it floods her mind with strange images. Tropical nights. Thailand? No, Peru. Yet she's never been there. She must have been dreaming. About a brothel, of all things.

She wanders disconsolately between the bathroom and the kitchen, putting the kettle on, sucking her pepperminty toothbrush, pondering, trying to hang on to her dream, coaxing it to stay and reveal itself. But it slips past her; it vanishes before she can catch at its trailing ribbons. Like the moon, it slips inexorably away, to be replaced by the solid shapes of things seen by daylight.

These include the wooden table she carries on to the balcony from the kitchen, the black cast-iron frying-pan, sizzling with tender pink bacon and the white flaps of eggs, the glossy yellow crocuses blooming at the foot of the apple tree. Helen settles herself on the wooden chair she has drawn up at the table, and is overcome by the smells and tastes of breakfast eaten outside. Hot coffee steam curls up in the sunlight, and there is hot sun on her face and on the piece of brown toast she holds in her hand. The bread is nutty and rich, a pleasure to chew and swallow, with a hint of molasses lingering afterwards on her tongue. Robert tasted sharp and salty. He is not here to taste the breakfast picnic, to see the light dancing through the glass of the marmalade jar on the strong, bitter strands of orange. She rolls her tongue around her mouth, going over in her memory all the moments of the night, and then abandoning them for the pleasures of the present.

147

This is her favourite place to sit. The distinction between outside and inside the house is blurred. She is still of the house, and almost of the garden, yet belonging totally to neither. She shares the privacy and the enclosure of the house with the openness and vegetation of the garden; she is the point at which they meet and overlap. She faces out, looking through the wrought-iron tracery of the balcony over the big garden beginning a few feet below her, at the crescent of the houses opposite forming her boundary on the other side.

Above her, very much defining her garden room, rears a fifty-foot weeping ash. It grows to the right of her, its trunk bent near its base so that the great mass of the tree drops to the left, its topmost branches reaching as high as the roof, waving graceful fronds to blind all the windows with green, and its lower branches drooping to form an umbrella-shaped tent between her and the garden. Joining house and garden in this way, acting as entrance pavilion and as resting-place, the tree has a special charm added to that of its size and height, its long slender leaves, its delicate constant movements, its shape.

Helen sits and gazes up along its slanting trunk, which runs like a dark brown road into a green forest, at the tip of which is the sun, dazzling through a play of leaves. When she sits here like this, she captures content. The tree drops bits of leaf and twig on to her head, on to the garden steps. She is in green shadow, and yet has a green sun dancing all over her.

She lights a cigarette, guiltily enjoying the acrid hit of the smoke, the nicotine, drawing it down. Last night still lies lightly like a shawl on her shoulders, persuading her that she is Eve on the first morning in Paradise.

Helen yawns with pleasure, and stretches, watching the ash burn like a flower at the tip of her cigarette. Smoke wreathes up blue and quick, hazy curls hanging and then dissipating in the sun, blue veils. She stubs it out as she hears the postman ringing at her front door.

How typically laconic of Felix. The cream lines pasted on to the yellow paper simply read: staying out here longer. Everything fine. Back in a couple of months. Love.

Helen paces up and down the little balcony. The pacing merely expresses her feelings, and does nothing to calm them. She feels as though she's had a tooth torn out, and at the same time there's an indescribable sense of relief. She's been set free from some sort of vigilance, and yet at the same time carries a burden of some sort of responsibility. Do I love my brother? she thinks: as much as I used to? New stirrings in the blood, new pores opening, it feels like, along her skin. No Felix. She will be alone. Living alone in his flat. Putting off, yet again, the moment when she starts looking for a place of her own, following the lures of freedom and independence that her own soul waves in front of her.

One autumn, when she and Felix are seven, the family has a week's holiday in a cottage in Norfolk, in a farm set in fields of potatoes, spinach and beet that stretch to the dunes hiding the sea, that roll flatly to all points of the compass, only churches pegging the brown stony land. It flaps as evening creeps up. Helen, dawdling home alone, comes through the shadows of a spinney of poplars and begins crossing the last field before the cottage, a huge field, seemingly endless, its edges creeping away in the twilight. Helen has never been out alone in the country at night. She stands in the middle of the field stockstill, feet planted in the wide ruts left by the tractor, arms outstretched, looking at the red barns hugging the horizon, their colours and shapes dwindling into the engulfing night, her extended fingertips feeling as though they go out for miles.

She loses all sense of her size, feeling at once like a dark dot in vast darkness, and like the darkness itself, bending protectively over the land and over the sea. Joy takes her over; she spins around, dances, and begins to run, round and round in ever-widening circles, blind in the night and not caring, one with the chill, salty air and the hard rutted ground. The thought of Felix, her inseparable companion, brings her back. She shouldn't be out without him. He is the cottage with golden windows lit, the voice that calls anxiously from the gate half a mile away, scolding, promising hot soup, a story before bed.

She's relieved, she fumbles, that Felix isn't returning for a while. It gives her a couple of months in which to organise herself for moving, to begin the arduous process of finding somewhere to live. She still has a room. And into this wide, clear, empty room swim other images, dislodging Felix's face: a typewriter on a desk, Robert.

She will write a novel at Felix's table. She will lie with Robert in Felix's bed. She didn't come with Robert last night. She hasn't come with any man since Steven, all those years ago. Only on her own. She wheels round, fetching up at the table again, and picks an apple out of the fruit bowl on her breakfast tray, sinking her teeth gratefully into its smooth green skin, enjoying the spurts of flesh and juice in her mouth. She remembers her English teacher at primary school, eccentric, beloved Miss Crane, making them all bring apples into class one day, eat them, and then write about what it felt like. Helen's piece was read out as one of the best, and she decided there and then, at the age of six, to become a writer. Three years later, she told her father, and he didn't mock. And look at me now, she thinks ruefully. Holding myself back, with a deep reserve. Why?

She catches a glimpse of movement out of the corner of her eye, and breaks her reverie, looking up. There's a man dressed in overalls standing a few yards from the balcony, gesticulating and coughing to catch her attention. He waves towards the weeping ash.

– Orders of the council, miss. That tree's got to come down straight away. It's too tall, it's coming out of the soil, and it's liable to fall over and damage the houses. Pity, but it can't be helped.

Helen retreats to the balcony's far end, shocked, holding her half-eaten apple in one hand. The council has sent three workmen to do the job. One of them holds a circular saw, a large flat blade mounted in a machine body. At his feet there are coils of rope, a blue metal tool box, a crumpled suit of blue overalls.

Another workman, a rope around his waist, swarms up the leaning tree-trunk, almost to the top. Helen cannot see him perched up so high, but she can hear the whine of the saw as it is opened up to full throttle, buzzing with a deeper note than a dentist's drill, roaring maddeningly like a motor-bike engine constantly revved on the same spot. Each branch, as it is sawn through, is slowly, carefully lowered to the ground by means of a rope and pulley.

The third workman stands underneath the tree, guiding each large, swaying and lurching branch, and letting the wood fall with a crash, which he seems to enjoy. From the top of the tree come snappings and cracks, as the workman up there breaks off smaller branches, half sawn through, with his hands. Then the saw begins again, and another large branch is lowered.

It takes the men three hours to lop off all the branches from the fifty-foot tree. By lunchtime only the main trunk is left, its majesty stripped, its nakedness pathetic. The ground to its left is springy with debris, piled knee-high with branches and foliage.

Helen shivers, looking at the poor nude tree. The workmen now tie two ropes around the tree's waist, then throw the heavy coils to the ground. The first workman picks one up and carries it over to the apple tree some yards away, twists the rope once around its trunk, pulls it tight, and stands there, holding the taut rope. The second workman does the same, picking up the other coil of rope and going in the other direction at an angle of forty-five degrees and twisting the rope around the sturdy trunk of another apple tree. The third work-man now stands at the base of the tree and picks up the circular saw for the last time.

He begins to slice through the tree three foot above its roots. He pokes at the slit he has made, he pokes with his terrible fang tongue as calmly as if he were cutting through fresh butter rather than live yellow wood. When he has sawn almost right through, he stops, turns off the saw, throws it to the ground, and leaps down.

All three workmen, and Helen, cowering in the corner of her balcony, stare at the tall, bare weeping ash imprisoned by ropes. Then the first workman counts up to three, and shouts, and the other two haul on the ropes. One two three, pull. Over and over again. Sweat bursts out on their foreheads, and blisters on their earthy hands; their feet carve up the grass into clefts of mud.

The tree groans. The split in its trunk, facing Helen, widens like a smile. The workmen's shoulders are thickly powdered with sawdust; they wipe their brows, and shout, and pull again. For an hour they wrestle with the tree, which fiercely resists them. Nonetheless, the gash in its trunk widens, bit by little yellow bit. Helen, who is trembling, and unable to move from the balcony, is reminded of bullfights, of huge puzzled beasts tortured to death, their blood spurting on to the sawdust which covers the shoulders of the work-men. The latter grin, and spit on their blisters. They are not brutes; they are merely doing their job.

And then the tree gives a final loud crack, and topples to the ground, thudding with a great tearing, splintering sound on to the mass of branches and leaves. It is a clean break. The stump shines, yellow and flat.

Helen springs to her feet, suddenly remembering all the details of her dream the night before. The brothel. Herself and her brother there. She goes running away over the grass, tripping over her dressing-gown, a long smear of red on the peaceful green view, the half-eaten apple rolling behind her down the steps. God and Adam and the angel stand under the apple trees, wiping their hands on their dungarees, jeering at her, and their faces are those of Felix and her father and Father Briggs.

– You're a whore, their voices call after her as she sprints out of Eden: nothing but a whore.

Fourth Visitation: Summer

One

    – Of course, Robert says: I have a difficult mother, I mean a difficult relationship with her.

    – Does she love you too little or too much? Helen asks: I find it's usually one or the other.

It's Sunday, two in the morning. They have drunk two bottles of wine, and smoked several joints. Helen is now bored by their conversation. She wants to establish a different contact, and make love: her insides are liquid with desire, her flesh jumps and fizzes at accidental contact with Robert's leg. But his thoughts are elsewhere.

She has begun to recognise this *of course*. It precedes certain wishes of Robert's that become enshrined for her heavy as stone tablets brought down from a mountain top. The law. Of course I need my freedom. Of course I need to be spontaneous. Of course I'll never settle down. In the beginning, she saw these wishes as orders, as utterly reasonable, and strove to comply with them.

    – It's not a matter of being loved, Robert says, shocked at her misapprehension: it's a question of her trying to *control* me.

    – Men rule the world outside, Helen snaps: and women rule the home according to male dictates. Is it so surprising that they sometimes abuse that power?

She looks at his wide mouth, his black hair.

    – Anyway, you were a boy. I bet she adored you. I bet she spoiled you to death.

She stops, hearing her voice green with jealousy and envy, fierce weeds springing up and poisoning the words of love which are all she wants to speak. She rushes on, unable to stop the bitter flow.

    – You weren't taught to think of anyone's needs but your own, and you need to control any woman who loves you.

    – D'you mean you? he asks in a small voice.

She sits up and turns round to face him, reckless on drink, dope, fatigue, her body's crying need.

    – Sure. You ring up on the nights you want to see me and take it for granted I'll be there. Then you want to pack me off again as soon as you've had enough. You refuse to make arrangements in advance. Your precious spontaneity is completely at my expense.

– You don't understand, he begins defending himself: I've been having a difficult time at work recently. My needs–

– *Your* needs. Always *your* needs. What about mine? she cries.

She looks at the curtains of his room, their deep green velvet glow. Her envy burns there. She's done it, the thing she's most frightened of: asserted her own needs.

The first word that she utters is *more*. It's a demand, a despairing plea, a shout of rage and frustration. Her mother has twin babies to feed. It's a lot of work, having two. Helen is all mouth, a gaping hole crying out to be filled. Her mother consults the words of doctors on the printed page. Fifteen minutes per baby, per breast, at specific intervals. No demand feeding in between. They'll have to learn, just like their mother does. If only I'd been able, she shyly tells Helen years later: to trust my own feeling rather than the books, I'd have fed you at night when you cried. I used to walk with you up and down the room, and I knew you were hungry and I didn't dare to feed you, because the doctor in the book said it was wrong. Instead, her own daughter later vilifies her. Helen's all impatience, hunger turning to a greed that's never known satisfaction, the pleasure of lying back, full and content. She strains for the forbidden breast, crying and red-faced, she gulps eagerly, too fast, and chokes. She distrusts this food, this thin, short-lived love given too abruptly and taken away too soon. She knows pleasure only by its absence. Instead of sweet milk, she is full of bilious hate: wind and emptiness. Oh, she's bad, a bad baby, there's no doubt of that. The baby book cracks like a whip.

– *Your* needs, Robert says uncertainly: I've not thought about them. I never knew you had any. You're always so happy.

She releases her breath.

– I need a lot, she mutters, turning over and addressing the pillow rather than him.

– You never show it. You're always so cheerful and independent, with your work, and all your friends, and your women's group. I've never thought I mattered to you particularly.

She thinks about this for a minute, angry and astonished.

– Really?

– You are a bit like superwoman, he says cautiously: you're so unselfish and patient and cheerful all the time.

She has on a short paper skirt in red, white and blue, a silver wand in one hand, an enormous red smile attached to her ears with elastic. Robert reaches over and holds her hand. His words touch her as firmly as his fingers do.

– I don't find it easy to trust men, she blurts: that makes it lonely, being a woman who wants to have love affairs with them.

She has opened herself to any attack he cares to make: you are neurotic, frightened, frigid, immature.

– I don't help you much, do I? he says: sometimes I reject you and put you down. I know I put you down the other day when you were talking about your writing.

– I shouldn't worry, she advises him drily: you're not unique. Every man I've ever been with has felt it necessary to put me down for being a writer.

Sooner or later, wham, it happens. Some comment, ostensibly joky, that hurts. So she withdraws, goes back to being on her guard, protecting the deeply private self that dances around on white sheets of paper. He can't come with her there, into that private place, he's not allowed into her hermitage from whence she issues strong cries, wails, love and battle songs. Is that what they mind, all these men, the exclusion? Or simply the fact that she lays claim to creativity?

– So what sustains you then? he asks curiously: if it's not a man?

– My work. And the love of women friends.

– There you are then, you see. You don't need me.

Other images immediately flick across Helen's mind. Robert taking her to music gigs at the Tabernacle, filling her up with salt fish and West Indian beer and fat joints rolled from home-grown grass, winding her up with his warmth and jokes and flirtatiousness and then releasing her spring and applauding as she clatters across the dance floor and spins for him. Robert looking so serious as she teases him and then catching her in a bearlike hug, scraping her face with his embryonic beard and then letting her go and beginning a serious discussion on spirituality. Robert, well, Robert. Sucking her breast as he burrows into her; making tea in silence early in the morning before dashing off to work; floating contemplatively in the bath, and then pacing, wrapped in a huge towel, up and down the room; embracing her at a party and then collapsing, wiped out on whisky, into an armchair; splitting his face into a huge smile; cooking her roast lamb and hovering anxiously as she eats it; snubbing her when she gushes; often completely forgetting she's there.

154

She rests her feet on his, and moves closer to him, curving herself against his brown satin back. The indescribable pleasure of that sensation, body on body. Nothing else matters at this moment except the fact that she can feel all of him against her skin. He wriggles his feet under hers. Then he turns over and clasps her in his arms. Very shyly, his hand moves down over her breast, her belly, her thighs. Then excitement takes him over, and the delightful slowness goes, replaced by urgency.

Too fast, she yells silently into his tightly-shut eyes: too fast.

– It's not a matter of technique or anything like that, she remembers once saying to Beth during a discussion on sex: I can't bear all those expert men who've read all the books and treat me like a machine with buttons to be correctly pressed as though my body belongs to them.

That's why she likes Robert so much. He's no expert, no robot. He's human, uncertain in many ways as she is, yet at the same time weaving about her as purposefully as a bee searching for honey.

– Buzz buzz, she suddenly says to him, giggling, and then closing her teeth gently over his earlobe: buzz buzz.

She takes his hand in her own. Immediately, he lies still against her, tense with the desire to understand what she wants. She can feel him trying to respond to her, and begins to open up to him like a flower. Nobody, she says sternly to the father in her head, ever calls flowers promiscuous when they part their petal skirts to welcome passing bees.

She came all the time with Steven, and she would like to with this man. She's on the ice floe again, waiting for winter to pass, waiting for the cracking, rending sound as the glacier begins to melt a little and to crash through the mountains, waiting for the first green tips of spring to show, the thaw, the water's mighty rush.

Earlier in the same day, she attends a meeting of her women's group. It's well into July now, deep summer. It's been hot for three days running, heat enough to ripen raspberries, swell melons, plump figs. People dress in loose cotton clothes, leaving shoulders and arms and legs bare, so that their skin, after these three days of luxurious lunch-time abandon in parks and on lawns, has turned apricot, and, in some cases, soft terracotta. The heat makes Helen happy. She walks slowly away from her meeting through Highbury fields, reluctant to enter the dim, stuffy tube, lingering to feel the deep warmth of the sun press through the thin cotton of her floppy shirt, turning her head to watch the children and dogs at play on the grass. Couples and families loll under the great lime and plane trees; older people sit on wooden benches on the broad walk fringing the wide sweep of green, shadows and sun lacy on their shoulders like collars of light.

The women have their meeting in the garden of the shabby collective house of one of them, tall brick walls enclosing them, and the tossing fresh green of lime trees. They begin at eleven in the morning. As the sun rises, they grow gradually hotter, and remove more and more clothes. They wail theatrically: their skin is pallid and pimply; their waists are flabby and slack; their breasts droop. This ritual of humorous complaining over, they forget about their bodies except to enjoy the heat of the sun on their skins, an occasional scratch of fingernails on calves or in armpits. They lounge in comfortable positions, bellies and thighs allowed to swell and spread, voluptuous.

She remembers a family summer holiday at Frinton-on-sea, when she was about nine. Those two middle-aged women looking at her with shocked and disapproving expressions as she ran past them up the steep concrete steps from the beach to the esplanade wearing nothing but a scanty pair of green bloomers. She pitied them, as she darted past and understood what they thought of her, but she despised them mostly, and knew, with a spurt of triumph, that she would never be like *them*. Prudish, living in their own little narrow world, and venturing out occasionally in order to be shocked. Lying next to Robert, she looks at her knees pressed primly together, and is swept by a chill of terror. And yet that summer was nothing but glory. Having Felix all to herself, the two of them wet, sandy and barefoot all day long, running half-naked at the sea's edge through the frills of waves along the clean sweep of the bay, the shining sand coloured pale brown and mauve and patterned with ribs and fans left by the shaping waves as the tide went out. In places the sand was flat, as smooth as glass, and in these large patches it reflected all the colours in the sky, so that when she looked out to sea she saw layers of tints, pale blue, bright blue, deep blue, and then a little olive-grey strip which was the sea itself, and then all the blues repeated in bands in the gleaming brown and purple mirror of the sands. She and Felix swam and embraced in the water, chasing each other and sliding over and under each other like a couple of dolphins; they fished, beach-combed and hunted for shellfish, day blurring into day in a splendour of sea, sand, sun and brown bodies, indecipherable. Putting her clothes back on at the end of each long afternoon was an intolerable jar. It felt all wrong.

Robert waits for her to tell him things just like the women in the group do, just like Beth does. She is nervous, not being used to this in a man, not expecting it. She's got used to not being seen or heard, is that it? She lies next to him, under his blue duvet the colour of the summer sea, holding his hand.

There are a lot of witches now, meeting in groups. There were six of them this afternoon, sitting in an untidy garden in Highbury, and somewhere, hovering about, the spirit of her grandmother, the feeling of Beth. They expose their lives to one another, they talk of their contradictory needs, for solitude and for sociability and for children, for work and for love and for cash, for women and for men and for mothering, the drives that pull them apart, in different directions, within themselves, and that make them disagree with one another. Helen has so much that she wants to say that she remains practically silent. And in any case, her thoughts keep wandering off to an insistent beat: tonight; with him. She's behaving, suddenly, like an apprentice witch, not listening properly, not able to learn. They are talking about female power, and her mind keeps wandering off.

The women's voices drone like insects. A thrush throws loops of clear notes out from the depths of the pear tree thick with leaf where it perches, invisible. Traffic rushes past, muffled by vegetation and brick walls. When Helen looks up, she is dazzled, and everything is bleached white: the top of the beech hedge, her old canvas espadrilles that once were khaki. The whiteness reminds her of that garden in the south of Thailand between the white wood hotel and the white sand of the beach, where the gardener sat on a circular bench under a tree dropping curved white petals, little boats of perfume, and stroked the white hotel cat intently and intimately. Steven's hand began to imitate the gardener's, in the fur between Helen's legs, and she swore afterwards that she came at the same moment as the cat.

On a day as hot as this, she suddenly remembers, my middle-aged cousin Dorothy confessed to me how she would sneak to the fridge and eat an entire bowl of mayonnaise. With what scorn did I, aged ten, regard her silently, and with what shock did I learn that a woman as old as my mother was capable both of greed and of something deeper and more atavistic still: a need for comfort, for communion which obviously her husband could not, or would not, provide. It scared me, tomboy with scarred brown knees, pitiless amazon in short back and sides.

– Helen, one of the other women says irritably: I don't believe you've been listening to a single word anyone's said for the last half-hour.

She looks up guiltily.

– It's true, she admits: I was thinking about something else.

– What? the other woman asks crossly.

Helen gulps.

– Food and mothers and sex.

They all burst out laughing, some unwillingly, resenting her distance from their conversation.

– Well, go on then. It's your turn, anyway. Talk to us.

She guides Robert's fingers, teaching them to dance, teaching them new rhythms, subtle and complex. But she feels awkward, a little resentful and absent, and her ears catch the sound of someone walking along the pavement outside, a woman hurrying through the summer night, the soft tap and click and shuffle of her high-heeled shoes. Most passionately, that's where she wants to be: outside, alone in the night, roaming the streets. Not here in this intimate bed having to teach a man how not to be a stranger. Fear springs up, and she doesn't understand why. Coming feels dangerous, and she doesn't know why. The pleasure, mounting up through her in waves, is too strong. She can't bear it, can't contain it.

– Come inside me, she murmurs to Robert: come inside.

He looks surprised at her impatience, but accepts her invitation. His pleasure, stiffened, wriggles into hers, and she laughs into his shoulder. They lie on their sides, cradling and climbing all over each other. They are wet under the blue quilt, and sticky, and warm. She begins to lose all sense of time. She begins to recognise this landscape, one she has visited before. It's suddenly so easy, being here, like stepping up one step higher, saying a word in a foreign language, beginning to run not walk. The pleasure mounts inside, almost unbearably, and she begins to cry out. Robert, assuming she is coming, lets go, and she feels him sizzle up inside her till she tingles all over.

They lie on the soft mattress, his body collapsed into hers, her flesh thudding and thundering, still sending out undulations of warmth. Nearly there, but not quite. She hurried, and then stopped on the brink. His head is on her breast, and she can hear his heart beat, his breath come in gasps. Outside the window they can hear the summer rain begin, the trees drip. Inside their cave of tangled limbs they are no less damp, sweat streaming between their bodies. Their joint smell rises like that of wet ferns, the undergrowth deep in under the trees.

– There's this lovely valley I'd like to show you, Robert says contentedly into her ear in his growling voice: in Ireland, on the west coast. You come into it really suddenly, you don't know it's there, and it suddenly opens up in front of you and you drop into it. It's really deep, with these high mountains all around it, and it's completely wild and uninhabited, just the most beautiful green and trees.

He kisses her ear.

– I'd like to go there with you, he says shyly.

Then he stops with a grunt, listening to what he is saying, and glares at her.

– Romantic rubbish, he says hurriedly in his deep voice.

She hugs him, laughing.

– I adore you.

– Go to sleep, he says, patting her shoulder.

He falls asleep almost instantly, snoring loudly as usual. She is used to this by now. She slips her arm under his back and pulls him round and tries to turn him over. He resists, catching her in his arms and holding her tightly.

– Don't go away, he says sleepily, half-awake: stay here.

– Turn over then, lie on your side so that you don't snore.

He turns over obediently, and she fits herself along his back, so that they lie like twin spoons packed together in cottonwool, her arm over his body and her hand clasped between both of his, her face laid between his shoulder blades, their legs laced together, a sandwich of white and brown feet. Helen falls forward happily into the black pit opening up in front of her. It's a valley, stony mountains rising up on either side of her, no green. She knows its name: the Valley of the Twins. Under her feet is sopping moss, silky black sponges, springy mounds. The wind rages at her through this corridor of rocks, scouring her ears. It is wintertime. Tiny streams trickle over gravel and between boulders, silver in the austere light. They inscribe themselves, a lacy script on the valley's floor, spelling out a word Helen peers at: *incest*.

Helen and Catherine are standing side by side in the lane dipping down from the common at the village's back, a mile from the house, picking hazelnuts. They stand on tiptoe, and grasp the slender branches, and bend them down, and gather the pale, polished nuts from the frills of leaves.

One way for Helen to manage some time alone with her mother is to suggest a walk. Catherine rises eagerly from her armchair. She loves to walk, whereas Bill does not, so she rarely goes.

– Just let me change my shoes.

The lane is muddy and soft after the storms of the past two days, a tunnel of bronze, vibrant green, gold. The two women work in a contented silence, filling a plastic carrier bag with nuts.

– I used to love doing this when I was a child, Catherine says suddenly into the silence: picking nuts. Every autumn. Then one year I stopped. I'd been given a new pair of roller-skates, and I spent every minute I could out roller-skating. I was the neighbourhood champion.

Her face, that normally is tense, reflecting her busy mind planning how best to organise the multiplicity of tasks that lies ahead, is relaxed, smiling. She hums as her fingers wander over the branches and between the leaves, searching for nuts. She's a little off-key, as usual. That's another family game, to mock Catherine for being unable to sing in tune. She doesn't sing or hum often, except in church, where no one laughs at her.

Helen looks at her mother enjoying herself.

– I never knew you were a champion roller-skater, she says wonderingly: you never told me that before.

– You never asked, Catherine says, stripping the hazelnuts from their twigs and dropping them into the carrier bag that Helen holds open: did you?

It's cold in the lane now, a wind springing up, the warm glow of the afternoon light beginning to fade. It will soon be time to retrace their steps home, wake Bill from sleep, make the tea. Catherine turns to face her daughter.

– What do you know about my life? she cries: almost nothing.

Going home slowly, picking their way through the puddles and the mud, they are quiet with one another, companionable, a bond created between them by a tired accusation, resigned words. At the stile leading from the last field into the back garden, Catherine pauses.

– I was sorry to hear you broke up with George, she says with difficulty: it must have been hard for you.

– Put my hair up for me, Helen suggests to her later that same day: go on, show me how to put my hair up like yours.

In the morning, Helen is sleepy after a night broken by nightmares, the need to get up several times and drink glasses of water, to reflect on the strange images swimming towards her out of the dark. She sits in the little kitchen of Robert's flat, holding his cat on her lap, wearing

160

his dressing-gown, dreamily watching him cook breakfast for the two of them.

– Helen, he sings out: wake up. I've already asked you once, how d'you want your eggs?

She starts, and the cat in her lap digs his claws into her thigh in protest. She comes sharply back to the present out of mists, and peers at Robert brandishing a wooden spatula.

– I don't know, she says uncertainly: a fried egg is a fried egg, surely.

– You can have them, he says patiently: winking or shut.

– Oh, she says: oh, winking, certainly.

Still half-asleep, she starts thinking about fried eggs.

That was the one dish her father ever cooked, fried eggs for Sunday breakfast, except one time her mother was ill and he made them lunch and supper too. Perverse, unnatural children that they were, they adored the rare treat of their father cooking for them, his gravy full of lumps and his slices of liver charred on the outside and raw inside. Now here's Robert cooking fried eggs too.

– Men, she declaims to the cat: are creatures of tradition and ritual, far more than women are, though this is not generally recognised to be the case. Robert always has fried eggs for Sunday breakfast. What can we deduce from this? Why, that he is a timid, obsessive creature, incapable of decisions on the spur of the moment, enslaved by routine, frightened of sudden change. Why not porridge today? Why not haddock, or poached eggs, or yoghourt, or peaches?

– Because you know I hate going shopping, Robert shouts at her: and you know I never have anything in the fridge. I made a big effort because you were coming over. I bought some eggs. I went shopping on Friday in my *lunch-hour*.

He is really offended. She shuts up, pushes the cat off her lap, and begins to slice bread to make toast for both of them. Robert and the breakfast simmer together on top of the stove.

– You don't have to do that, he says crossly: I'll do it.

She stands behind him, puts her arms round him, then puts one hand inside his nightshirt and caresses the curly carpet on his chest.

– Peace? she asks.

– If you'll stop behaving like a lunatic, he snaps: and sit down, we can have our breakfast.

They split the newspapers between them, and sit munching and reading, occasionally lifting their heads to smile at one another, read out bits from the paper. Robert finishes his fried eggs first, and begins to wipe a crust of toast methodically around his plate. Then he puts it down, takes a sip of coffee, clears his throat.

– You busy today? he asks: got time to go for a walk or anything?

She looks hastily down at the wooden table to hide the rush of pleasure to her face, her involuntary beam. On weekday mornings, they part early and hurriedly to get to their respective jobs, and on previous Sunday mornings he has usually announced his need to work. Her eyes caress the smooth grain of the table, the worn yellow handle of her knife, the soft pyramid of salt at the side of the blue and white plate.

– Oh sweetheart, I can't, she says regretfully to the marmalade jar: Beth's down this week-end, at her mother's. We've planned to spend today together.

Robert looks snubbed.

– Don't ever say, he says to her sharply: that I asked you to give up anything for me.

She pushes back her chair and rushes round the table to where he sits, and hugs him fiercely.

– I won't, she assures him: you don't clip my wings, and I'll try not to clip yours.

She pauses. That's not totally true.

– You try to clip my wings sometimes. But I don't let you.

– That's quite enough of that, he protests through her kisses: the coffee'll be getting cold.

She sits down in her place again.

– What about tonight? she asks: after Beth's gone? Are you free?

He considers.

– Yeah. I could manage that. Now listen, if you've finished, I'll get on with clearing this lot away.

He doesn't want help with the washing up. She watches his serious, methodical back, his fingers wringing out the dishcloth, folding it neatly at the edge of the stainless-steel sink.

As she is going, and turns to say goodbye to him, he surprises her with a kiss.

– Go on then, he says, raising his head: be off with you. Be off. I'll see you tonight. Give me a ring when you know what time Beth's going back.

He pushes her out of the door and closes it behind her. Helen bows her head to the cold rain, which is still falling, but she walks singing down the street, in transit between her two dear friends.

162

Two

– Beastly English summer, Beth grumbles: I hate it.

– It's only turned nasty today, Helen defends the London climate: it's been lovely, most of the week.

– I want a holiday in the sun, Beth sighs: and I want this baby to be born. I'm tired of waiting. Lugging this huge weight about, it makes me tired.

She carried herself according to the new need of her body, the swell out front, balancing herself with her back braced, her shoulders curved backwards, her belly tipping forwards and up like a giant acorn. She sits down heavily on Helen's sofa-bed and breaths out: whew. She does look tired, lines visible under her eyes for the first time.

– It was sweet of you to come over, Helen says: but you look worn out. You should have let me come to see you at your mother's.

– I'm not ill, Beth snaps: pregnancy's not a disease, you know.

Helen begins to laugh.

– Same old Beth. Pregnancy hasn't changed you nearly as much as I thought it would.

Beth looks back at her, uncertain for once, her blue eyes fierce.

– There is something I wanted to tell you. And somehow, it's easier to talk to you here than at my mother's. I couldn't say it in front of her.

Helen comes to sit next to her, and takes her friend's hand.

– Well, go on, then. What is it?

Beth pulls her hand away, so that she can beat her fists together in her lap.

– It's Pete. He's chosen this time of all times, three weeks before the baby's due, to freak out. He says he never really wanted the baby, that it was my decision not his, and that he's not sure he wants to be a father at all.

– That's just last-minute panic, Helen says firmly: he'll get over it. He hasn't freaked out about the baby before, has he? So I suppose it was bound to happen sometime.

– D'you think so? Beth says, looking miserably at her: I'm not so sure.

Helen hasn't seen Beth this unhappy for a long time. The look on her friend's face pulls at her heart.

– The thing is, Beth mutters: he hasn't been home for a couple of nights. He rang me yesterday, before I got the train down to my mother's, and said he was staying at Ruth's for a while. That's the woman he was with before me.

She lowers her face as the tears begin to slide down her cheeks.

– Why does he have to do it now, just when I need him? Why does he assume it's only him who can feel rejected? Those bloody baby films they show you at the clinic, you should see them. There was one glossy colour one with the doctor saying: take especial care of your husband during your pregnancy, make sure he feels loved and wanted and not left out.

She is weeping openly now.

– Who'll take care of me? Who'll help me look after the baby?

– I've heard, Helen suggests: that men often go a bit funny when their women get pregnant. They're jealous, that's all. It reminds them that there's something they can't do.

– I thought Pete was feeling really involved with it all, Beth says, wiping her tears on her pink cotton sleeve: he hasn't been able to come to many of the birth classes with me because of his hours at the hospital, but I didn't realise he might resent that. I suppose we didn't talk about it enough.

She sniffs loudly.

– Have you got a handkerchief? I need to blow my nose.

Helen takes one out of her bag and passes it across. She sits thinking while Beth wipes her eyes and snorts into the clean linen.

– It's not just that men are jealous, she says suddenly: it's also that they've got these really weird ideas. Some of them really don't seem to recognise that they're involved in conception at all. It's sort of magical thinking, women as goddesses make it rain babies and the men just sitting there feeling astonished.

– Ha, Beth says viciously: that's just a rationalisation for the bloody old status quo, if you ask me, to keep up the division of labour. Let the women get on with rearing the kids, while the men get on with making the bombs.

– Sometimes I think men are such idiots, Helen says with great bitterness: I can't see why I ever think I could love any of them. Worse than idiots. *Wilfully* wrong. Power-mad fools.

She gets up and walks to and fro across the room.

– I can't stand it. They make me *so* angry.

Beth sighs.

– I could kill Pete right now, d'you know that?

She starts to laugh bitterly.

– Doctor crushed to death by pregnant girlfriend. I can see the headlines.

– You know what I think we should do? Helen says: go out for a walk. Are you too tired? Why don't we go to a park or something?

She waves her hand at the room.

– I spend too much time in here, working. Let's go out somewhere and see some trees. I'm fed up with staring at the walls.

You'll look so beautiful when you're pregnant, Steven used to repeat to Helen: we'll have the most beautiful children together, you'll see. She couldn't stand his smug assumption that that was all that she wanted from life. Couldn't admit to herself, either, how much she feared it. She offered him poems instead, fragments of prose woven out of their experience together, and he rejected them, saying: too complicated, too difficult to understand, too intense. Why can't you just, he cried: be happy with me? We'll live in the country, and have our babies, and you can do your writing. I'll support you. We'll be so happy. She spat back at him: I need to live in London, and your job's in Bangkok. So forget it.

– I'll tell you what, Beth says: would you do me a big favour?

– Of course.

– You shouldn't say that. You should say: what?

– All right. What?

– Would you see me back to my mother's? I'd rather go for a walk out there, it's more like the country anyway. And it'll be easier to be near home when I'm tired after the walk.

She stops, considering.

– That's funny, calling my mother's house home. I haven't done that for years.

She watches Helen's face uncertainly.

– Will you mind? It'll mean taking the train from St Pancras. But there's quite a nice park when we get there, some old estate that's been taken over by the council. You could stay the night, if you wanted. I'm not going back to Leeds till tomorrow morning, we could travel back into London together.

Helen hesitates. Suddenly, it seems to her, the room is full of witches, whirling in bright silky frocks. They are Beth and herself, she realises, and all the women in her women's group.

– I'm going to see Robert again tonight, she says cautiously: that's

165

what I've arranged to do. But I'd love to come with you out to your mother's. Of course I'll come for a walk there. And then I'll come back here afterwards.

The train from St Pancras carries them north from London, half an hour's ride through the towns that once were completely separate, as villages, from the capital, and which now serve as its dormitory suburbs. Helen and Beth have donned coats, for even though the rain has stopped and the day is lit again by pale golden sunshine there is a nip in the air, as though, Helen drearily thinks, the summer is dying before it has even properly begun. They rub their hands together to warm them as they alight at their destination and stand outside the little station and peer around for a bus. Behind them is the red brick arch that carries local traffic over the railway lines, and in front of them a half-circle of asphalt broken at intervals by small flower-beds, a wooden shed serving as cafe and selling hot soup and tea over its window-sill, a bus stop and a taxi rank.

– That's the bus stop, Beth exclaims: that one over there.

The bus that obligingly turns up almost immediately speeds them out of the station forecourt and into the little town's high street, and then from there into the countryside.

– Don't worry, Beth says, catching Helen's eye: you won't have any trouble getting back. These buses are regular, even on a Sunday.

– You might have told me it was so far from the station, Helen grumbles: where does your mother live, for heaven's sake?

– Back where we've come from, Beth says, waving her hand at the bus window: I'll get the bus back with you. It's just a really nice park. You'll see.

She sounds far more contented than earlier on, so Helen subsides in her seat. Yet for some reason, her mouth is dry, and her ears pop and ring. She swallows, feeling as though she is on an aeroplane dropping sharply, in need of barley sugar.

– Here you are then, the bus driver sings out, swerving around a final sharp bend and pulling up on the side of the road next to a pair of wrought-iron gates: Gettering Park.

They stand on the verge for a moment, watching the bus turn the next corner, and then themselves turn in the direction of the gates. There are two council workmen there, dressed in overalls, busy earning Sunday overtime by repairing the gate-posts, and they smile wordlessly at the two visitors without stopping their work. The two women halt, listening to the tap, chink, ring of hammers on stone,

166

and then walk on. Pleasing, but slightly melancholy, the sound dies behind them.

– It's never crowded here, for some reason, Beth explains: even on a Sunday.

She sounds guilty about not wishing to meet a lot of people.

– I feel the summer's already going, says Helen, sighing, and looking about her.

Inexplicably, yellow leaves dangle from branches above them, and are scattered in ones and twos along the drive. This should not be the case. It is only July. Helen suddenly feels that she *wants* it to be autumn. Summer is somehow dangerous. So she sees the light wind lift the leaves; they rise up a little way into the air, and then drop down again. Some of them stick, curled, to the damp tree-trunks. The sky has changed, towards further rain, to the same colour as the gravel under their feet, a grey expanse just visible through the great lime trees arching overhead. Helen shivers, not so much at the chilly air, as at vastness and emptiness, at the trees letting the sky leak through. The drive ahead looks endless, and they are walking slowly, Helen setting their pace, pretending she is solicitous of Beth, but in reality her feet reluctant to go forward, constantly stopping to kick at stones and twigs. Beth and herself feel very small compared to the ancient, massive limes.

– I'm over thirty, Beth says suddenly: I'm ageing. I notice it now. A certain roughness of skin, lines under my eyes, lines around my mouth.

Helen turns and studies her.

– I know what you mean, she remarks: I've seen you change. But to me you look, well, beautiful. You know I've always thought that about you. And the older you get, the more beautiful. The character expressing itself.

– I'm frightened, Beth says, gesturing vaguely with one hand: you know? Whether Pete'll come back or not. Whether the baby'll be all right or not. Whether or not I'll cope. Whether there'll be a nuclear war.

She bends her head and pulls her coat tightly around her body.

– The pregnancy's so big, Helen whispers: when you emphasise it like that.

Knowing Beth will soon be a mother, and trying to understand her fears, makes Helen feel dizzy. Or else it is the fact of walking down the long drive and feeling as though she is in one of those dreams where you know what will happen next, placed in a landscape that at first seems utterly strange, but then reveals itself as familiar. Mists may swirl about your path, but, if you listen hard, you hear your own voice as narrator, warning you what lies just around the corner.

– This does feel odd, Helen says, stopping, and looking from side to side: it feels *odd*.

She glances at Beth, at her catlike face with its high cheekbones and long eyes, her scarf tucked into her upturned collar and her hands stuck into her pockets. Beth has accompanied her this far, but somehow, from here it is up to Helen alone. This landscape blurs. Soon, it seems to her, the trees will be bare, skinny black branches mushrooming out and up like lungs in anatomical drawings. The earth, her fragile skin, is the wrong side out. She will die from exposure. Around the corner, along the next stretch of the drive, everything may change.

Time slips, recommences, slips back. Helen's brain whirrs and clicks like an alarm clock ready to strike. These clothes they are both wearing, surely they are far too warm for a summer's day? What is it that recalls to her bare legs and ankle socks, and the sun pressing down like a flat-iron onto her head?

The wind in the lime trees echoes her mother's voice: Helen, Helen, put on your nice white shoes.

– Come on, Beth says: let's go on. I'm cold standing here like this. Come on, Helen.

– Come on, her mother calls faintly from the end of the drive: Hurry up.

Helen walks obediently, dreamily forwards accompanied by her friend. The summer day has turned really cold now, spots of rain beginning to patter on the leaves and on the ground. She is walking down a wide avenue of limes, in obedience to memory not maps, towards a house which she knows should be imposing, solid, but which, at this distance, is dwarfed by the chilly grandeur of the sky as the trees on either side thin out and they reach the end of the drive. The gravel under their feet grinds and squelches as the rain increases and drips on the laurels and rhododendrons marking the beginning of what was once a tidy formal garden, now hopelessly overgrown.

The shutters of the house are freshly painted, and thrown back. They were blue once, and white now. She knows where to find the bell push hidden in the rose bush clambering around the front door, and her eyes mark the bootscraper at the side of the porch, the white tin box for letters still in its place. She presses her forefinger firmly on to the bell, and, just as before, waits a few seconds and then hears it clang deep in the recesses of the house.

– What are you doing that for? asks Beth, puzzled: can't you see the notice? The house isn't open on Sunday. They only open the cafe during the week.

– I haven't been inside here for a long time, Helen murmurs: the door was stiff to open when I came before.

She shakes herself like a sleepwalker, and looks at Beth in bewilderment. Then she remembers what comes next.

– We need to go around the side of the house.

– I suppose you'll tell me in your own good time, Beth grumbles: what's going on.

They sit in the little copse at the side of the house. The fallen tree-trunk on which they perch is slimy and dark as mushrooms in the gentle rain, and their feet rest on cushions of moss. They huddle together for warmth, while Helen tries hard to capture whatever elusive memory stalks her, mocking, from behind the trees.

– No, she says at last: it's not here. Let's walk a bit more.

Rain is cupped in every glossy, every crinkled leaf. Through the trees the sky is dirty yellow, and above, bright grey. They pick their way out of the copse again, and back around the front of the house. Helen studies the high, thick fence of rhododendrons separating her from the garden, and decides, with a sudden excited curiosity, to push through. She treads from the gravel sweep over the white pebble edging of the path, over long grass, and parts the bushes with her hands.

She doesn't know what she will find. She is used to town parks, primly cropped and trimmed, where trees, flowers, grass are all cut back, where notices say keep off. She hopes for something different, completely unexpected, for a ravine, perhaps, to open up before her, so wild is the aspect of the day and so dramatic her mood.

In front of her, below her, banked with steep grass slopes, is a sunken garden. Overgrown, it has obviously not been touched for years. The tall banks of shrubs that enclose it emphasise its privacy, its seclusion. No one, it seems, comes here now, to walk in it and find the soul refreshed, the senses revitalised, to tend it, to sit for hours and find content. But all her life Helen has been journeying, and the end of her journey is here. Soaked through and shivering, she is sorrowful. The last thing she dared hope for was female companionship on her journey, a woman walking with her and watching over her. She didn't know that women liked and trusted one another. She thought that it was only boy children who were wanted, that girl twins were exposed to die on the mountainside. She has always been a hero on a

169

quest, for in the legends it is always the hero who finds the monster and slays it, and it is the hero who is given the love of women as a reward.

This garden is a physical enacting of memory, the past. When you look long and hard at it, you can begin to trace how it formerly was. All its divisions are blurred, flower beds merging into one another in a riot of green, weeds no longer distinguishable from cultivated plants. The path itself along which they step is indistinct, blurring into the flower-beds it fringes, furred with thick moss, weeds springing and flowering in the cracks between paving-stones. Buried beneath all the teeming plants and shrubs long since gone to seed is merely the suggestion of a planned wilderness, branches trained to droop and trail as though by nature not by a cunning artifice, rose bushes coaxed to clamber up stakes and spread down curtains of bloom, palms set in lofty clumps at the curve of the path. Now, nettles pick at their knees as they go, and thickets of michaelmas daisies, not yet in flower, obstruct their view.

The path twists in a series of loops and complications around trees and in out of flower-beds like little forests, turning back on itself constantly, pulling the garden together in a tightly tangled knot, like a maze, like a labyrinth.

Beth stands at the entrance to the labyrinth; she holds the threads of Helen's words that she unwinds like a ball of string and pays out as Helen goes on, and she tugs gently sometimes, so that Helen knows she is there, so that she knows she will find her way back from her chaos and will not be lost.

Helen's words are like statues set at intervals along the garden path, mossy plinths bearing figures from legend and myth. She tiptoes forward, examining them one by one.

The first statue is very old, the stone crumbling in places under the onslaught of weather, ivy gripping the cracks. The legend on the plinth simply reads: Adam and Eve. There they are, the two lovers, entwined in one another's arms, so closely interlinked that they seem to be one. It is hard to see where their bodies separate, so closely are arms wrapped around arms and legs around legs; even their heads look like twin flowers on a single stalk. Though their bodies are those of adults, their faces, turned towards Helen, are those of children: Felix and herself. Look, the calm, detached expressions seem to be saying: we are in our right place. This is how things should be: the

170

masculine and the feminine so tightly joined that they are inseparable one from another. Both have graceful, white stone limbs; their features are identical. A hermaphrodite bloom. Plato's double-bodied human, before the axe of separation falls.

The second statue is around the corner, half-hidden in a thicket of rhododendrons. Helen works patiently, pulling aside branches and tripping over roots, until she has penetrated to the heart of the mystery, past the huge purple flowers and the thickly bunched leaves and can stand before the statue face to face. She bends to rub away earth and moss from the base, so that she can read the inscription carved there: the lost brother; the twin. Naked, indolent, Steven lolls on his plinth, as though waiting for her to join him there, his eyes amused, one finger arrested in the act of scratching his bony nose. His mouth gives him away, its reproachful droop. Why did you reject me and send me away? it asks: after I was ready to give up everything for you and claim you as my own? Why did you turn against me and screech that I had to go away and never return? Helen looks at him in supplication. It was too dangerous, she whispers: but you couldn't understand. I was protecting us both from sin, can't you see that? He continues to look past her, and she knows that he always will, now. They have turned away from each other for good.

Incestuous wishes, for which she was punished with blood. Blood beginning to flow suddenly like the words of a curse uttered by God. The mark of the forbidden apple on her hands. Her mother a long way away, keeping Felix with her, throwing food to Helen that spatters on the ground. Helen is the evil one, and the axe has descended, God's axe, severing Adam from Eve, twisting their sinful heads round so that they look in opposite directions now, away from each other, over one another's shoulders, towards exile, opposition, strife.

All she wanted was her companion back, the lovely boy of the days before the Fall, before she knew his name or hers or that they were different from each other, different from animals and plants. All she wanted was that unity, that silence, that connection; which was punished with blood.

Helen's tears fall and fall, as the knot inside her unloosens, the hard knot melts into water. She has reached the pool at the garden's centre, thickly fringed with weeds, its edges scummed with green. Beth has followed her along the corridors of her perplexity, and has come with her into the deepest cavern of the labyrinth, where the pool lies, formed from the tears that she has wept inside herself and has not known were there. Beth bends with her over the pool, standing next to her at its edge, and touches her. She says: don't be afraid. Look into this pool of tears that you have wept. What do you see there: monster, or self? And being there by the pool, having reached the end of her journey, Helen sees herself: a woman, no minotaur. And she cries, hanging on to Beth's hands, for Beth has birthed her, she has brought her out in water and pain, and she has shown her how, when she tried to be a hero, she killed off that deepest part of herself, because she called it monstrous.

Giant rhubarb rears over their heads, and bamboo spears tower to the heavens. In some places the grass comes up to their waists, and the shiny leaves of the fig tree are larger than the body of a child. Helen has only a baby's size: plant stems are sturdier than she is; she could climb into a flower and cradle herself. Here, in this wild wet garden, jungly as the foreign territories that explorers seize, and heady like them with spice and green, Helen has rediscovered Eden: which is paradise. Halting, and leaning her hand guiltily on Beth's swollen belly, she recognises it for what it is.

Paradise is the mother's body, the orient that travellers wish to plunder, rape, explore. Paradise is that time when it is the twins inside their mother, alone with her. Paradise continues after birth: it is fatherlessness, the time before language; it is not-separation and not-speech. Paradise is before puberty, it is the twins together, one perfect whole.

Yet Eve eventually feels desire, feels curiosity. Expelled from paradise by her own longing to explore and name the world, she knows that she must dwell forever in the place outside, no leaving-present except to be cursed as body, evil, putrefaction, death and whore; no puberty rite except that which other women give her: the stumbling into speech and writing so that she can mourn.

God said to Adam: you will toil by the sweat of your own brow to bring forth fruit. And he said to Eve: you shall labour to bring children forth, in pain.

There was a hole in the heart of her, a place of loss, a gap crying out to be filled. She ached to speak, and to be listened to. She ached for redemption, for a saviour to come. She ached for mothering, the love that listening gives, the love that a woman now gives to her. Beth has nourished her in her need, before Helen knew what that need was. She came to Beth dumb, with hands outstretched, crying out silently

172

in the depths of her, and the other woman answered, saying, I am listening to you, saying, I am here. This is the precious gift another woman gives her, taking her words in, wanting to be fertilised by words. This is their loving labour, performed with one another, and it brings forth children, a mutual pregnancy, as they embrace and listen to each other, and the words inside them leap for joy.

Spreading her hands over Beth's little world, Helen feels the child inside her friend jump, leap, kick, roaming happily in an enclosed green garden, ignorant for a long while yet of difference, and laying her head on Beth's shoulder she holds her in her arms, and weeps for the loss of paradise.

And then Beth ceases to be Ariadne, holding the magic ball of string. She drops it, she becomes midwife. She cuts the cord, and declares Helen separate, loose, free, baptised by tears. She commands her to sing of her redemption, her life, to speak, to write. She orders her: now define *self*, now define *woman*. The heart of the labyrinth is not the end, but another beginning. Start to write.

Three

The following morning, Helen sits again at Robert's kitchen table, sipping strong tea, listening to the sounds of splashing from the bathroom as Robert washes his hair. The cat, who likes to be comfortable, twists about in her lap, stretching up to rub his face against hers. It's seven-thirty, and Monday, and she ought to be making a move, but she stays indolently where she is, not wanting to disturb Robert by urging him to hurry up so that she can drop into the bath, wanting to hang on to being in his flat.

– Little monster, she whispers to the cat: little beast. Strange little thing, nuzzling at her in an ecstasy of contained violence, seeking her armpit, her breast, dipping his head between her legs and burrowing through towelling. Last night, she and Robert played at monsters, taking it in turns, fighting to see who could snarl and growl most, and then purr loudest. Helen showed Robert the monster who lives in a mountain cave, leaping up and down with a grin, and a sandwich clasped in one scaly paw. She showed him the monster called mino-taur, who dwells in the labyrinth, in the depths of a dark still lake. And she showed him the monster Ariadne, who one moment is the princess handing the hero a ball of twine so that he will not get lost, and the next is the spider spinning her labyrinth web and winding the innocent hero into her jaws. And she danced for him, in a whirl of skirts, and he laughed and clapped, and then he put on his hat and danced for her too.

This was being together, and it was also circling around each other before they engaged, their arms tying each other up like string around parcels that only their movements asleep will undo, their tongues licking at skin that does not dissolve like sugar, but remains instead endlessly renewed and enjoying. They feel a mixture of pleasure, being in the right place, which means together, and great nervousness. How different are they from one another? How much does it matter? The sex is to explore that.

Now Adam too, and not only Eve, is allowed to be curious, to want to find out, with no slapping-down or needing to blame afterwards. He can discover her, how her lips curl, just so, in a certain way, how her tissues inside are ribbed and soft, how her breasts rise and fall, how her nipples are brown and pink and sturdy like raspberries, how she rises, all of her, how her deep heart comes right out to meet him and take him in.

And now Eve can look at Adam with desire, she can describe him with words and summon up images, no longer silent. His skin, she tells him, is the colour of apricots, and breathes with the smells of spices and earth when her mouth moves across it. She praises his short black hair, which has silver threads in it, and smells of sweat and of sun, and his thumbnails, which are lined with sweet green dirt. She celebrates him, all his beauty, part by part, and the whole, she sings of him standing up to greet her and wave at her, and she holds him, and takes him in.

There are no words in the language to describe her embrace of him, and so they are forced to become poets, giggling, inventing new ones. This is what Helen's mother meant, then, when she used to say: it is very beautiful. When a man darts like a humming-bird and leaps like a salmon, and a woman flies up and out to meet him, and encloses him in mid-air, in the depths of streams. Only Helen, convinced she was a sinner, did not want to remember, did not want to know. But now there are words, and words, which flash across the darkness of her mind. Doors open, close, along the corridor. She is a violent, a blue flower, that beats its fleshy wings, that claps, she is a drum of blood, a shout, a city street. She presses down and down and down, as waves of blue sensation eddy up and up and up.

Robert is letting her move him down strange paths, to places where they have not been together before. He lets her guide him, he listens to what her body says, he follows her slow dance, learning new steps very different from his former ones, a gentler rhythm. They let the body take over. Their bodies decline for them the verb to be: I am, you are, he is, she is. We are. And Helen comes, comes in response to him who responds to her, and is no longer frightened of you, me, and can let her body say with his: we are.

She is whole, she knows that now, and she can see all the different sides of herself: the masculine and the feminine; the productive and the reproductive; the receiving and the creative; the light and the dark; the rational and the irrational; the active and the passive. She needs to embrace all these parts of herself if she is to live without being maimed. Here are the twins after all; not, as she once thought, bright separate meteors flashing across the sky; not, as she once thought, warring archetypes exhausting her energy. The twins lodge simply, deep inside her, as images of different parts of herself, as needs for different sorts of activity. She begins to smile with delight at this recognition of what makes herself: wholeness dependent on twin capacities and twin needs. Out of the tension, the meeting between the two, she forms the synthesis of who she is today.

She cradles Robert's sleepy body in her arms. Do you know this already? she wants to ask him: have you also worked this out? Is it the same for men, or different? Tell me, please tell me.

– Let me live, she whispers: I want to create, wholly, with all of myself, not just half.

Robert in her arms shifts and grunts.

– I'm an honorary woman now, aren't I? he murmurs: wouldn't you say?

– I love you, she says, kissing him: I love you, I love you.

– Hmph, he mutters, and falls asleep, and begins to snore.

Helen drains the bitter brown tea in her cup, looking up as Robert comes into the kitchen. She knows that it's Monday morning, and that he likes to be left alone to get himself ready for school, but she can't resist getting up and hugging him.

– There I was last night, she tells him: making up poems to the exotic smell of your skin. I recognise it now, it's garlic.

She registers his stiffness, and, looking up, his abstracted face. What about last night? she wants to tempt him back: don't you remember it?

– I must go, love, he says, hastily pecking her cheek: be seeing you.

The front door slams behind him. He's better than she is at cutting off when necessary, at separating. Her work waits for her, as his does for him, yet she's still lolling here in his kitchen, wrapped around in the closeness and pleasures of last night, unwilling to leave them, unwilling to go away from his flat, from him. There's a time for everything, her grandmother whispers in her ear: and everything in its own time. Be off with you, now. Don't waste time. The surge of resentment for Robert dies. To indulge it would be to find an excuse not to get down to work. She collects her clothes from where they lie scattered all over the floor, and goes into the bathroom.

Helen writes all day, only stopping to cook herself lunch and supper. There are problems to solve.

In solitude the mind opens up under the pressure of reality. The mind spreads itself wide like the petals of a white flower under insistent rain. Solitude is a necessity which we enjoy too rarely, like a luxury. Peace at night, alone, the supper plates and saucepans piled in the kitchen sink to be washed up tomorrow or the day after, whenever she so chooses, the plants watered, the gas fire lit, the table cleared. There is the blue night of the street beyond the uncurtained windows, the typewriter and the sheets of blank paper waiting for her, eager companions. She is not going to fall asleep, or drink too much wine, or ease herself out on dope. Her mind is clear, scoured and ready like a bowl in which eggs are to be beaten, like a board on which green herbs are to be bruised and chopped.

Welcome, visitors: the thoughts and images which do not come in through the front door, but which seep through window cracks, which sidle up from the soft recesses of the bed and split the eiderdown. Her room is a jungle, a larder, a temple, a zoo. And the only thing that matters is to begin, over and over again.

Last night, she slept in Robert's arms, and dreamed. She and Beth have made a date to meet in the graveyard next to Anna's house, only the graveyard has been turned into a park where children can come and play. The church is long since gone; the backs of factories and schools enclose the park on three sides, and iron railings separate it from Anna's garden on the fourth. Seventeenth-century tombstones, florid with arabesques, strange angelic faces backed by shoulders and wings, scrolls, and curly, almost indecipherable lettering, are ranged side by side around the walls and the large flower-beds. A path loops between the latter, underneath the trees.

Up and down pace the two women, their heads bent towards each other, their hands in their pockets, their long woollen scarves flying out behind them in the damp wind, up and down. It is autumn. The trees poise themselves and stand on tiptoe to eject leaves, which flutter down, wide brown and yellow crinkly flags. Leaves on the ground are a soft mass, pink and amber, and leaves still on the branches hang like peaches and burn russet and bronze. Beech trees are thin and red, quivering like the ghosts of flames; each chestnut leaf is a little warm fire.

Their boots crunch over the gravel and sand of the path, their hands come out of pockets to stroke glossy black twigs bare of all but the latest rose blooming hot, strong and pink. Dark yellow streaks, and dark red, and pale brown. Beth's face is sad. Helen halts their walking under the tall, half-bare trees, and turns to her, and takes her in her arms. She lays her own cold cheek against her friend's, and feels wetness between them, whose tears, Beth's or her own, she cannot tell.

They walk on again, arm in arm, towards the white stone statue in the middle of the central flower-bed. Delicate stone body dancing on pink and brown fallen leaves, trampling them into a rich compost for the soil to feed upon. In winter, lone stone body, chilled and knifed by winds, shoulders clad only in the plush of snow. Then, snowdrops and crocuses will dart green shoots between her toes, and swallows will hang in her armpits, young green hedges springing around her waist. The names on the plinth underneath the statue are theirs, and so are the names on all the gravestones round about. Aeroplane smoke tears the sky in two, grey cartridge paper. The precursor of nuclear bombs. There is something that Helen must do, if only she can remember what it is. The trees' sharp quills scrawl words on the sky to help her, and the earth of the flower-beds hums an invitation.

She walks away from Beth, over the sopping green lawn and past the brightness of beeches, to the wall at the far side of the park. Felix's front door is made of grey glass, and she peers through it eagerly, trying to make out his shape. He takes a long time to answer the bell. She crumples his letter of invitation to her in one hand. While she waits, the sky explodes, and trees shrivel to skeletons of black lace, bony ribs enclosing lungs that pant, a bellowing heart. She hears his footsteps shuffling on the other side of the door, and when she leans forward again to beckon him, through the glass, to hurry up, she sees her own face hanging there as he steps through it, down the corridor.

Michèle Roberts
A Piece of the Night

Michèle Roberts' first novel was acclaimed as a landmark in
feminist fiction. It concerns Julie Fanchot, French born, English
convent educated, who has learned to please. The seductive
daughter, Virgin Mary, romantic heroine, perfect wife and mother
— she knows how to be all of these. But she knows that she is also
the witch, the whore, the madwoman, the insatiable, the lesbian.

'Her prose is rich and sinewy and invigorating and her ideas are
stimulating and thought provoking'
The Sunday Press, Dublin

'Uncompromising in its feminism and confident and original in its
style…Its language is our own — angry, analytic, harsh and poetic'
Women Speaking

Joint winner of the *Gay News* Book Award, 1979

Fiction: £3.95
ISBN: 0 7043 3830 0

Joan Barfoot
Duet for Three

Aggie is eighty, and dying. Helpless, unwieldy, incontinent, her
body is slipping out of control, and she can only remember the
heady independence of those happy years after the death of her
husband. Now she is dependent on her ageing daughter June, a
woman who can neither accept nor offer love. Her consolation is
the passionate love she feels for her granddaughter Frances, a free
spirit whose dreams and desires, this time, will perhaps not be
destroyed by the forces of circumstances and convention.

Joan Barfoot is the author of two much loved previous novels
Gaining Ground and *Dancing in the Dark* — both of which are still
in print with The Women's Press.

Fiction: £3.95
ISBN: 0 7043 3981 1

Alice Walker's Short Stories
You Can't Keep a Good Woman Down

Fourteen stories that explore the contradictions of modern
America, the sexual, social and racial prejudices that fuel the
dream of individual success; and at the same time celebrate the
vitality of black women, and their capacity to transform suffering
into energy for change.

Fiction   £2.95
ISBN: 0 7043 3884 X

In Love and Trouble

'One of the most important, grieving, graceful, and honest writers
ever to come to print ... this is a powerful, big, even a wild book'
June Jordan.

These spellbinding stories are Alice Walker's tributes, moving,
angry and loving by turn, to the black women of the rural
American South in which she grew up.

Fiction   £2.95
ISBN: 0 7043 3941 2

Charleen Swansea & Barbara Campbell, editors
Love Stories by New Women

'Feminism gives us the strength to do a lot of things — even to write about love, without drowning' GLORIA STEINEM

Here are 18 stories about women in love: with themselves, with men, women, liquor, horses, sex. These stories buzz, shriek, purr, tickle, weep, entertain, inform.

'*Love Stories by New Women* is a collection as diverse as women themselves. There are some short ones and fat ones, some short tempered and some languid ones, but most of these stories bite into the heart' Bertha Harris

'A rich and varied and spikey collection of short fiction by a group of able young writers: a bouquet of roses and lilies and tire irons and harpoons running from the sensual to the anecdotal, the ribald to the stark deathshead' Marge Piercy

'*Love Stories by New Women* is a shocker and should be required reading for any man who has experienced women as obtuse, fickle, mysterious or dangerous...With some of these secrets out, we might love better' Pat Conroy

Fiction: £2.25
ISBN: 0 7043 3847 5

Marion McLeod & Lydia Wevers, editors
One Whale, Singing
and Other Stories from New Zealand

This volume of stories from New Zealand is distinguished by a
freshness in the writing, and a liveliness in the telling, that hooks
the reader almost as soon as she dips into its pages.

Some of the writers' names are familiar: Janet Frame, Keri Hulme.
But most are not. It is their themes that we recognise, the themes
women write about everywhere, childhood and friendship, love,
betrayal, childbirth, anger, pain, ambition, death. It is a view of the
world from its vulnerable underside, where actions have
consequences and women have too often to bear them. We meet
Amelia Batistich's Dalmation Mama, Phyllis Gant's terrorised wife,
Rosie Scott's crazed and abandoned woman, the child Olive who
has to milk the cow, the bewildered daughter in 'Duncan'....

Fiction: £3.95
ISBN: 0 7043 4014 3

Hardcover: £8.95
ISBN: 0 7043 5006 8

Janet Frame
Scented Gardens for the Blind

'A brilliant outburst of a book' *Kirkus Reviews*

In this haunting novel Janet Frame leads us to inhabit in turn Vera
Glace, the mother who has willed herself sightless; Erlene, the
daughter who has ceased to speak; and Edward, the husband and
father who has taken refuge in a distant land. She bids us consider
the pain – impossibility? – of closeness, of love, among human
beings; and the beauty, and danger, in the world of the senses.
Then, behind this parable of human relationships, she springs
another level of meaning upon us: a study of a mind that has burst
the confines of everyday individual consciousness and invented its
own colourful and tormented reality.

Fiction £3.95

ISBN: 0 7043 3899 8